CI LIA

# CHECK YOUR TRIGGERS

Your mental health and emotional well-being matters to me. You can find a list of possible triggers on the book's page on my website at katerandallauthor.com or by scanning the QR code below.
Xoxo

For Matt. Always.

# CONTENTS

# Chapter One
## Cillian

THE GIRLS WE RESCUED from the clutches of those asshole skin traders we took down had been gone for barely twenty minutes when the distant rumble of engines broke the silence of Viktor Petrov's wooded property. When I got the call from Finn that his brother's woman had been taken, I strongly suspected it was going to be a bloody night. And so far, I've been proven right. Fortunately for all of us, Liam Ashcroft was in Boston with his brother Jude, who happens to be good friends with Finn's brother, Eoghan. As soon as Liam heard who we were going after, he was all too happy to offer his particular set of skills to our cause.

When Liam showed up with his team and wanted to seize the opportunity to eliminate some of the worst humans who've been freely walking the planet, I was more than eager to help. Scum like this deserves to be wiped from the earth, and if it helps my best friend and his family sleep better at night knowing these assholes are dead then I'll gladly add some manpower to the cause. I certainly won't lose a wink of sleep over killing these fuckers.

"Two black Sprinter vans. I make out a driver and passenger in each," Sawyer says through the comms in our ears. Sawyer is Liam's resident computer genius and hacker extraordinaire, at least according to Sawyer himself. With quick efficiency, he had cameras set up about a quarter mile up the road, transmitting to the military-grade laptop sitting on the desk inside Andrei's office—the dead man on the other side of the room whom we haven't had time to dispose of yet. This asshole thought being Petrov's second-in-command would protect him. He thought wrong.

"I have eyes on the vehicles," Abel says through the earpieces we're all wearing.

Abel and Hendrix are concealed in the thicket of trees surrounding the house where Viktor Petrov conducts the sale of kidnapped girls to the highest bidder. Apparently, Liam and his team have been looking into Petrov for some time. Though Liam is known in most circles as a security expert and fixer of otherwise sensitive situations that need to be kept from the prying eyes of law enforcement, his passion lies in a side project funded by the exorbitant fees he charges his wealthy clients.

"Both vehicles have parked outside the back door," Sawyer explains, looking at his computer. "They're opening the cargo doors now."

"Do you have a visual on the inside of the vans?" Liam asks, and Sawyer rolls his eyes.

"Of course. One man in each, but they're getting out."

"So, six total?" I ask, and Liam grins.

"Easy pickings," he says with a cocky smirk on his face.

I walk to the other side of the desk where Sawyer is monitoring their movements. The six men are stretching after their journey, three of them lighting cigarettes and inhaling deeply as though they have all the time in the world and nothing to worry about.

I just love ruining these assholes' day.

"Where are Andrei and his men?" one asks, looking around the property.

"Probably inside testing the merchandise, the horny bastard," another replies and they all bark out a callous chuckle.

It makes me fucking sick to my stomach.

"I'll go find him," one of the nonsmoking men offers, and two of the others follow him to the door that leads to the basement.

"On my word," Liam whispers into the comms.

The pounding footsteps of the men coming down the stairs can be heard from where Liam, Sawyer, and I wait in the office. Sawyer closes his laptop and quickly shoves it under the desk before the two of us move to stand against the wall on the other side of the doorway opposite Liam.

"Andrei, get off the girl and come out here," one of the men calls into the cavernous basement. The three men snicker and the adrenaline flowing through me kicks up a notch. I'll be happy to see these sick fucks dead at my feet.

Two sharp knocks sound at the door before it opens. "Andrei?"

Liam steps from the other side of the doorway with his gun raised. "Nope." He fires his weapon before the man has time to blink. "Now," he says into the comms and gunshots explode from outside.

The two other men who are inside the basement begin firing into the small office, causing pieces of wood to splinter and fly off from their wild shots before we hear footsteps pounding back up the stairs.

"Not today, motherfucker," Sawyer growls and stalks out of the office with me right behind him. We step in front of the stairwell and fire. Seconds later, a dead body rolls back toward us, landing at the bottom of the stairs with a bullet in his head and several in his back. I rush up the stairs and find the other man crumpled and unconscious against the wall. After kicking the gun he holds loosely in his grip, I check for a pulse.

"He's still alive," I call to Liam.

"Keep him that way for now," is Liam's answer.

Grabbing the man by the collar, I drag him down the stairs before dropping him on the cold basement floor.

"Hendrix. Abel. What do you have?"

"All dead," Hendrix answers.

Liam nods, then turns to Sawyer. "Keep watch on the cameras. I doubt anyone followed, but we can't be too careful."

Sawyer holsters his 9mm before returning to the

office. "Can someone remove the corpse? He's starting to freak me out," he calls from inside.

Liam shakes his head and chuckles. "Like you've never seen a dead body before," he mumbles under his breath as the other two men reach the bottom of the stairs.

"You know how Princess is," Abel teases.

"I can hear all of you," Sawyer says through the comms we still have in our ears.

"I know," Liam replies.

"What about this guy?" I kick the leg of the nearly dead man who has a bullet wound in his shoulder, arm, and stomach.

"I'm going to see if we can get some answers." Liam looks at Abel. "Grab the bag from the truck."

Abel's hurried footsteps have him returning with a medic bag in less than thirty seconds.

"You'd better hurry," I tell Liam as he opens the bag and pulls out a syringe and a vial filled with liquid.

Abel carries out a chair from the office while Hendrix finds an old extension cord from a darkened corner of the basement. After they have the asshole tied in a chair in the middle of the room, Liam plunges the syringe into the man's neck. His eyes pop open and he struggles for a moment, his wild eyes scanning the four of us standing in front of him.

"You're all fucking dead," he spits out.

Liam chuckles, completely nonplussed by the man's threats. "If I had a nickel for every time some asshole tied to a chair said that to me, I'd be a hell of a lot richer than I already am." Hendrix and Abel let out a huff of laughter as Liam stands in front of the man, pulling a mean-looking hunting knife from his belt. "Really, the only question is how painfully you want to die. I have plenty of shit I can pump in your veins to keep you alive and in excruciating pain, or you can answer my questions and I'll put a bullet in your head and end it quickly. Your choice."

"Fuck you," the dumbass answers with his chin tipped high in a show of absolutely ridiculous bravado.

"That's what I thought you'd say," Liam says with a gleam of excitement in his eyes. "Let's begin, shall we?"

"Well, this certainly isn't the day I had planned when I opened my eyes yesterday," Liam says, taking a long drag from his cigarette.

"Those things will kill you." I tilt my head toward the cigarette he has at his lips once again.

Liam's eyes are full of mirth as he throws the cigarette to the ground and stomps it out with his foot.

"What did you find out?" I ask while he leans back against the truck we're standing next to.

"Not much. He doesn't work with a buyer directly. More like the buyer for the buyer for the buyer. Seems Petrov has made quite a name for himself in the industry for having some of the most beautiful women.

You have to be rich as fuck to go through that many channels."

My mind wanders to the girls who we found in cages when we arrived. That sick piece of shit was going to sell off his own daughter to some unknown man that would likely have her locked away halfway across the world. His own flesh and blood. I can't wait until we catch up to him just so I can spit on his grave.

"So you aren't any closer to where you were in finding out who is buying these girls?"

"It's not always about getting closer to the buyers. Sometimes it's simply about saving women and putting a few of those slimy arseholes to ground. If we can get information, great. But nothing we do is going to get rid of every single human trafficking ring on the planet. The best I hope for is putting a dent in the operations by taking out one outfit at a time."

Looking around the property, I ponder what he's saying. We saved nine women today, including Gemma, Eoghan's girlfriend and Alessia's best friend. I didn't come with the intention of saving anyone other than her, but when I saw the helpless women who were dirty and scared for their lives in that dank room being held in cages, I was glad as fuck we were all there. Those women had experienced horrors that no one should have to face, and God only knows what would have happened to them had we not shown up. That idea makes me understand Liam's point of view. Even if you aren't taking out the heads of these operations, you're saving girls from a fate worse than death. It may not seem like much of a win to some, but to the women they rescue, it's everything.

"He did have an interesting tidbit of information. Said they were transporting the girls to New Orleans. Some Italian guy named Massimo had a crew there waiting for them. Know anyone by that name?"

Only one comes to mind, and it's rumored he still has connections to Petrov. In fact, we know his dead son had ties to another asshole we took out a few months ago who was making some serious money in sex trafficking.

"Could be Massimo Farina. His son worked with Carlo Cataldi, who was also working with Petrov to take control of Boston back from us. There were rumors that Carlo was making money from the sale of women, but we didn't have any proof until Ozzy and his woman were kidnapped."

Nearly a year ago, Finn got a call from his cousin telling us that something was going down at one of the Cataldi warehouses. It had to do with the president of the MC we work with and his woman who had just won a case that put Carlo's father away for life. We called the VP of the Black Roses and busted into the warehouse before Carlo could enact whatever sick plan he had for the couple. That was the confirmation we needed that Carlo was involved in the skin trade and the first time I had a hand in saving a woman from it.

"Your outfit has some business ties to New Orleans,

no?" Liam asks, his tone all too casual.

"We do, though I'm not entirely sure how you know that."

"You'd be surprised what I know." The smirk on his face tells me it's a lot, but if I know anything about Liam Ashcroft it's that he would never use the information he has against various criminal organizations unless he has a reason to. "Though I don't know much about the Farinas. For instance, I'd never heard the name connected to trafficking until today."

The Farina family has control of everything in Massachusetts, from Springfield to New York. If Massimo Farina has been dealing in human trafficking like the dead man in the basement suggested, then his days of having that power are numbered. There are few things the Monaghans refuse to tolerate from any family in Massachusetts, and at the top of that list is selling women. The Cataldis already tried to dip their toes in that business and were handled accordingly—meaning they were wiped from the planet and their former capos now answer to Finn.

"Neither have I," I reply. "If I had to make a guess, it sounds like they're picking up where Carlo left off."

"Like I said, we don't always get the big fish, but I think if we work together, we could fry the fuck out of that one. You have a long-standing relationship with people in New Orleans, specifically at the ports, which I don't. If they're moving women in and out of there, those relationships could come in handy."

I nod in agreement while I consider what he's saying, still surprised that he has that information. Though, I probably shouldn't be. "You want our help in taking out Farina's operation?"

Liam shrugs. "I mean, I think you and your boss would be inclined, considering he's in your backyard."

Looking around the wooded area and at the house—which will be charred wood and nails in a matter of minutes if the amount of C-4 that the others are rigging up is any indication—I consider his proposal. Of course, I'll need to loop Finn in on Liam's plans, but he's always trusted my judgment when I've been in the position of making a deal here and there without getting his permission prior.

I turn back to Liam, needing to make a couple things perfectly clear before I decide on anything. "If we agree to this, we aren't turning them over to the authorities. In our world, we take out our own trash."

Though Liam skirts the letter of the law when he sees fit, he has connections to every alphabet agency across the globe. The last thing I'll ever be is a rat, and I want Liam to know exactly where my boundaries are.

The smirk he's perpetually wearing kicks up a few notches. "This operation is completely off the books."

I reach out my hand and he grabs it. "Then we're in business."

# CHAPTER TWO

## CILLIAN

"OKAY, KEEP ME UPDATED."

I slip my phone back into my pocket as I look over the muddy waters of the Mississippi River. My work as Finn Monaghan's lieutenant is never done. I decided to make some improvements to the security measures at the casino. Not that what we have isn't top notch, but with the issues recently with the Russians from New York and the Italian families in Massachusetts, there were a few areas I could see that would benefit from small improvements. Especially because I'm not on-site as much as I've been in years past.

I went to Finn about a month ago and told him about the offer Liam Ashcroft made me. And that I'd accepted without consulting him first. The thought didn't cross my mind that he may have a problem with it until after I'd agreed with Liam. But when I watched that house of horrors burn to the ground, I knew then and there that I was willing to do whatever I could to help Liam with his work, even without the backing of the Monaghan organization, which is a first. I've been loyal to the family since I met Cormac Monaghan years ago. Hell, they *are* my family, but there was no way I was going to pass up the opportunity for that rush I got taking out those assholes in New York. When I went to Finn with the agreement I'd made, he saw the fire in my eyes when I told him that I was almost certain Farina was dealing in humans, and he backed me on my decision immediately.

It was exhilarating to be part of Liam's team, if only for that one operation, and incredibly satisfying when we put bullets in the men who came to that dingy little house to buy girls. There aren't many lines I'm not willing to cross, but sex trafficking is a nasty business and Liam is making some headway against those who profit from it. And I wanted in. More than that, I *needed* in. Needed to do something that wasn't centered around gaining more power but was instead focused on stripping power from those who used innocent women for their sick proclivities.

"Hey, Cillian." I turn to see one of our contacts at Port NOLA make his way over to me.

The Monaghan organization used this port often before we had control over the Port of Boston, thanks to Finn's marriage to Alessia Amatto, whose father is head of one of the Italian Mafia families in Massachusetts. Their marriage gave us the power we needed to squeeze out the Cataldis and take over illegal operations in and out of that port. We had a good little setup here in New Orleans, even though we rarely use it anymore. But it seems other people do for nefarious reasons, which is what brings me here.

"Sampson, good to see you," I say, offering my hand to the port escort who we've had on our payroll for years. "How are the kids?"

His smile beams like it does any time I ask after his family. "Good, good. We have another one on the way. Due in about a month."

"Wow, congratulations. I had no idea."

"Yeah, I don't see you much down here anymore. What brings you today?"

"Need some information and someone to keep an eye on a few things for me."

"Well, I've got two of 'em that work pretty well. What am I looking for?"

"Italians. Specifically, anyone throwing around the name Massimo Farina."

From the cautious digging Liam has done since the day at the Petrov property, it seems I was right—Massimo Farina has taken up where Carlo Cataldi left off. Though human trafficking isn't his main source of income, it doesn't mean he hasn't started building a reputation, especially since Viktor Petrov was killed. It left a void on the East Coast, and Farina seems to be trying to fill it.

"Shouldn't be too hard. You East Coast boys tend to wear suits like a second skin, even in the summer."

A chuckle rumbles in my chest as he eyes the dark-gray suit I'm donning. He's right. It's rare I leave the house in anything but, and the Italians from Farina's outfit are no different.

"Thanks, Sampson. If you see anyone or hear of anything, give me a call." I pull a money clip from my pocket and peel off a few hundred-dollar bills, handing them to the man in front of me. "For the baby."

Sampson smiles and slides the money into his pocket. "You in town for a couple days?"

"Nah, not this trip. I have to get back to Boston."

"Anyone ever tell you that you work too hard? You need to enjoy life. You're in the Big Easy. *Laissez les bons temps rouler.*"

"I may have heard it a time or two." I shrug and offer him my hand. Sampson grabs it and shakes his head, offering me a rueful grin.

"Why do I feel like I'm talking to a brick wall?"

"Because you're a smart man," I reply, returning his smile

Sampson clicks his tongue before waving his hand in my direction. "Don't go blowing smoke up my ass now."

One thing I appreciate about Sampson is the casual attitude he's always had with me. Most men are on their toes in my presence, seeing as I'm the right hand of the head of the Irish mob, but not Sampson. He's an old street kid like me, except he found himself a woman and went *mostly* straight before I met him. But like recognizes like. There's respect among thieves, even if he makes his money with hard work now.

Well, most of the time.

"I gotta head in. You take care. Maybe have a night on the town, and see what New Orleans has to offer other than a smelly port on the Mississippi." He runs his gaze over me once more. "Maybe even change out of that suit."

I can't help but laugh at that. "I'll talk to you soon, Sampson."

When I get into my car and turn the air conditioner on full blast in an attempt to cool off from the sweltering Louisiana heat, the last inclination I have is to go back to my hotel room. My flight doesn't leave until morning, and there isn't anywhere else I need to be tonight. Usually I'd head to my hotel, order room service, and treat myself to a few whiskeys in the quiet of my room. It's not often I have an evening free, and when I do, I tend to enjoy my own company rather than be out in the bustling city streets. But Sampson's advice echoes in my ear as I hit Finn's contact information and the ringing sounds through the speakers of my rental car.

"Cillian. What's going on?" Finn answers.

"Just leaving my meeting with our guy at the dock. Says he'll keep an eye out."

"And the security upgrades?"

"Ronin is overseeing everything."

I've spent the last few years with Ronin under my wing, teaching him the ins and outs of our security protocols. Some may say I'm a control freak, but there's only one way to make sure a job gets done right, and that's by doing it yourself. The fact that I'm willing to hand some of the tasks over to Ronin says a lot to Finn about how much I trust him to handle everything the way I would. It hasn't been a particularly easy transition for me, but it's the only way I can keep all the plates spinning if I want to work with Liam.

"Are you breathing down his neck to make sure he does it exactly as you would?" Finn chuckles. "I can practically hear you rolling your eyes."

He isn't wrong. Finn has always appreciated my commitment and dedication to what I do for the Monaghan organization. It's changed throughout the years since he took over for his father. He's also told me, on more than one occasion, that I don't need to actually do everything myself. He was more than happy to have Ronin take over some of my responsibilities, especially with things at the casino. It's the one part of my business where I allow someone else to handle certain aspects—but I've never let anyone else take charge of it.

"Ronin's a good kid. He knows what's expected from him and doesn't deviate from his instruction, so no, I don't have to breathe down his neck."

"That's high praise coming from you."

"Fuck off," I say with no actual heat behind my words. Finn is the first to point out my workaholic tendencies—and the first to give me shit about them.

"Where are you off to now? Back to your hotel for another lonely night in?" There's that damn laugh again.

"Nope. I ordered three hookers and a bunch of blow on your dime, so I'm going to be partying all night in the suite you're also paying for."

Finn snorts out a laugh. "If it were anyone else, I might believe them. But all I hear is you're going to get room service, a glass of whiskey, and read some financial reports before going to sleep at ten p.m. on the dot."

"Again, fuck off."

"Why don't you at least go have dinner somewhere other than your room? Maybe wander into a bar and have a nightcap there instead of holing up like you usually do. Even my eighty-seven-year-old grandfather had more of a life than you do; God rest his soul."

Why is everyone so invested in what I do with my personal time today?

"Jesus, will it get you off my back?"

"I'd be even happier if you got some leggy brunette on hers. When was the last time you had an actual date, or even a casual fuck, for that matter?"

"When did me not spending the night alone in my room turn into a dissection of my sex life?"

"Or lack thereof."

"Don't act like you know what I do when you're not around."

"I don't have to. You're either working or sleeping. How about you go out and act younger than the senior citizen you're pretending to be half the time."

Is he wrong about my dating life? Well, no. I've always taken my role in the family seriously, and that has left little room for meeting a woman, let alone dating one. But it's not like I'm a monk who took a vow of celibacy for Chrissake. There have been a few women in the last couple years who I've had arrangements with, but it's never anything more than scratching the itch when it arises, and it certainly isn't something I've felt the need to broadcast. They all knew what the score was and were perfectly happy keeping emotional entanglements out of the equation.

"How would your wife feel if you were trying to get your friend to go out and get laid?"

"Trust me," Finn laughs out. "Alessia thinks you need to let loose as much as the rest of us."

"Is marriage already so boring for you that you two discuss my sex life?"

"Don't be an idiot. You've met my wife. You think she doesn't keep me on my toes?"

"Then why are you two sitting around talking about me?"

"Fuck off."

I let out a snickering chuckle as I pull up to the front of my hotel. "Not so fun when the shoe's on the other foot, is it?"

"Jesus, you're a twat."

"I know you are, but what am I?"

"Oh, I see the conversation has reached its peak of maturity," Finn gripes.

"Hey, you started it." Egging him on is too much fun at this point to stop.

"Case in point. Speaking of boring wives,"—I hear Alessia shout something about his boring wife kicking his ass in the background—"I'm taking my beautiful, sexy and the epitome of *not* boring wife out for dinner."

"Okay. The hookers are going to be here soon, so I should probably shower."

"Yeah, you have fun with those financial reports."

We hang up, and I hand the valet the keys to my luxury rental before walking from the car to the air-conditioned lobby of my hotel. When I get into my room, I look around the empty space, and suddenly the idea of staying in all night doesn't seem as appealing as it did when I left Port NOLA. The heat and humidity of the city cling to me, making my suit feel less like the high-end bespoke fabric it is and more like one of those rubber getups people wear to work out in.

Cormac Monaghan always said the suit makes the man. He would tell us that when we walked into a meeting, we'd better be dressed to kill—and he wasn't referring to the pieces we carried under our jackets. No one would respect some punk kid who walked into a meeting in jeans and any old T-shirt. The first thing I did when I started making some real money within the organization was schedule an appointment with his tailor and have a custom wardrobe made. No one blinked an eye at the tattoos that peeked out from the sleeves of my jacket or the scars that lined my knuckles when I became Finn's lieutenant after Cormac retired as boss. When we walked into a room to do business, they knew I deserved the respect my position entitled me to.

After peeling the layers from my body and hanging the suit in the small wardrobe in my room, I step into a cool shower and start to relax. It feels good to wash the layer of sticky moisture from my body. Boston can be hot and humid in the summer, but it's got nothing on New Orleans. Wrapping a towel around my waist, I step out of the cool shower and head into the bedroom, picking up a room service menu and immediately tossing it back on the desk.

Fucking Sampson and Finn are getting into my head.

Sitting on the edge of my bed in a towel, I take in the room before lying backward and letting out a long sigh. Over the last few years, I've been laser-focused on my job within the Monaghan organization. Don't get me wrong...I'm as loyal to that family as the day I was when I met Cormac Monaghan—back when I was fourteen. But something is missing in my life. If I'm honest with myself, something has been missing for quite some time. I'm not naive enough to think it's the love of a good woman—or a slightly homicidal one like Finn has found—that I'm missing. That's never been a driving force for me, much to the dismay of Maeve Monaghan, Finn's mother. But when I helped save those women from being sold and played a part in taking out their buyers, something inside of me was unlocked. A part of me wants to have more—*make* more—of an impact. Killing those responsible for the nightmares that too many women face filled that void. Despite knowing I want a change, I haven't made one, and that feeling of being bored with the mundane is rearing its head again.

Fuck it. What can letting loose for one night hurt? Maybe a nice dinner and a bar with some music is what I need to stave off this growing feeling of discontent.

Getting up from the bed, I pull another suit from my garment bag and dress in gray slacks and a button-down, dark-blue shirt. I strap a small revolver to my ankle, having learned long ago that it's better to be safe than sorry. I'm about to throw a jacket over my shoulders but think twice about the stifling humidity of the city and decide to go without.

Tonight, I'm not on business. I'm simply Cillian Doyle, a man with a night to kill in New Orleans.

When the valet brought my car around, I asked him for recommendations for a good restaurant with authentic New Orleans cuisine and a bar that was off Bourbon Street with some live music. I know the street is a staple in the city, but I'd rather not be running into drunk tourists while I'm out. He put the locations in the car's navigation system and sent me on my way.

As I finish the last of my crawfish étouffée on the patio dining area of the restaurant the valet recommended, the waiter comes over, and I decide...fuck it and order a banana Foster and a glass of whiskey. When in Rome, and all that. He clears my plate, and I lean back in my chair, enjoying the brass band playing on the corner across the street. Sampson was right. There's much more to New Orleans than a port and my hotel room. Enjoying a night out is rarely a luxury I indulge in, but so far, I'm glad I allowed myself to be goaded into it.

The bar that the valet suggested is within walking distance of the restaurant, so after I finish the decadent dessert and my whiskey, I decide to take a stroll along the street. Though we're close to Bourbon Street, there is definitely a different feel here. The citrusy scent of sweet olive bushes surrounds me instead of the cloying stench of piss and vomit that many people associate with the famous street only a block or two away.

I easily find the bar and dip inside into the open space. Instruments are arranged near the small stage set up on the patio, but no one is playing, so the band must be on a break. The bar has a darker, more sophisticated feel with its brick walls and low ambient lighting, but splashes of colorful paintings in bright reds, greens, blues, and yellows hang throughout the space. As I slide onto a stool, an older man walks over with a friendly smile on his face. Maybe there's something to this whole Southern hospitality thing. It's much different than the gruff attitude of the bartenders in Boston, that's for sure.

I order a whiskey and hand the man a couple bills before settling into my seat. Then, just because I feel like being a dick, I turn around so my back is facing the bar and take a selfie with a one-finger salute and send it to Finn.

**Me:** *See, asshole. I left my hotel room.*

He replies a few seconds later.

**Finn:** So *the hookers were a no-show, or you just couldn't keep up?*

**Me:** *Fuck off.*

When I lay my phone on the bar, a blonde sits one seat down from me and lets out an irritated sigh before the bartender takes her order.

"I'll have a daiquiri, please—strawberry, if you don't mind," she says in a breathy Southern accent. She glances at me and smiles, but it doesn't quite reach her eyes. I hate seeing a woman in a bar look upset, and there's something about her green eyes that say she's had a shit night and could use someone doing something nice for her.

"I'll take care of it," I say as the girl reaches for her purse.

"Oh, you don't have to do that. I'm quite capable of paying for my own drinks."

"Please, allow me." I pull my wallet from my pocket and hand the bartender a few more bills when he returns with her fruity concoction.

"Thank you..."

"Cillian."

"Thank you, Cillian. It's been an absolute hellish night, and it's nice to meet a gentleman. Lord knows they're in short supply."

"Sounds like there's a story there." I'm not one to talk to random women in a bar. That was for a younger and less jaded version of myself that I grew out of years ago. But I figure, fuck it, why not? Again, I'm running with the whole *when in Rome* philosophy.

"Just your typical 'come to New Orleans on a girls' trip, meet a guy who wants to take you to dinner, go to dinner, guy thinks him paying for said dinner means he can grope you under the table, you storm off, then none of your friends answer their damn phones so you can meet up and salvage the rest of your evening.'" She pauses for a moment before finishing with, "Or, you know, at least tell them you aren't dead in a ditch somewhere."

My eyes widen as she inhales a much-needed breath after that tirade before she blows it out and swipes her blonde bangs from her mossy-green eyes.

"Well, the drink comes without any expectations, and I'll keep my hands to myself."

"See," she says, pointing at me. "Gentleman."

"If something as simple as not pawing you after paying for your drink makes me a gentleman, I hate to think about the guys you usually meet. That's bare minimum in my book."

"You'd be surprised," she says, nearly under her breath. "I'm Charity." She holds out a dainty hand, and I take it in my much larger one.

Charity looks down at our clasped hands and notices

the ink on my wrist peeking out of the long-sleeved shirt I'm wearing. "Tattoos? Why, Cillian, maybe I was wrong about the gentleman thing. Unless you really are one with a bad-boy streak."

She's obviously flirting with me but the little giggle is endearing, and what can I say? It's been a while since I've been in a town where no one knows who I am, sitting in a bar with a sweet Southern blonde. Well, the last part has never happened.

"I'm just a businessman here until tomorrow who didn't want to sit in my room. The tattoos are from a life lived that's long since passed." If three hours is long.

"What do you do?" she asks before slipping the black straw in her mouth and taking a healthy sip of her drink.

"Vacuum salesman."

Charity nearly chokes on her drink when she laughs and playfully swats my arm. "Liar."

My smile widens and I raise my glass to my lips before taking a swig of the Irish whiskey. "I'm in textiles. Was here for a meeting, but I head back tomorrow. You're on a girls' trip?"

"Yup. I start graduate school in January and decided to have some fun before it's all work and no play."

I can understand that.

"Where are you going to school?" I ask.

Just then, the band gets on the stage and begins their set. They aren't overwhelmingly loud, but Charity leans over the seat separating us so we're not having to yell over the jazz playing in the background.

"I'll be moving to California to attend Stanford." When she says the name of the school, her face lights up with pride—and she damn well should be proud of herself.

I let out a low whistle. "Impressive."

She smiles in that bashful way I imagine has been ingrained in her as a Southern woman.

"What about you?" she asks.

Though the music isn't deafening, it's still a challenge to have a conversation over the brass instruments.

"May I?" I ask, pointing at the empty seat between us.

Charity nods and I slide over. "I live in Michigan. Work for my father's company. We're securing a new contract in New Orleans, so I'm down here to dot all the *i*'s."

"Cold winters up there," she replies. "I don't think I could ever live in snow like that."

"I don't know. I'd take winters over this humidity any day."

Just then, her phone lights up with a text message notification. She grabs it from the bar top and lets out another little huff before looking at me. "That's one of the girls I'm on the trip with. I should go meet up with them." A sweet smile crosses her pink lips before she waves at the bartender.

"Yes, ma'am?" he asks and she beams.

"Would you happen to have a pen back there I could borrow for a quick minute?"

I don't know if it's the whiskey or the slow jazz, but I wish she weren't leaving so soon so I could hear that sweet Southern lilt just a little longer.

When the bartender hands her the pen, she grabs a napkin and writes down a phone number before handing it to me. "If you ever find yourself in California, give me a call."

I smile and take it as she stands. She turns to leave and steps wrong, causing her ankle to buckle. My hand reaches out to grab hold of her before she falls, but her purse drops from her shoulder, causing the contents to spill on the floor. We bend down at the same time to pick up the items and end up knocking our heads together.

"Ouch," she says, rubbing her forehead with an embarrassed giggle before I take one of her hands and she anchors her other on my hip for balance. "I'm so damn clumsy."

I hand over her purse with a grin. "Happens to the best of us."

Charity leans in and gives me a hug. "Thank you for being so sweet, Cillian. I wish we had more time to get to know each other."

When she releases me, I smile at her. "Take care, Charity."

With that, she walks to the front of the bar where the door is and turns, giving me a little wave. I'm not going to lie and say my mood hasn't turned a little melancholy with her departure as I signal to the bartender for another drink. When I reach into my pocket to pull out my wallet, I'm hit with the sudden realization that it isn't there. I look at the ground to see if it fell out of my pocket, but all I see is the checkered linoleum of the worn floor. I know I had it here. I paid for my drink, then Charity's dacq—

*Son of a bitch.*

She just fucking stole my wallet.

# CHAPTER THREE
## NOVA

T HE TRICK? STAY OFF Bourbon Street. Most people tend to be a bit more mindful of their belongings on the busy street, other than the drunk twentysomethings, but lifting from college-aged partiers isn't exactly going to net much profit. They're probably close to broke to begin with, and finding that out when you attempt to get cash back on a purchase draws too much uncomfortable attention from the tired cashiers. It's a real fucking letdown when you spend the night pickpocketing only to find out all the wallets you lifted are full of nothing but a few singles and useless plastic—not to mention there're cameras everywhere nowadays. It's not hard to track credit card purchases and get the police to make a call and look at the footage to find the thief. Most people will simply cancel their cards and dispute the charges with their bank, but it's still risky on my part.

That's why I hit up the places off Bourbon where the nicer restaurants are; it's a bit more low-key. The places that still get the tourists, but they're a bit older, carry cash, and on a good night, I can pick up several hundred dollars. Especially if I spot the single guys who look like they're here for a night out between meetings and whatnot. There are plenty of those.

The sweet Southern belle act has worked wonders the last few months. I'm either damn good at pretending to be an innocent woman who's had a bad run with assholes, or these men are as stupid as can be. Maybe a combination of both. Worked like a charm tonight, at least.

I'd already performed my song and dance three times before walking into the little jazz bar. Fortunately, my best friend Harper is off from her bartending job tonight, so she's been able to send me texts or call me to give me an excuse so I can make my exit. She's not the biggest fan of how I make my money, but working a regular nine-to-five or at the million restaurants and bars in the French Quarter isn't going to get me out of this town. Dreams cost money and mine is to someday live carefree on a beach with a little oceanside bar and a place to call my own. Something no one can ever take from me.

Walking into Geraldine's, the busy bar where Harper works, I hurriedly make my way to the bathroom at the back of the building. Her ex, Damon, is working tonight, but I make sure to blend into the crowd of women who look to be part of a bachelorette party so he doesn't spot me. At a glance, I look like any other run-of-the-mill blonde in a light summer dress and wedges, all dolled up for a night out. But Damon actually knows me, so he might recognize me, and I'd rather not see the judgmental stare he generally casts my way.

I head to the door marked *employees only* and unlock it with the key I copied from Harper. This is a great place to stop when I'm on this side of town, to change out of my getup and into my normal clothes. I've never been caught out on the street by a target or the cops, but if anyone were to suspect me, they'd be looking for a sweet-looking blonde in a cute summer dress. Not my usual fare.

First thing I do is take the wig off and let my long black hair fall to the middle of my back before brushing the strands into a manageable mess. The sweltering heat of New Orleans is stifling tonight, and the humidity is doing a number on my natural waves. There's a small set of lockers where employees can put their personal belongings. It's not uncommon for the girls to have a change of clothes or extra makeup stashed in here. I open the locker that Harper uses and pull out my clothes and makeup. The summer dress slides off my body and is quickly shoved into the bag. I pull on my favorite pair of distressed black jeans and the old band tank top I got from a guy I dated a couple of years ago. The relationship didn't last for more than a few weeks, but this top is pretty damn comfortable and makes my tits look fantastic. Pro tip, never date the drummer of an indie rock band. The intensity is great in the beginning, but it burns out just as fast.

After I swipe on a line of black liner and swap the

pale-pink lipstick for the bright red I usually wear, I'm ready to leave "Charity" behind me for the night. Maybe I'll grab a drink at one of the local bars where there's no chance of running into any of my marks from tonight. Though Geraldine's is a favorite, I'm not much for sticking around unless Harper's working. Damon likes to blame me for the demise of their relationship a couple months ago, but it was his sanctimonious attitude that ultimately had Harper walking away. I'm not saying anyone should lose their morals or anything, but he never missed an opportunity to talk bad about me and what I did to earn a living. He wasn't one to rat—this is New Orleans, after all, and no one is a hundred percent aboveboard—but he was always going on and on about how someday shit would catch up to me and he didn't want Harper caught in the crossfire. He'd tell her she was too good of a friend and that I took advantage.. What he seemed to forget is Harper and I are as close as sisters, and there isn't a damn thing he could say to make her turn her back on me. As for him? Yeah, not so much.

Since Damon hasn't come pounding on the door yet, I pull out the wallets I lifted from the crocheted boho bag I matched with my sundress. The first three have around two hundred dollars each inside. Not bad. When I open Cillian's wallet, it doesn't escape my attention that his driver's license was issued in Massachusetts—not Michigan. I also notice he doesn't have a single business card in his wallet. Shouldn't he carry around a couple cards at least? He also doesn't have a single business credit card. I have a strong suspicion the man does not deal in textiles. I'd expect at least one business credit card, especially if that's what he's in town for. I pull out the cash and count seven hundred dollars. Very nice. Serves the asshole right. He's probably got kids and a wife at home in Massachusetts or some shit, and he's down here for whatever business and was hoping to hook up with a stranger in a bar. I don't know, and I don't really care.

I put the crocheted bag in the locker with the rest of my "work" uniform and stuff the wallets in my black leather bag before zipping it closed with the plan to dump them a couple blocks from here.

I open the door right as Damon is about to use his key to enter.

"I've told you a million times, Nova, you can't use the employee bathroom just because your roommate works here. How did you get in anyways?"

"It was unlocked," I reply innocently.

"The hell it was."

I simply shrug and move past him to the bar that's thinned out since my entrance.

And that's when I spot him.

Cillian is sitting at the bar with a glass of brown liquor in front of him. His eyes meet mine from across the room, and I swear I see recognition in his gaze. That's impossible, though. The girl he met had blonde hair with bangs and looked completely different than

I do now. I quickly look away in an attempt to make the moment seem as though I'm simply looking for someone while simultaneously trying to keep my heart rate under control. Acting as though I don't see the person I'm not actually looking for, I make my way to the entrance of the bar after pulling my hair to the side and looking down at the blank screen of my phone in an attempt to hide my face from a side view as I pass Cillian. I'm almost to the door when a pair of black leather shoes comes into view. I stop and look up. Directly into the piercing bluish-gray gaze of the man I was trying to avoid.

"Hello, *Charity*," he drawls with an amused tilt to his lips.

"Charity?" I ask with confusion lacing my voice. "I'm sorry, I think you have the wrong person." My regular voice lacks the sweet Southern twang I use when I'm talking up a mark, but from the look on Cillian's face, I'm not fooling him. Doesn't mean I'm not going to try, though. "Excuse me." I try to step around him, but he moves to stand in front of me again.

"I suggest, if you don't want to cause a scene, you have a seat with me at the bar."

"I don't know who you're looking for, but it ain't me."

His grin widens, but his eyes hold some sort of dark intent and the two don't quite match but are a compelling combination nonetheless.

"Oh, I think it is," he says, pulling his phone from his pocket. "But have it your way."

"Who are you calling?"

"Who do you *think* I'm calling?"

Probably the fucking cops, if I had to guess.

"If I sit down, will you put your phone away?" I ask, holding his gaze.

The last thing I want is the cops showing up here and finding the wallets in my bag. It would be bad for me, seeing as I haven't spent a day in jail and hopefully never will, but it would majorly screw over Harper. I doubt her boss would be too keen on the fact that her best friend and roommate was arrested in his establishment. I look toward the door, thinking maybe I'll have a shot if I push past him and run. The quirk of his brow and slow shake of his head tells me not to even try.

Cillian is staring with his phone in his hand, waiting for my next move. I nod and turn toward the bar. This isn't a situation I've found myself in before, but probably should have prepared better for. The fact that Cillian recognized me has me wanting to know what the hell I did wrong or—and maybe more importantly—who the hell this guy is. Most people, men in particular, aren't that astute. I took him as any other guy off the street who saw a pretty face. Guess I fucked myself on that one.

I have a seat next to him as Damon returns from the back. "You staying, Nova?" he asks, looking between me and Cillian. I see the question in his eyes. I may not be his favorite person, but he's not going to allow anyone to harass a woman when he's behind the bar.

Needless to say, there have been plenty of times he's had to step in, considering this is New Orleans, and drunken, unwanted advances from tourists happen pretty regularly everywhere.

"What would you like to drink, *Nova*?" the man sitting next to me asks.

I shoot Cillian a side-eye glare and curse Damon in my head for using my real name.

"Whiskey seven. Thanks."

When Damon turns and walks down the bar a bit, I face Cillian, whose eyebrows are raised in surprise.

"What?"

"You like whiskey? That's a far cry from a strawberry daiquiri."

My lip curls in disgust. "I actually hate daiquiris."

"Why'd you order one earlier, then?"

Since I'm already busted, I figure, in for a penny, in for a pound. "Helps with the Southern belle act. Not many *genteel* ladies shoot whiskey. What do you want?"

"Well, my wallet would be a nice start," he replies, leaning back in his stool.

"I don't have it." That will be true—as soon as I leave.

"I don't believe you. You didn't ditch anything before you came in here."

"How would you know? And how did you find me, anyway?" There's no bite to my tone, more like curiosity.

Damon walks back over and sets the drink in front of me. When I take a sip, I'm feeling more like myself and less like the Southern belle I was playing when Cillian and I first met. It's so much better than that nasty strawberry concoction from earlier.

"Took me less than a minute to realize my wallet was gone. Then, less than a second to realize you're a pickpocket." He sips his whiskey with a self-satisfied smirk playing on his full lips.

"Most people wouldn't automatically jump to that conclusion. Especially some guy from Michigan here on business for Daddy's textile company." My head tilts to the side as a grin similar to his stretches across my face. *Textiles my ass.*

Cillian is staring at me with those piercing blue-gray eyes I found so intriguing the first time he locked onto me. They remind me of dark storm clouds before a natural disaster, which is fitting right about now. This entire conversation could turn into a major disaster at any moment, especially if he decides to call the cops.

"I'm not most people," he replies with a quirk of his brow. "When I walked out of the bar, I saw you about a block ahead of me. I followed you and watched you walk into this fine establishment." Cillian takes a distasteful look around at the neon beer signs lighting up the brick walls. It's old and a little run-down, but regulars don't come here for some sleek craft cocktail experience. It's a place for people to get away from all that Bourbon Street bullshit.

"At least they have a decent whiskey selection," he says, nodding toward the back bar, where hundreds of liquor bottles line the shelves, backed by a mirror running the length of the wall.

"Fun fact. Do you know why there's a mirror behind a bar?"

Cillian's lips quirk in a smile. "Enlighten me."

"So the bartender can keep an eye on everyone when his back is turned. Back in the Wild West days, bars were dangerous; they put a mirror up so bartenders wouldn't get caught unaware during a robbery or some shit."

The expression on Cillian's face is a cross between confusion and curiosity when I finish my explanation.

"What?" I ask.

"This little confrontation isn't going like I expected. Most thieves would be scared I'm going to call the cops. Many would have tried to run out of here."

"Well, I'm not most thieves," I say, parroting his words from earlier as I flutter my eyelashes in his direction. "And I have a feeling if you wanted me in trouble with the police, you would have called them before walking into this bar."

He hums his agreement before taking a sip of his whiskey.

"Why *didn't* you call the cops?"

"Where I come from, we don't use the police to handle these types of situations."

"They don't have police in Massachusetts?"

"I see you looked inside my wallet."

"I thought it was interesting that a guy from Michigan who works for his family's textile company would have a license for an address in Boston and not a single business credit card or business card for that matter."

"It could have been true." He sips his drink with a small shrug.

A huff of laughter falls from my lips. "In another life, maybe."

He smiles and looks down at the glass he's holding, swirling the ice cubes inside. "Yeah. In another life."

"Tell me about this one," I say, curious as to why he lied in the first place. There's a story to Cillian Doyle, and I'm finding myself very interested in hearing it.

I'm not sure how this conversation went from me being afraid he was going to have me arrested to wanting to get to know him, but here we are. And I'm having more fun tossing questions back and forth—which neither of us are really answering—than I've had in quite some time with any other man. There's something about the way Cillian carries himself. He's not particularly worried about the fact he was stolen from, though for some reason, I get the distinct impression that's not something that happens to him often. Call it a criminal's intuition or some shit, but I've always believed like recognizes like, and there's a certain unexplainable camaraderie I'm feeling right now. It's fucking weird if I'm being honest with myself.

"I live in Boston."

"I gathered that." I sip my whiskey 7 and let the vanilla and butterscotch notes dance over my tongue before swallowing. "You aren't really from there, though?"

"Why do you say that?"

"Most people would say I'm *from* Boston, not I *live* in Boston."

Cillian nods. "I'm from a little town in Minnesota, but we moved when I was a kid."

"Who's we?"

"My mom and my stepdad."

"You didn't have a good relationship with him?"

"Jesus, are you psychic or some shit?" Cillian's shoulders shake a bit with a laugh.

"Do you really believe in all that woo-woo shit?"

"Don't you?"

"Listen, I know I live in New Orleans but that doesn't mean I think the spirits talk to me or whatever."

"You said *live* not *from*."

"You're a quick study."

We stare at each other for a few moments, both of us wearing matching smiles before Damon comes over.

"You okay over here?" he asks, but neither of us glances his way, perfectly happy in this little bubble as we study each other.

"Are you okay?" Cillian asks me.

"Are you?"

His smile widens at my nonanswer. He's having just as much fun playing this game as I am.

"Okay..." Damon drawls out before walking away, and we both laugh.

I rest my arm on the bar and turn fully toward Cillian. "How did you guess I stole your wallet?" Like

I'd told him, that's not something most people would have caught on to so quickly—if at all. Who would have expected that from a sweet Southern girl after all?

"It was a gut feeling. You aren't the first thief I've met in my life, but you're definitely the prettiest."

"Why, Cillian," I say in the accent I'd used with him earlier. "Are you flirtin' with me?" My hand presses against my chest as my eyelids flutter rapidly.

"Maybe I am, Miss Charity."

I throw my head backward in laughter, and when I look back at him, he's wearing a wide smile.

"You hang out with many thieves in your real line of work?"

"On occasion," he replies.

"Now I'm really intrigued. Let me guess. You used to be a juvenile parole officer, disillusioned by the system. So you quit your job and became a teacher in the inner city, hoping you could influence disenfranchised youth and steer them away from a perilous life of crime."

"I think I've seen that movie."

"It was a pretty good one," I reply.

"I don't know about the perilous life of crime bit, though. I've done pretty well for myself, even if some would consider me a criminal."

"Who's some?"

"The cops, FBI, DEA. Pretty much any law-abiding citizen." He shrugs in that casual way that says he isn't the least bit concerned about what anyone thinks of him or what he does—not even the law.

"I had a feeling you weren't a straight arrow." If he thought that little tidbit would scare me off or shock me in some way, he's wrong. Besides, it's not like I have much room to talk. "So what's the real story? Jewel thief? Computer hacker? Mob boss?"

"Not the boss."

My eyes widen and his smile remains. "You're in the mob?" I ask, leaning toward him a bit.

Man, I really know how to pick 'em.

"My family runs Boston. The Monaghans."

"Never heard of them." I wave my hand and lean back in my seat, having too much fun poking at someone who is certainly a dangerous man. There is something fundamentally wrong with me, but at this moment, with this man, I don't care.

Cillian's smile doesn't fall as he shakes his head. "You know, if most people found out they stole from the lieutenant of the Monaghan family, they'd be falling over themselves with apologies and promises of recompense."

"You're the lieutenant in the mob?" I ask, widening my eyes with my mouth slightly agape.

"Does that change things a little?"

I flatten my expression. "No," I reply before taking another sip of my drink.

Cillian shakes his head—he seems to do that quite a bit in my presence. "Why doesn't that surprise me?"

"How does one become the right hand to the boss of the...what's the name of the family again?"

"The Monaghans."

"Ah, right. The Monaghans."

"You looking for a career change?"

"Oh, do you think I have what it takes?" I sit straighter in my chair and try my best at a very stern expression, mimicking the one Cillian wore when he saw me trying to escape Geraldine's.

He outright laughs in my face, and I shoot him a withering look.

"I think you'd make a good secret weapon in negotiations," he says.

"Because I'm so intimidating, right?"

"Because you possess the fine skill of talking circles around people, and you're charming as hell. They wouldn't know what hit them."

I tilt my head to the side and sip my cocktail. "I think you *are* flirting with me."

"You should consider practicing law. Here I was, walking into a bar, ready to put the fear of God in you, and instead you have me buying you a drink and having what has strangely turned into one of the most entertaining evenings I've had in a long while."

I arch my brow. "You haven't bought me anything yet."

"Yes, well there is still the matter of you having my wallet."

"Drinks are on me then," I reply, smiling as I clink my glass to his. "But really, how did you find yourself in that line of work?"

"I pickpocketed the wrong guy. Or the right one,

depending on how you look at it."

"I knew you were a kindred spirit," I say, smacking him in the arm. Cillian looks at where I grazed him with my hand then back to me, raising one eyebrow. I shrug like I smack lieutenants for some crime family in Boston every day of the week before leaning in close to his ear and whispering, "You think you still got it?"

When he turns his head slightly toward me, the scent of whiskey and something else distinctly Cillian—bergamot and cedar, perhaps—fills my nose.

"What do you have in mind?" he asks, his breath floating over my lips.

"We could have a little fun, make a little cash," I shrug and lean back, finding the closeness to be sensory overload.

Our gazes hold as he clearly considers my proposal. I've known this guy all of ten minutes, and I can almost see the wheels turning behind his stormy eyes. Without knowing much about him, I get the distinct impression that he doesn't let loose and have fun very often. It's a good thing he met me tonight, then.

Cillian grabs his drink and finishes it in three long gulps. I don't watch the way his Adam's apple bobs with each swallow or the way his tattoos wrap around his forearm as he holds the glass to his lips. Nope. Not at all.

He sets the glass on the wooden bar with a thump and turns to me. "Show me what you have in mind."

# Chapter Four
## Nova

I STAND AND GRAB my bag from the back of my chair, pulling out a twenty for our drinks and sliding it under my glass.

When Cillian stands, he holds his hand out expectedly. "My wallet?"

"Oh, right." I grab it and slide it into his waiting palm, then pull the wad of cash from my bag. Leaning under the bar, I begin counting the bills—keeping it hidden so no one can see what I'm doing unless they're standing as close as Cillian.

When I try to hand him the cash I lifted from his wallet, he shakes his head. "Keep it. You earned it."

Not needing to be told twice, I shrug and shove it back into my purse before grabbing his hand, leading him out of the bar.

We walk the few blocks to Bourbon Street. Though these aren't my usual stomping grounds, I don't want to have an unfair advantage over Cillian for what I have planned. It sounds like it's been awhile since he lifted anything, so I figure the drunk tourists here will put us on even footing—even if we won't make much.

Standing on the corner, I turn to him and take in the amused expression on his face.

I lean in and wrap my arms around his neck so it looks to anyone like we're sharing a lover's embrace. Without missing a beat, his arms wrap around my middle, and he pulls me firmly against his chest.

"I'm not sure what you're planning, but I'm not hating it," he says, looking down at me with a smirk that would probably melt the panties off most girls.

I rise up on my toes so my mouth is against his ear. "You're going to walk to the end of the block behind me, and I'm going to walk to the end of the other block. We'll meet right over there." I tip my head down the street from the corner we're standing on. "Whoever has the most wallets wins."

Pulling back, I look into his eyes and catch the gleam of excitement in them.

"What does the winner get?"

"Bragging rights." My smile stretches from ear to ear as I wait for him to answer.

His answer comes in the soft brush of his lips against mine. "I'll see you in a couple minutes," he says, then pulls away.

"Don't think that's going to make me go all gooey and mess up my concentration."

"I would never." His hand covers his heart, and he looks at me with mock offense.

I roll my eyes. "See you at the finish line," I say, heading down the street and grabbing an empty daiquiri glass from the patio of a bar I pass, playing the part of a drunk tourist.

When I get to the corner of my street, I stand for a couple moments and let the crowd file past me before making my way back toward where Cillian and I parted ways.

"Whoops, sorry about that," I say, bumping into a middle-aged man walking in the opposite direction, sliding his wallet from his pocket before discreetly dropping it into my bag. Moving past him, I'm behind a group of college-aged girls, all with tall daiquiri glasses in their hands as they laugh and walk to their next destination. I smoothly slide a wallet out of the bag of the girl on the end, and she's none the wiser. I repeat the "drunk bump" a few more times before reaching the corner and turning toward the end of the street I told Cillian to meet me on. Usually, I wouldn't risk so many lifts in such a short amount of time, but it's late, and most of the people out on Bourbon are a few steps past drunk or well on their way.

As I hurry down the quieter street, I spot Cillian walking in the same direction on the other side. He sees me and smiles, waiting for a car to pass before jogging across to meet me. He grabs my hand and we dip into one of the many bars lining the sidewalk. There's a live band playing inside, but instead of jazz, it's an indie rock band with more of a reggae flare.

I lead us to the back of the building where the restrooms are and nod toward the men's while I head into the women's. Thankfully, no one is in here, and I close a stall door behind me before grabbing the wallets from my bag. Five total, but only three hundred in cash. Damn. This is why I stay away from Bourbon. No one carries cash anymore. Blowing out an annoyed breath, I open the stall and dump the wallets in the trash under a thick layer of paper towels. Since I still have the others from earlier—thank God those had more cash—I dump those as well. Even if someone were to find them tonight, there's no way to trace them back to me, and to be honest, there are probably stolen wallets scattered across several bars' trash throughout New Orleans. It never ceases to amaze me that people aren't more careful with their belongings in a city like this, but I suppose it would be a lot harder to make my living the way I do if they were.

Oh well. *C'est la vie.*

I open the door to find Cillian leaning against the wall in the hallway, waiting for me. I don't know why, but that brings a smile to my face. Most guys would have gone to the bar or found a seat somewhere, but there he stands.

"You making sure I don't skip out with my winnings?" I ask as the door closes behind me.

"Just making sure you're safe. I hear New Orleans can be dangerous. Never know what kind of criminals you could bump into."

"Yet I'm still alive and well." My arms stretch out on either side of me as I perform a little curtsy for him.

His eyes skim over my tight jeans, linger on my

exposed midriff, and then rise to meet my gaze, sending a shiver down my spine. Of course I would be attracted to him. He's like the ultimate bad boy or some shit.

"That you certainly are. Can I buy you a drink?" he asks with a tilt to his lips.

"God, no wonder you're bored and alone. Is that seriously how you try to pick up the ladies?"

Cillian barks out a laugh. "I'm not bored. Or alone at the moment."

"Well, of course you aren't. I'm here with you, and I'm a barrel of fun."

"You're definitely something, Nova."

"Why thank you," I reply, flashing him a bright smile.

"I'm not sure that was a compliment."

"*Pfft.* It definitely is." I tilt my head toward the bar. "Come on. I'll let you buy me a drink."

We head to the bar and have a seat in the high black vinyl chairs. Cillian orders us two Irish whiskeys—one on the rocks, the other with lemon-lime soda—and we toast before taking a hearty swig from our glasses.

"So, how did you do?" I ask, leaning toward him so he can hear me over the music.

"Six wallets," he says with a prideful smile on his face.

"Look at you, big man. Maybe you still got it after all."

"Unfortunately, it only got me about a hundred bucks and these." He pulls out two free VIP passes to a strip club and a couple condoms.

"The pitfalls of Bourbon Street. That's why I tend to stay away. Well, at least you have something to do tonight," I say, smiling and nodding to the passes.

Cillian looks at me with amusement. "I'm happy with my current company."

Those tingles I felt when I saw him waiting for me outside the bathroom are back in full force.

"What about you?" he asks.

"Five and a couple hundred."

"Looks like you won."

"The deal was who could lift the most. You beat me by one. It's not your fault your marks didn't have cash."

"Don't forget about the strip club passes."

"Yeah, I used to have a drawer full of those until I started hitting other streets." I laugh at the memory of when Harper and I first lived together and she went into the kitchen to look for a packet of sauce in a drawer and found those instead. She had a couple questions.

"Have you ever been caught lifting a wallet? Aside from me, that is," Cillian asks.

"Once. It was years ago, though. The guy must have felt a tug and looked down. I ran like my hair was on fire. That's when I started wearing wigs and things I could easily stuff in a trash can."

"Smart. The one time I got caught, I thought I was going to shit my pants when I realized who caught me. Turned out to be the best thing for me."

"Is this where you wax poetic about the guy who saved you from a life of crime? Because considering you work for a crime family, I think he failed."

Cillian huffs out a laugh and shakes his head. "No,

I pickpocketed my boss, or rather my old boss. He's retired, and now his son runs things."

"Holy shit! You lifted from a mob boss?"

"You lifted from a lieutenant. Most would have freaked the fuck out once they found that out."

"Yeah, but it was you. You don't intimidate me. Not like an actual boss would."

"I don't know whether or not I should be offended. In some circles, I'm considered quite dangerous if you land on my bad side."

He shoots me what I assume is his angry glare, but all it does is make me laugh. "Sorry," I wheeze out. "Yes, you're a very intimidating, scary man."

A rueful smile plays on Cillian's lips as he sips his whiskey. "What am I going to do with you?" he asks, shaking his head.

"You could dance with me," I answer as the band plays one of my favorite covers, adding their own flare.

"I'm not much for dancing, but go for it."

I shrug and stand from my seat, dancing my way into the crowd that's formed. My hips move to the deep bass of the song, and when I spin around, Cillian is watching me with his head slightly tilted and a smile tipping the corner of his mouth. I stay out on the floor for a few more songs before heading back to the bar. Instead of sitting, I stand next to Cillian, still swaying to the beat of the music while I sip my whiskey. Cillian's face rests in the palm of his hand as he gazes at me, that smile he's been wearing all night still on his face as he studies me.

"What?" I ask, leaning just a tad closer.

"I was just thinking this was not how I saw the night turning out. I thought I'd be having a nice dinner and a nightcap outside of my hotel rather than in my room like I normally do. Instead, I got stolen from, tracked down the thief, got roped into a pickpocketing challenge with said thief, and ended the night drinking with one of the most interesting, charming women I've ever met."

"You think I'm charming?" I ask, leaning even closer. There's attraction here, and though it's probably one of the worst ideas I've had in a long time, I can't stop imagining what his whiskey-slick lips would taste like.

Cillian's gaze holds mine as his finger traces up my arm. "And beautiful. I don't think I mentioned that."

"You didn't," I reply as he slowly leans toward me with desire sparking in his eyes.

Then his phone vibrates loudly on the bar in front of him, lighting up with the name *Ronin*.

"Shit," he breathes out and leans away from me. "Yeah," he answers and listens for a few moments before talking again. "My flight lands at ten in the morning. I'll be there for the install. Thanks for updating me." He hangs up and looks at me with an apologetic look instead of the one I much preferred from moments ago.

And the spell is broken.

"I should get you home. I need to get back to my hotel and get a couple hours of sleep before my flight."

"You're leaving in the morning?" I'm just going to

ignore the hint of disappointment that slipped out.

He nods. "Work."

"Ah, yes. The life of crime waits for no man."

He doesn't answer, instead, he stands from his seat and throws a couple twenties on the bar before handing me the rest of the cash in his hand.

"Uh-uh. You won that fair and square," I say, holding my hands up.

"I don't know about the fair and square part."

"To-may-to, to-mah-to."

"Come on, I'll give you a lift back to your place. Or do you have a car?"

"Nah, I cabbed it here tonight. I'm good."

"Come on, Nova, let me save you the cab fare. At least then I'll know you made it home safely."

I want to tell him that I make it home safely by myself every night, but I'm also not quite ready to say goodbye.

Instead of arguing, I nod and he smiles brightly, taking my hand and leading me out of the bar. We walk a few blocks back to where he parked and not once does he let go of my hand. Nothing is going to come from this night. We both know that. He has a life in Boston, and I have my reasons for never wanting to be anywhere near Massachusetts, but that's a conversation for another night that we won't have.

Cillian drives me the fifteen minutes it takes to get back to my little bungalow I rent with Harper and parks in front before getting out and walking to my side of the car to open the door for me.

"Such a gentleman," I say as I get out. Cillian doesn't move when I stand, which brings us chest to chest for a few moments. He looks like he wants to say something but thinks better of it and steps away, allowing me to walk past him.

"Unfortunately," he mumbles as we head up the sidewalk to my house.

We stand in front of my door, and all of a sudden, I'm feeling more awkward than I have the entire night. If Cillian were to bend down and kiss me like I can tell he wants to, I'd make his last few hours in New Orleans unforgettable. I'm no stranger to a one-night stand. If you have an itch, I say scratch it. But there's something about the man standing in front of me that says that particular itch won't be scratched so easily if he's involved. And I have a feeling he's thinking the same thing. What do you do when you meet someone who you have an instant chemistry with, but they live thousands of miles from you and everything you want?

"I guess this is good night," I say. "I'd say sorry about the whole trying to steal your wallet thing, but I'm not."

When Cillian smiles, it lights up his entire face, and I'll be damned if I don't wish I'd be able to see it tomorrow, and the next day, and the next...

"You should do that more. It's a good look on you," I say, pointing to his mouth.

"Night, Nova." He leans down and brushes his lips against my cheek before turning and heading down the stairs. When he gets to the bottom, he turns back around and jogs back up the cement steps.

"Hand me your phone real quick," he says, holding out his hand. When I place it in his, he asks for my password.

Before thinking better of it, I reply, "072599."

"I hope that isn't your birthday."

"Not mine."

Cillian types away and hands the phone back to me. "Give me a call if you ever need anything."

"Like what?" I can think of a few things I need at the moment, but that's not what he's offering.

*Jesus, get a grip, girl.*

"I don't know. If you find yourself in hot water or anything, I know people who would help you out. I just...I just want you to have a way to get a hold of me."

For the first time tonight, Cillian seems slightly flustered. And damn if I don't find this side of him adorable.

"Thanks, Cillian. Have a safe trip back to Boston."

He holds my stare for a beat before nodding and heading to his car. When he's pulled away and makes a left at the stop sign back to the French Quarter, I unlock my door and head inside. Harper is curled up on the couch with a book and looks about ready to head to bed.

"Good night?" she asks, setting her book on the coffee table and rubbing her tired eyes.

"Best one in a long while."

"Damon texted me all pissed off because you have a key to the employee bathroom."

I roll my eyes. "No, Damon said that because he

wanted a reason to text you."

Harper laughs and shakes her head. "Probably true. He also said you left with some guy he's never seen before."

I smile, remembering the way Cillian's eyes lit up when I told him my idea for our little game. "I did."

"That's all I get?"

I lean against the doorframe that separates the hallway from our small living room. "I met a guy, we hit it off, his life is in Boston, and mine's here. That's pretty much it." As I say the words, they almost feel like a lie. Sure, it's a true statement, but it's also so much more, which is fucking weird and unexpected and, unfortunately, never going to be anything more than tonight.

"You have that look on your face," Harper says, twirling the finger she's pointing in my direction. "It's been a while since I've seen it. Actually, I'm not sure I've ever seen this particular one."

It's been a long time since anyone gave me these kinds of butterflies. There have been a few guys since I started living with Harper, but they burned out as quickly as they started. Then, in the last year since...yeah, I haven't even had the slightest inclination to get involved with anyone.

"Nothing to do about it, I'm afraid." I shrug with an unfamiliar feeling of a missed opportunity settling in my gut. "I'm going to bed," I say and turn, walking down the hall to my bedroom at the end. "Night Harpy," I call.

"Night, Chevy," she replies, and I smile at the silly nicknames we've used since the first night we met.

Harper is like a sister to me. She's really the only family I have left after my brother took off to Massachusetts, where he's now buried in some small town outside of Boston. I have no interest in anything having to do with that place or the people who reside there. Well, save for one. We'll just have to chalk it up to one of those nights suspended in time. He has his life and I have mine, and that's all it's ever going to be.

# CHAPTER FIVE

## CILLIAN

I T'S BEEN A MONTH since I met Nova on my last trip to New Orleans. Since we don't use that port as much as we used to, I haven't needed to make my presence known. For the first time since we took over the Port of Boston, I find myself wishing I spent as much time at Port NOLA as I used to.

I'm still baffled by the fact I didn't simply take my wallet back from her and threaten her within an inch of her life for stealing from me. They would have been empty threats, but she wouldn't have known that. Or maybe she would have. There was something about her that I still can't put my finger on, but it was as though she saw the man I am. Instead of running scared like most would if they were to find out what I did for a living, she was intrigued—and anything but intimidated. We played cat and mouse with each other, having to glean answers from each other through the questions we volleyed back and forth. It was more fun than I'd had in longer than I can remember, and dammit if I wasn't completely enchanted with the little thief. Like so many things about her, that simple fact confounds me and would have me chasing my tail trying to figure it out. Normally, I detest unanswered questions and loose ends. Instead, I've accepted that I'll never understand how and why I was delightfully disjointed for an entire evening in her presence.

There was something about her that reminded me of who I used to be before I was taken under the wing of Cormac Monaghan. She possessed the same wild fierceness I had when I was a kid who was pickpocketing my way through Boston to make ends meet.

When I was fourteen, my mom was diagnosed with late-stage breast cancer. We'd moved from the small town in Minnesota years before, and though my mom had friends, she didn't have family around. Not that she had much back in Minnesota, save for a drunk brother-in-law and a nephew who turned out to be one of the worst men I'd ever known. Honestly, had one of the members of the Black Roses MC not taken care of him, I would have—blood or not.

After my stepdad took off after my mom's cancer diagnosis, we were left completely unprepared for what life would be like without his income. The lack of emotional support for me and my mom was never an issue. I'm pretty sure the man had one foot out the door for years before he finally left, but if we didn't figure out a way to make some money ASAP, we were going to be more fucked than we already were. Being that I was fourteen, there wasn't much I could do legally. Sure,

I had a couple part-time gigs washing dishes in a few restaurants under the table, but since it wasn't exactly on the up-and-up, I couldn't complain about the less than minimum wage I was making to the labor board.

My life of crime started innocently enough. I had a friend in school who used to brag about lifting wallets and how easy it was. We were hanging out one day, and I watched him do it. He pretended to trip over himself and fell into a distracted businessman in a nice suit. The guy was kind of a dick about it, and when my friend righted himself, he came away with the wallet from the man's pocket. He dared me to try, but I said hell no.

*At first.*

A couple weeks later we got the eviction notice on the small apartment we moved to when my stepdad bailed.

The next time I hung out with this particular friend, I peppered him with questions. *How did he pick his targets? How much did he usually get? How did he get rid of the wallets?* All the things I thought I needed to know to become a pro and fast. I studied every move he made when he showed me on another unassuming person on the street.

Then I tried.

And I got away with it.

There was a rush that came along with the theft. A rush and a sense of relief. Maybe I could actually bring home some real money to keep the roof over our heads. So I did it again. And again. After school, when I was supposed to be washing dishes, I was out lifting wallets.

I had nimble fingers and was quick on my feet. Being in downtown Boston, there were plenty of people on the street who were distracted enough from either being on their phones or hurrying from one place to another. It was easy pickings.

Until I lifted from a man who would ultimately change my life.

*The good thing about the Boston streets late on a Friday afternoon is everyone around is in a hurry to get home and start their weekend. Devon, my friend who started me on pickpocketing, had to stay late at school to make up some assignments he missed, so I'm on my own.*

*I usually stick to a five-block radius and switch those up every few days. I don't need shop owners getting used to my face—just in case. As I sip the soda I bought from a corner market, I spot two guys in nice suits making their way down the street. One is talking animatedly on the phone while the other listens intently. They step into a florist shop, and I spy the man who isn't on the phone pull his money clip from his pocket and pay for a bouquet before sliding his clip back in.*

*Bingo.*

*They walk out of the shop with one of the men still on the phone. I flip my ball cap around so it's covering my face and quickly begin walking toward them with my head down as though I'm in a hurry to get somewhere.*

*"Tell the asshole if he knows what's good for him, he'll have Cormac's money by end of day tomorrow," the guy says as I slam into the man carrying the flowers.*

"Shit, sorry." As I crash into him, I lift the money clip from his pocket, smashing the flowers between us.

"Watch where you're going," the man on the phone says to me, and I throw him the middle finger before hurrying off.

Fucking prick.

I'm about fifty feet from them before I hear the man with the flowers. "That punk stole my wallet."

Looking behind me, I see the angry faces of the two men in suits as they push their way through the busy sidewalk, making a beeline toward me.

Shit.

I take off in a sprint, sure that I'm faster than the two guys behind me. Without wasting the time to turn around, I bolt around a corner...and straight into a delivery man with a case of whiskey. How do I know it's whiskey? Because when I collide with the man, the case goes flying out of his hands as I'm launched backward, falling on my ass. The bottles crash to the ground, several smashing open, causing a rapidly growing puddle to soak into my jeans as I lie flat on my back, only cushioned from the fall by my backpack. Unfortunately, it doesn't stop the wind from being knocked straight the fuck out of me. The smell is familiar, and memories of my deadbeat stepdad with a rocks glass in his hand while sitting in an old recliner race through my mind.

The delivery driver is flat on his ass as well, stunned by the collision as I sit up and try to catch my breath.

"You okay, kid?" he asks, gingerly hauling himself from

the pavement.

He walks over to me, his boots crunching through the glass, and extends a hand to help me up. I grasp his forearm on autopilot—and because I don't want to cut my hands to shit on all the broken glass surrounding me.

"Grab him," one of the men I was running from calls as he turns the corner.

I try to rip my arm free from the delivery driver, but his grip is too strong.

"You little shit. Do you have any idea who you just stole from?" the asshole who told me to watch where I'm going spits at me.

Seconds later, the man with a now crushed bouquet of flowers turns the corner.

"You know this guy, Mr. Monaghan?"

"No, but I have a feeling we're going to become acquainted real fucking quick."

He walks over to me, the delivery driver's grip still holding tightly around my forearm, and rips the hat from my head.

"Jesus Christ, how old are you?"

My jaw is clenched tightly as I refuse to answer.

The man, Mr. Monaghan, simply shrugs. "Have it your way." He then turns toward the delivery man. "You okay, Mickey?"

Mickey nods. "I'll clean this up."

"Come on, you little punk," the other man grits out, grabbing my other arm and yanking me from Mickey.

"Let go of me, you prick." My attempt to wrestle my

arm away from this guy is futile as he drags me through the back door of a bar and into an office, away from the prying eyes of its customers.

"Don't be too rough on the boy, Sully," Mr. Monaghan states as Sully yanks me into a chair.

"Stay," Sully directs, pointing one of his meaty fingers at me.

Mr. Monaghan casually strolls around the wide oak desk I'm sitting at, then takes a seat in the high-back leather chair behind it. Sully takes a stand in front of the door, probably to ensure I don't make a run for it. I'm not small for fourteen by any stretch, but these guys each have at least fifty pounds on me, and by the looks of it, they aren't afraid of knocking a few skulls together. Since I'd rather those skulls don't include mine, I decide to sit quietly. My eyes flit around the small office while Mr. Monaghan studies me. It's not much to write home about, just a brick-walled space, two chairs in front of his desk, and a few pictures on the wall. There's a framed photo of a couple who look to be old as shit. Two men are holding shotguns in one picture, and there's another that has the man in the first picture with who I'm assuming are his wife and two sons. Below that one is a more recent photo of a couple. I recognize Mr. Monaghan with a woman and two boys—one who looks about my age.

"Do you know who I am?" Mr. Monaghan asks.

"Mr. Monaghan," I reply, shrugging my shoulder. What does he expect me to say?

"You're a disrespectful little punk," Sully hisses from his

*place in front of the door.*

I turn my head toward him. "Better than a glorified guard dog," I reply, indignation lacing my tone. They grabbed me and shoved me in this office, but I'm the one who's supposed to show respect? Yeah, fuck that.

"Sully, cut the kid some slack," Mr. Monaghan says before turning his attention back to me. "How old are you?"

I stay silent.

"Come on, kid, it's a simple question," Mr. Monaghan says.

"Fourteen."

"I have a son that age. You in school?"

I nod.

"Live around here?"

I nod again.

"Real talker," he chuckles to himself. "You got a name?"

"Yeah."

Mr. Monaghan rolls his eyes, but his lips twist as though he's trying to hide a smile. "You mind sharing it?"

I take a deep breath. The guy obviously isn't going to call the police on me. Thank God, because that's the last thing my mother needs to deal with.

"Cillian Doyle."

Mr. Monaghan smiles and sits back in his chair. "Well, Cillian Doyle. I'm Cormac Monaghan. Since that name doesn't seem to hold any weight with you, I'll tell you what I do. I run the Irish mob in Boston."

Fuck me. I just lifted the wallet of a goddamn mob boss.

He must see the look of surprise mixed with fear on my face, and he shakes his head.

"Don't worry, I'm not in the habit of cutting fingers off thieves. That was my grandfather's way of handling things." He nods toward the pictures on the wall I was just studying.

I don't know if he thinks that statement is supposed to make me feel more at ease because it most certainly does not.

"Why are you on my streets stealing wallets?"

"Why would anyone? I need the money."

"You trying to save up for some new video games or something?"

I wish my life were that simple. "My mom's sick and my dad took off." Maybe if I'm honest with him he'll cut me some slack, as in let me go with nothing more than a warning. One can hope.

Mr. Monaghan tenses his jaw a few times and shakes his head. "What kind of father would abandon his kid and wife like that?"

He doesn't seem to be asking me that question, more like he's disgusted with the entire idea of it, but I answer anyways. "To be fair, he was my stepdad. And a shitty one at that."

The look he gives me isn't pity, which I'm grateful for. It's thoughtful, as though he's trying to figure out what to do with me. I suppose being a mob boss means you have to make examples of people who steal from you, but I hope to God I met him on a day when he's feeling lenient as far as punishments go.

"You make much doing it? It's pretty risky to steal from people without eventually getting caught."

"That thought has crossed my mind several times in the last ten minutes, yeah," I reply.

"What's wrong with your mom?"

"Cancer."

Mr. Monaghan thins his lips and looks at one of the pictures on the wall. "My grandmother died of lung cancer," he says.

We sit in silence for a few moments as he looks at the picture of who I'm assuming is his grandmother before he sets his hands on the desk and folds his fingers together.

"Listen, the last thing you should be doing is some penny-ante shit that could get you pinched. So, I'm going to make you a deal. You're going to work for me."

My eyebrows shoot up my forehead in surprise. What the hell does the head of the Irish mob expect me to do?

"I'm no drug dealer." I've heard stories about other criminal organizations having high school kids selling drugs at their schools to their classmates. I'm not interested in that shit. I could care less if people like to party, but I'm not trying to get kids addicted to the shit that's floating around the streets.

"Good to know. But that has nothing to do with what I'm offering. You're going to be my personal messenger and collector. Run errands that I need, things like that."

"You want me to be your errand boy?"

"Better than a pickpocket who's liable to get arrested.

*Where would your mom be then?"*

*I think about that for a few moments. He's not wrong. What I do is risky, but it keeps a roof over our heads and food in our fridge. "How much you pay?"*

*"How much do you make?"*

*"Usually eight hundred a week." No, I don't, but it would be nice if I did.*

*"I'll double it," he says with a shrug.*

*"Just for running errands?" There's no way that's all he expects of me with that kind of paycheck.*

*"Yup. If you keep your nose clean and stop running around stealing wallets, we have a deal."*

*That kind of money is tempting as hell, and I'm not exactly in a position to turn it down. "Okay, Mr. Monaghan. You have a deal."*

*He stands from his chair and holds out his hand for me to shake. "Glad to have you on board, Cillian."*

I don't know why Cormac decided to take a chance on me all those years ago. Maybe he saw a little bit of himself in me like I did with Nova. Maybe I caught him on a good day, but from then on, I became a member of the Monaghan family, not just the organization. Once Maeve found out that my mom was sick, she took it upon herself to send me home with home-cooked meals anytime I had to stop by the house to meet with Cormac. Then, not too long after that, Finn and I started working together. Cormac wanted his son to learn the business from the ground up since he would be taking over at some point. We hit it off right away, bonding over our love of the Yankees, which was a rarity considering we lived in hard-core Red Sox territory. My mom and I had a standing invitation to join the Monaghans at church every Sunday, followed by brunch at the Monaghans', and Sully would usually come pick us up at our little apartment on the south end, then drop us back in the evening. And when my mom died right after I turned nineteen, it was the Monaghan family standing next to me at her funeral, with Maeve on one side of me and Cormac on the other, keeping me from falling apart.

A knock sounds on the security room door at the casino, startling me out of my thoughts, and Finn peeks his head in as I turn in my chair.

"When do you take off for New Orleans?" Finn asks.

I check my watch. "About seven hours."

Finn blows out a breath. "What are you still doing here then? Go home and get some sleep before your flight."

"Just finishing up a few things, *Dad*," I reply with a smile. About a week ago, Finn let me in on a little secret he hadn't announced to the family yet regarding him and Alessia expecting a mini Monaghan in a few months.

"Don't start with that shit. I've been telling you for years that you need to get more rest."

I wave off his concerns as he steps further into the room and has a seat next to mine in front of the monitors.

"Fuck, I hope this shit with Farina gets settled soon," he says, rubbing a hand over his face. "I'd rather Alessia give birth during a time when we didn't have to worry about an all-out war with the remaining Italian Mafia in Massachusetts."

Since killing off the head of the Cataldi organization a few months ago and partnering with the Amattos, Alessia's family, things have been quieter, almost peaceful. Well, if you don't count taking out the head of the New York Bratva. Thankfully, the new head of the Bratva out that way has a strong connection to us, considering his sister is living with Finn's brother, Eoghan.

"It's a dangerous life," I say.

"Yeah, but this shit with Farina makes it more dangerous."

"It's not like you're directly involved. I'm working on this with Liam."

Finn shoots me an annoyed look. "Seriously, Cillian? This whole little operation might be between you and Liam but don't think for a second you wouldn't have the backing of the entire Monaghan organization if shit went sideways and Liam needed us there. I won't stand for the shit Farina seems to have himself involved in any more than you or Liam. I don't give a rat's ass if I'm not directly involved. You're my lieutenant and a brother to me. Plus, when you guys take out Farina, I'll be stepping in. That's the agreement we have with Liam."

Though my work with Liam is something I felt the

need to help with any way I could, Finn had some stipulations when it came to Liam using our contacts in New Orleans. Nothing in this life is done out of the goodness of our hearts. As soon as we figure out how to dismantle Farina's rings, everyone will be better off, and our organization will hold the power in all of Massachusetts. Not a bad concession for me dividing my time between the Monaghans and the Ashcroft Agency.

"If we play our cards right, this won't come anywhere near you or Alessia," I tell him. Though my involvement could cause complications, Liam has assured me that his team will be the ones to deal with the blowback. Truth be told, I don't know that he can keep that promise, but we'll all be better off with Farina out of the picture if our suspicions turn out to be accurate, which it's looking more and more like they are if the phone call I received from Sampson is any indication.

"One can hope. I'll see you when you get back."

Finn stands and heads out, presumably to get home to his wife since it's so late. Or early, depending on which side of the bed you're on. I close my computer and pack my things, deciding to take Finn's suggestion to crash for a few hours before my flight.

"So there were a few guys in suits hanging out around

here?" I ask Sampson as we sit in his escort vehicle.

"Yup. This is where the international cargo comes in. Specifically from Eastern Europe and Russia."

"Did you catch any names?"

"There were three guys, and one mentioned talking to Massimo. Told him three weeks from today."

Fucking Farina.

"Did they say anything about if the cargo was coming in or going out?"

"Nope. Don't even know what the cargo is. Told you everything I overheard. I wasn't about to look like I was listening in on their conversation."

"You did right, Sampson. We have a name and a port location. If you happen to see anyone else or hear anything else, let me know."

We drive away from the port and back to the parking lot. When he stops in front of my rental car, I peel a few hundreds from the clip attached to my wallet and smile. If running into Nova last time I was in New Orleans taught me anything, it's to keep a backup stash of cash in the safe in my hotel room.

"For the baby," I say, handing him the bills.

Sampson nods. "The baby thanks you," he says with a wry smile.

We say our goodbyes, and I drive back to my hotel. I've always found comfort in routine, so I stay at the same hotel outside of the French Quarter. When I open the door to my room and set my bag on the bed, I pull back the heavy red curtains hanging over the window and look out at the New Orleans skyline. Nova is out there somewhere doing God knows what, and there's a rather large part of me that wishes I would have gotten her number instead of only giving her mine so I'd know, too.

Instead of changing from my suit and heading out to Geraldine's with the hope of running into her like I've considered a million times since my plane touched down, I pick up my phone to call Liam.

"Cillian, what did you find out?"

"Hello to you too," I say in response.

"Sorry, didn't realize you needed sweet words before getting down to business," Liam quips.

"It's a standard nicety in this country."

"Very well, then. Hello dear. How was your day? Did you happen to find out any new information from your friend regarding a certain Italian fellow who has been doing rather intolerable things as of late?"

"You can be a real prick. You know that?"

"I've been told a time or two, yes," Liam lets out an amused chuckle. I'm pretty sure I could go tell this guy to fuck himself on a daily basis and he'd laugh it off. If I hadn't seen firsthand how he handles these assholes, I'd have serious doubts about how committed he is to this cause.

"I spoke with Sampson, and he confirmed three guys at one of the docks were hanging around a couple days ago. Said he overheard them talking about informing Massimo, but didn't refer to him as Farina, not that it matters. Knowing they were Italian and used Massimo's name is enough for me to go on."

"I agree. Anything else?"

"We have an approximate date, but don't know if they were speaking of a shipment going out or coming in, or what exactly is supposed to be in the shipment."

"With the chatter I'm hearing, I'd say it's safe to assume it's of the human variety," Liam says.

One of his guys is all over the dark web finding pieces of shit who sell girls and those who buy them. Fuck, I'd hate to have that job.

"Okay. I'll make sure to have a few of my guys in New Orleans keeping an eye on what's going down. I'll send in Abel to set up surveillance in that area too."

"Sounds good. I'll make sure to be back down here as well."

"Got a taste for bloodshed, did you?"

"Depends on who's blood."

"Good, good. We'll firm things up in the next couple weeks. Let me know if your guy hears anything else."

"Will do," I reply and disconnect the call.

It's been a long day already and as I'm thinking about a shower and ordering food, my phone notifies me of an incoming text. It's from a number I don't recognize, but the picture that comes through of the woman in the blonde wig is a sight for my sore fucking eyes.

**Nova:** *I was just thinking about you.*

**Nova:** *I know you said to call if I needed anything and I don't. Everything is fine.*

**Nova:** *It's just that the band we saw that night is playing tonight at the same bar, and I don't know, it made me think of you.*

**Nova:** *Okay, that sounds pathetic. Delete this from your phone and memory. Thanks, bye.*

I may be laughing to myself at her embarrassment, but I'd be lying if I said she hadn't crossed my mind a time or a hundred, especially knowing she's so close, but I have no way of getting ahold of her. Well, I didn't.

**Me:** *I'll do no such thing.*

**Nova:** **stares at floor* please swallow me now.*

**Me:** *Why are you embarrassed? I know I'm unforgettable.*

**Nova:** *And so humble.*

**Me:** *You look beautiful, by the way.*

I see text bubbles appear and disappear a couple of times before one of her responses comes through.

**Nova:** *Flattery will get you nowhere, sir. Especially when you're over two thousand miles away. But thanks.*

**Me:** *I'm not...*

**Nova:** *Not what?*

**Me:** *Thousands of miles away. In fact I'm currently in a hotel room overlooking the New Orleans skyline.*

Nothing comes through for a few minutes, and I wonder if the reality of me being in New Orleans rather than a safe distance from her would have changed her mind about reaching out. We can't find ourselves in trouble if we aren't within reach of each other, and I have a feeling being close to her again would not end with me leaving her at her door with a kiss on the cheek like last time.

Finally, another text notification pops up.

**Nova:** *Any plans tonight?*

**Me:** *Yeah. I hear there's a reggae band playing at a little bar off Bourbon. Thought I'd check it out.*

**Nova:** *Hmm. Interesting. You taking anyone?*

**Me:** *Yup. A black-haired little thief who I haven't been able to stop thinking about for the last month.*

When I'm met with silence again, I wonder if I've gone too far. A month is plenty of time to make the night we had bigger in my mind. But she was the one who reached out to me. That has to count for something.

**Nova:** *Interesting. I have a feeling someone matching that description plans to be there around 10.*

**Me:** *I'll be sure to keep an eye out for her.*

**Nova:** *You do that. And maybe keep a better eye on your wallet tonight, too.*

**Me:** *Will do.*

But I know damn well it's not my wallet I'm in danger of losing.

# Chapter Six
## Nova

I F YOU ASKED ME why I decided to text Cillian, I would tell you it was because I was out of my mind. At least, it felt that way when he didn't respond at first. Not like I gave him much of a chance before bombarding him with my embarrassment.

We shared a night a month ago. A night where nothing really happened between us. It's not as though we shared some passionate moment. I only felt the brush of his lips once during our game and then again when he said good night, but damn, I wish I would have felt a lot more. It would have been more if whoever called him hadn't interrupted and brought both of us back to reality. It would have been a bad idea to pursue anything further. If I'd had him in my bed that night, it wouldn't have done either of us any good. Well, it probably would have done both of us a lot of good several times over, but not in the long run. I'm still not clear on why he was here to begin with, but it doesn't matter, I doubt the Irish mob has a remote field office set up in New Orleans, and I'm not interested in some long-distance romance.

But there's something about the way Cillian looked at me that night that I can't get out of my head, which is far beyond status quo for me. I don't obsess over looks and soft touches. I don't get tongue-tied, or in this case text-tied, over men. My dating past is lackluster to say the least. Maybe I've never prioritized relationships—or I've prioritized the wrong ones. That full smile he gave me at the end of the night has played on a loop and has me thinking of things I never considered before, wanting things I have no business wanting...

Jesus, what am I even talking about? No one said anything about having any sort of romantic relationship. I mean, him living so far away definitely takes the pressure off...and here I go again. It was one night. I probably imagined the looks he was sending me and the way I reacted to his closeness.

Yes, that's why I texted him. To convince myself it was all in my head and there wasn't some insane spark of chemistry that I don't ever remember feeling with anyone else. I certainly didn't expect him to be in New Orleans today or to want to see me. In reality, I saw the poster for the band we saw playing at the same bar, and the temptation was too strong to resist like I had so many times before. Then, when I put on the wig and was ready to head out to work as Charity, I thought about the look of recognition—and dare I say, amusement—when he caught me trying to sneak out of Geraldine's. The way he wore a little smile for most of the night, the corner of his lips quirked upward. How he finally let loose with a full, wide smile and that laugh. God, that was a good sound.

So I threw caution to the wind and texted him. Then immediately regretted it. You'd think with all the technology out there they'd have come up with a way to unsend texts in cases of total and complete mortification. But no. Instead, I went and decided to try to explain away my reaching out, like that was going to make anything better.

Turns out, I didn't have to worry. Cillian made a few vague attempts at showing me his interest the first night we met, but I'd chalked it up to being in the moment and nothing more. Maybe I shouldn't have. It's not like I held out hope to see him again. Goes to show what I know.

After working three restaurants and a bar tonight, I head over to the local venue where the band is playing. I stopped at Geraldine's to change since Harper was working, and I didn't have to deal with Damon or go home before meeting Cillian. When she poured me the whiskey 7 I desperately needed before meeting up with Cillian, we chatted for a couple minutes, but she was distracted with the new guy she'd been dating for the last week who stopped in with a couple friends to say hi. After waving hello to her new man and his group, I left Geraldine's to make my way to a certain bar with a certain guy for a date I'm still ridiculously nervous about. No, *not date*. He didn't say anything about a date. Just two people who had a fun night together getting together again for some more fun. Jesus, I sound like a complete imbecile.

Now, I'm standing in front of a bar, too chicken shit to go in.

Thoughts are tumbling through my head, making me nearly dizzy with anxiety. What if I built him up in my memory and am sorely let down when I see him again? What if he thinks the same about me? What if the connection I felt was a figment of my imagination? What if it wasn't? I have plans in the works to get me out of New Orleans and get me closer to that little beach bar. My plans certainly don't include a six-two lieutenant for the Irish mob. *Then why did you text him?* That's an excellent question and one I don't have an answer for—except to tell the little voice asking it to shut the hell up. It was a moment of weakness, then excitement, that he was in town and wanted to see me.

*Alright, Nova. Time to put on your big-girl panties and walk into the damn bar.*

I take a few steps toward the brick building and hear the band playing from the front door. Stepping into the crowded space, I look toward the bar. Sitting in a seat with his back turned toward me is Cillian. I take a moment to drink in the muscles of his back and shoulders that are visible even through his shirt. He lifts what I'm assuming is a drink from the bar and tilts his head back in a quick movement like he's taking a shot. Maybe I'm not the only one who needs a little liquid courage tonight.

Cillian turns his entire body around in the stool he's sitting on and locks eyes with me from across the room. The half smile he wore for most of the night we spent in each other's company last time sits on his perfect lips while he studies me with a glint of mischief in his eyes. Now I know I wasn't making up how damn gorgeous this man is in my head. His blue-gray eyes sparkle with amusement as I make my way through the crowd until I'm standing in front of him.

"Was wondering if you were going to make your way in or not," he says, drinking me in like I did to him before he spotted me.

"I'm not that late."

"No, but I saw you standing out there for at least five minutes before you walked in here. You afraid I bite?"

*More like hoping he does.*

I shake my head, my eyes rolling toward the ceiling. "Does nothing escape your attention?"

He shrugs. "Not usually, no."

"How about the fact that I don't have a drink?"

Cillian turns toward the bar and hands me a glass. "Whiskey 7. I had him use the Irish whiskey this time. Though I think it should only be drunk straight or on the rocks."

I sip the delicious cocktail, then tilt my lip in a smirk. "It's early. This is just my warm-up."

"I don't know if I should be offended that you need to be lubricated to spend an evening with me." His throaty chuckle sounds over the music playing, and it does a certain something to my insides.

"I'm perfectly happy to spend the evening sober, but it looked like you needed a little something too, if the shot I saw you take when I walked through the door was any indication."

"You don't seem to miss much either."

"Part of the job, I guess."

I slide into the seat next to Cillian, causing our legs to brush against each other. The heat from his thigh instantly seeps through the tight jeans I'm wearing—the ones that happen to make my ass look fantastic. Not that I wore them for him or anything.

"So, how was work, dear?" he asks, sending me a little wink.

"It was a good night. So good, in fact, drinks are on me."

"Not in this life," he replies, shaking his head. "I invited you out. Therefore, I'm paying."

I could argue, but I have a sneaking suspicion it wouldn't do me any good, so I nod instead, then turn around in the stool to watch the band.

They begin playing the song I was dancing to the first night Cillian and I were here. When he gets up and stands in front of me, holding out his hand, I shoot him a questioning look.

"Dance with me," he says, a smile gracing his way too gorgeous face.

"I thought you didn't dance."

He shrugs but doesn't put his hand down. "You made

it look so fun last time, I thought I'd give it a shot. What, you afraid I'll step on your toes?"

I look down at the black wedge sandals I paired with my outfit and move my foot in a circle. "I'd hate to have my shoes ruined."

"Live on the edge a little," he replies with a smirk.

"That's all I do." We stare at each other for a few moments, the tension growing thick between us. It's just a dance, for God's sake. "Okay, fine."

I take his hand and he leads us to the middle of the makeshift dance floor with everyone else. When he turns to face me, he pulls me into his body, covering one of my hands against his chest with his own and sliding his other arm around my waist. It's not a particularly fast song, but we sway to the smooth beat, never taking our eyes off each other. The rest of the room disappears. Cillian's distinct scent of cedar and bergamot envelops me as he holds me close. His stormy gaze is just as intense as I remember, but right now, I can barely think of anything other than the way the heat from his body is pressing into me or the feel of his heartbeat under my hand. It's thumping hard and fast, like mine. Yeah, there's no way I simply imagined this chemistry.

When I lift my hand to the back of his neck and gently scrape my nails over the short hair, he inhales a sharp breath before his hand flexes around my waist, pulling me tighter to his front. It's like we're picking up right where we left off a month ago. Except this time, I'm hoping to God, the devil, or any deity that will listen that he doesn't take me home and leave me with nothing more than a good-night kiss on the cheek. If the heat in his gaze is anything to go by, I'd say that isn't in his plans for the rest of the night.

"My flight is supposed to leave in the morning," he says, still swaying to the music. The song has changed, but we're still moving together, never missing a beat.

"Okay..." I'm not entirely sure where this is going.

"But I can change it."

Oh.

"Change is good." What does that even mean? I swear my brain is turning to mush with him pressed against me.

His deep chuckle vibrates through me.

"You seem to have that effect on me. Have me changing the way I usually do things."

"How's that?" My voice is so low and breathy; it's amazing he hears me over the music. But just like the first time we met, Cillian and I find ourselves in our own little bubble where we're the only people who exist.

"Well, normally when I come to New Orleans, I don't leave my room except for whatever meeting I'm here for. I certainly don't go to bars or dance with beautiful women on a random Tuesday night."

"But you dance with women on other not-so-random nights?"

He stares into my eyes, picking up on what I'm really asking. Not that it matters. There's no expectation of a relationship here.

"Not in a while. I've had this raven-haired thief running circles in my mind. Can't seem to get rid of her."

"Must be tough."

"Only because I can't make any promises or plans for a future, but fuck, I wish I could."

"Maybe she isn't interested in any of that. Maybe she's perfectly willing to take what you can give when you can give it. Not everything has to be about a future. Maybe she wants to live in the now and not worry about the rest of that shit."

Cillian tilts his head down so our lips are barely a breath apart. "Maybe."

I close the small gap between us and crash my lips to his. The taste of his whiskey invades my mouth when Cillian's tongue plunges in, teasing and twirling with mine. This kiss is everything I spent the last month imagining it would be. Cillian kisses with his whole body, his hands roughly moving over my back before one lands just above my ass and the other tangles in the back of my hair, pressing my body tighter against his. When I let out a quiet moan, he rips his mouth from mine and presses his forehead against mine, his chest heaving with every inhale before a rough exhale.

"Fuck, Nova. I wish we weren't in the middle of a bar right now."

"Where are you staying?"

"Same place I always do. About twenty minutes from here."

"Then let's get the hell out of here."

Cillian stares into my eyes for a few brief moments as though he's thinking something over in his head before he nods and steps away from me, grabbing my hand and hauling ass out the front door.

"Wait, what about your tab?" I ask before an excited and uncharacteristically girlish laugh bursts from me.

He chuckles as he walks up to his car and unlocks it then opens the door for me. "You're worried about me skipping out on a tab right now?"

I step around the door to sit in the passenger seat. "Well, I like this bar. I don't want to be eighty-sixed for not paying. The bartender will have to pay for our drinks."

"I paid before you got here. Though, I do find it amusing how worried you are for the bartender."

I give Cillian a small smile as I slide into the plush leather interior of his black rental car. "What can I say? They make an honest living."

"You're something else, Nova." Cillian shuts the door then walks around the hood of the car. As soon as he gets in the driver's side, he leans over and grabs me by the back of my head, slamming his lips to mine. I lean into the kiss as best I can, considering there's a center console blocking me.

"Fuck, this is going to be the longest twenty minutes of my life," Cillian states when he tears his mouth from mine and starts the car.

"Let's see if you can make it there in ten."

"What do I get if I do?"

"I think you know what we both get when we get there. Let's see if we can get to it faster."

"Works for me," he replies, peeling away from the curb and flooring it down the street as I let out a yelp of surprise, followed by another excited laugh.

"Thirteen minutes. Not bad," I tell Cillian when we park in front of the swanky hotel he's staying at. The valet walks to my side of the door and opens it for me before another valet opens Cillian's car door and hands him a ticket when Cillian hands over the keys.

"Not like I could mow over the group of pedestrians at that stop sign," he says, grabbing my hand to pull me through the doors of the hotel.

I let out a low whistle while taking in the giant marble fountain and expensive flower arrangements covering nearly every surface. I look up and gawk at the glass cathedral ceiling throughout the entire lobby. "Jesus, it must pay well to be in the mob."

"I do alright for myself," Cillian says with a wink before stopping at the elevator and swiping a card in front of the reader.

When the door opens, he quickly pulls me inside and presses me against the mirrored wall of the elevator. His mouth crashes against mine as he holds both of my hands over my head, pinning me to the wall.

"There's probably cameras in here." My voice comes out as a breathless moan as Cillian works his lips down the column of my neck.

"Don't give a fuck," he replies before his lips find mine again.

Honestly, neither do I. I've never felt so damn needy and out of control in my entire life. I'm no blushing virgin, but the way Cillian makes me feel is completely out of the realm of anything I've ever experienced. From the way his mouth consumes mine to the feel of his hands pressing mine to the wall of the elevator. There's something to be said for feeling trapped in this kiss with him as though if I wanted to escape I couldn't. Not that I would ever want to.

There've been a few times in my life when I've felt this kind of passion from someone. But it has never been coupled with a burning desperation like the way it feels with Cillian. I may live a certain type of unconventional lifestyle, but I've always maintained control and never allowed myself to get swept away in whatever this is. But holy hell, if I'm not one-hundred-percent ready to throw all that control away for a chance to spend the night wrapped up in him.

The doors open, and Cillian breaks the kiss before letting go of my hands then gripping just under my ass. When he lifts me, I wrap my legs around his waist and my hands grasp his shoulders. It feels as though fire is running through my veins. I'm burning from the inside out and so fucking desperate to get into his hotel room. In four long strides we're at the door to his room, and he pulls out the key card to open it. Our lips meet in another brutal kiss the moment the door opens, just before he steps through. Once on the other side, he kicks the door closed, and I'm spun around against the wood before he rips his mouth away and presses his forehead to mine.

"You make me feel so goddamn out of control," he pants as I grind myself against him.

"Same." I don't know why he affects every cell in my body this way, but I'm also not going to question it too much right now.

"This isn't something I usually do."

"You mean you don't have a woman in every port?"

Cillian huffs out a laugh and shakes his head. "Hardly. Until a month ago, I'd barely seen anything other than the port here and this hotel."

I take the opportunity to let my gaze wander around the room. There's a couch in the center, a small oak desk against one wall, and a giant television on the opposite wall. Then, I spot a door that I'm assuming leads to a bedroom. Directly in front of us is a large window with the curtains open. The twinkling lights of New Orleans shine through the window. From what I can tell, the suite is huge. Lots of available surfaces.

"You sprang for a suite. For some reason, I would have imagined you in a little hotel room with a bed and not much else."

"It was a last-minute decision," he says, bringing his lips to my shoulder where my shirt has slipped down.

"You don't have to impress me, you know?"

"I did it for me. I like the view from here and wanted to see you naked with New Orleans behind you." He spins me around and carries me to the window before setting me on my feet. "You and New Orleans will always be interconnected in my mind, Nova. I need to watch you come undone with the city behind you."

I mean, how could I possibly argue with that logic?

Cillian rips my shirt over my head and tosses it behind him before his lips find my peaked nipple under the fabric of my pink lace bra. He sucks hard through the fabric and the scrape of his teeth, along with the lace, sends a shot of warm tingles down my spine. Cillian kisses his way down my body as he lowers to his knees in front of me. The cool glass against my back is such a stark contrast to the feel of his hot tongue as he licks and sucks all the skin on display. I'd say it's helping with the raging inferno that my body has become, but I'd be lying. Every kiss—every sweep of his tongue—sets off little explosions deep inside of me. Honestly, I'm a little worried at this point. There's no way this can be normal, right?

When his lips find the waist of my jeans, he lifts his head and spears me with his dark gaze as he removes my sandals. His fingers find the zipper of my pants, and too fucking slowly, he pulls the tab down. The sound of my zipper coming undone is loud in the otherwise quiet hotel room, ratcheting up the tension tenfold.

"Are you trying to kill me?" I breathe out, and all he does is give me one of his half smiles.

When he has the zipper open, he yanks my pants down my thighs. I have no idea how I'm still standing at this point. Having this man on his knees before me is a sight I've fantasized about plenty of times, but to see it real and in person is on a whole other level that even my dirtiest fantasies couldn't have conjured. He holds my stare a few more moments while he strokes the seam of my pussy with his fingers. When he glances down, a wide smile stretches across his face.

"You're so wet for me. I can't wait to taste you."

"No one here is stopping you," I tell him, my voice shaking with anticipation.

Cillian doesn't wait another second before his tongue takes a long lick through my center. When he groans, my knees buckle, and I nearly fall to the floor. He lifts my leg over his shoulder so that some of my weight is balanced on him.

"Stay." He dives back in and begins eating at me like a man starved and the only thing that will satiate him is my pussy.

"Yes, sir," I breathe out, grabbing his hair as he absolutely devours me. I'm no wilting wallflower, and this isn't the first time I've had a man go down on me, but holy shit. The way Cillian uses his entire mouth with his teeth scraping over my clit to be soothed by his tongue moments later over and over is nothing I've felt before. It's barely been a minute, and I feel the orgasm building already. There's nothing slow and steady as I erupt into his mouth. I don't have to concentrate on the sensations as they've overtaken every part of me. My hands clamp into fists, and my fingers pull at the strands of his hair so forcefully I'm sure he's going to have two matching bald spots as I let out a shout of pleasure so loud I'm afraid the people walking on the sidewalk below are going to hear me.

Cillian follows me down, his licks becoming softer and more languid as I catch the breath that was stolen from my lungs.

He looks up at me from his kneeling position with a wet grin covering his face.

"That's one. You're getting an orgasm for every time I had to fist my cock to the memory of you dancing in that bar the first night we met."

"How many times was that?"

"Considering it's been a month since I've seen you last, neither of us will be getting any sleep tonight."

"Guess it's a good thing you changed your flight then." My voice is breathy as a result of the postorgasmic haze, and I have a feeling it won't be clearing tonight.

"Good thing. Now turn around so I can watch your ass as I fuck you from behind against the window."

# CHAPTER SEVEN

## CILLIAN

"I T WAS THE JEANS, wasn't it?" Nova asks, her voice slightly slurred when I stand and press her against the window with my body.

My hands cup her cheeks while I tower over her. "It's everything about you, sweetheart."

Her nose scrunches into an adorable grimace. "Sweetheart?"

"Not a fan of nicknames?"

"Not a fan of being called *sweet* in any capacity. Seems a little disingenuous."

"How about the sexiest woman I've ever laid eyes on?"

"Better." Her lips tip up in a half smile.

"Or I could go with tempting vixen who has me so damn hard my cock is ready to punch itself out of my pants."

"That's a mouthful."

"I'd like to give you a mouthful."

Nova laughs. That feeling I had in my chest earlier, seeing her smile at me when I laid eyes on her at the bar, comes rushing back. I fucking love the sound of her laugh and the way her face lights up, even when she's laughing at me.

"I walked right into that one," she groans out.

I bend my head down, needing to taste her smile. Nova lets out a moan as our tongues tangle in a dance that feels like we've been doing forever. Maybe it's all the times I fantasized about what she would've tasted like if I'd let myself indulge when we met. I've pumped my cock so many damn times to the thought of being on my knees and eating her cunt. I couldn't wait to get her back to my hotel when she was pressed against me as we were dancing at the bar.

After we texted earlier, I truly had no expectation to come back here with her. Desire? Yes. Did I change my hotel room with the hope that she would be here with me tonight so I could finally taste her and sink into her like I've been dying to do for the last month? Fuck yes, I did. What do they say about luck? It's when preparation meets opportunity or some shit. I prepared, and I sure as fuck wasn't going to let the opportunity to have Nova naked against the glass as I ate her out pass me by.

Her hands find my shirt and she begins undoing the buttons as we continue to explore each other's mouths. The taste of her on my tongue mixed with the whiskey she drank earlier is something I will never get enough of. When she finishes with my shirt, her hands move to the belt buckle of my pants, undoing the leather and ripping it out of the loops with a flourish. Her deft fingers then find the button of my pants, and she opens it before pulling down my zipper. Nova breaks our kiss to trail her lips down my chest and over the hard planes of my stomach, her tongue licking between each groove of muscle on display before she kneels in front of me.

"Your turn," she tells me with that damn smile on her face—the one I haven't been able to get out of my head.

"This isn't tit for tat."

She looks up at me, her brow arched in question. "So, you're saying you don't want me to suck your cock?"

"I am absolutely *not* saying that. I would never say that. I'm just letting you know I didn't make you come with my mouth expecting you to return the favor."

"Why did you, then?"

"Not a day has gone by since meeting you that I didn't wonder what you tasted like. Your mouth, your pussy...I needed to know."

"Did you consider maybe I was wondering the same thing?" Her hand reaches into my boxer briefs, and she pulls my hard cock out. Stroking her hand along my thick shaft a couple times before reaching forward, she slides her tongue from root to tip before she puts me in her mouth and sucks me back deep into her throat.

"Oh, fuck," I breathe out, reaching to place my hand against the window behind Nova. "Goddamn, baby, your mouth..." I can't even form words to express how amazing her wet mouth feels as she nods her head back and forth.

Releasing me with a pop, her green gaze meets mine. "Are you done trying to talk me out of this?"

"Yes, yes. God, don't stop." My other hand tangles in

her hair, guiding her back to my cock for her mouth to take me in again. She lets out a little laugh that turns into a deep moan when she sucks me in deep, her tongue swirling over the head every time she moves back. The intensity of pleasure flowing through my bloodstream is so overwhelming I almost lose myself to it. But her mouth isn't where I want to come inside her for the first time. I take a step back, and she releases me before looking up at me with a questioning stare.

"I'm not going to last long in your mouth."

I grab her under her arms then pull her against my body, taking her mouth in another bruising kiss before pulling away suddenly and turning her toward the window. Nova's hands slap the glass as mine comes down on her ass, leaving a red handprint. When I lave my tongue over her stinging flesh, she lets out a needy moan, tilting her ass higher in the air.

Bending down to grab my pants with one hand, my other moves to her front, and I begin strumming her clit with my fingers. I open my wallet, but my fingers have to leave her perfect pussy for a moment so I can pull out the condom inside. Once I have the condom in hand, I toss my wallet behind me somewhere, not giving a shit where it lands and tear the wrapper open.

"Fuck, Cillian. Hurry." Her voice is so fucking needy it sends shivers of excitement through me. I'm making her feel this way. She's as desperate to be filled as I am to finally sink inside of her.

When I'm sheathed in the latex, I grab her hips and

bend my knees a bit before slamming into her waiting pussy.

"Oh, my God!" she yells and slaps the glass with her palm.

The sensation of being inside Nova for the first time is nothing I could have prepared myself for. Her tight heat swallows my cock over and over as I pump into her like a madman. Sweat drips down my back, and I catch her blissed-out gaze in the window. She's fucking stunning with her eyes half-lidded and her mouth parted as moan after moan falls from her lips. Watching her ass shake with every thrust is so goddamn erotic. I never considered myself an ass man, but she was right—when she showed up to the bar in those skintight jeans, it was everything I could do not to run my hands over every mouthwatering curve in front of the whole damn place.

"God, I'm so close," she moans.

I slide the hand grasping onto her hip around and begin stroking her clit as my cock slides out and slams in.

"Get there, Nova. Fuck, you feel so good."

Something primal overtakes me as I lean down and bite her shoulder. Nova screams in pleasure as her pussy clamps down around my cock, the noise echoing off the glass. I can't hold back any longer and my cock jerks inside of her as I come inside the latex. The power of the orgasm nearly knocks me to my knees, but I steady myself, placing my hand over hers against the glass with our fingers locking together in a tight hold as we ride the wave of our orgasms. My lips graze her shoulder where I've left a bite mark.

"Sorry about that."

"I'm not," she pants. "But just so we're clear, you aren't some kind of vampire or blood-sucking demon, right?"

My laugh is raspy as I pull out of her. "Um, no. I'm not a fictional creature that hunts victims in the dead of night."

Nova turns and wraps her arms around my neck, a smile playing on her lips. "I mean, I've never seen you in daylight. It's a fair question."

"It's a weird question…"

"It's New Orleans. Weird shit happens here."

"You have some interesting ideas."

Nova laughs before pressing her mouth to mine for a too-brief kiss. "And you're fun to fuck with."

She drops her arms from around my shoulders and walks to the door leading to the bedroom, her delectable hips swaying with each step she takes.

"Where are you going?" I ask.

When she reaches the bedroom, Nova turns the handle and lets it swing open before turning around and leaning against the frame. "You said you were going to give me an orgasm for every time you had to fuck your hand the last month. I figured we'd move into the bedroom. I think New Orleans has gotten enough of a show for the evening."

Nova cocks her head to the side as she waits for my next move. I don't make her wait long. In four long strides, I'm at the threshold of the doorway. I stop in front of her and bend down, pick her up, and lift her over my shoulder. She squeals in surprise as I continue into the bedroom.

"Brute," she laughs out, slapping my bare ass. I turn my head and bite hers in return before bending over and placing her on the bed. Her face is red, and laughter spills from her as I position myself over her, covering her body with mine.

When her lips find mine again, the kiss turns just as heated as it was from the start. The orgasms haven't seemed to tamper our desire for one another in the least. Nova's pussy grinds against my hardening cock, and I'm so fucking tempted to slide into her completely bare, but somehow find the will to tear myself away and stand from the bed. I head to my suitcase and pull out a full box of condoms, minus the one I put in my wallet.

"You sure that's going to be enough?" she asks with a cheeky smile.

"Between my fingers, mouth, and cock I think I can make it work."

Nova's eyes widen a fraction before she blows out a long breath. "Fuck me. We're in for a long night."

The sun was peeking through the curtains of the hotel room before Nova and I finally closed our eyes. We didn't make it through the entire box of condoms, but damn if we didn't put a significant dent in the count. One thing I realized—when she was lying on her back, and I was covering her body with mine, sliding in and out of her tight heat—was there was no way one night was going to be enough to reenact all the fantasies I had about her over the last month. Shit, I'm not sure how long it would take, but probably longer than I have in New Orleans.

My eyes peel open, and I'm met with the sight of Nova lying on her stomach with her face toward mine. Her black hair is covering her closed eyes, and I swipe the locks back. She lets out a very loud and very unladylike snore, which wakes her from her slumber. Her green eyes meet mine, and I smile.

"Jesus, I think you broke my pussy last night," she says in a raspy groan.

A snort of laughter escapes me as my hand trails over the curve of her naked back and over her ass before brushing my fingers over her center. Nova shifts her legs wider as I gently glide them through her wet flesh.

"How about I kiss it better?" In the one night we've been together, I've become thoroughly addicted to her taste and the noises she makes when I make her come on my cock or in my mouth—it doesn't matter. It's music to my ears either way.

"Mmm, I think that might be a good idea."

Nova rolls to her side and looks behind me. "Shit. Is that the right time?"

I turn my head and see the clock on the nightstand reads 1:46 p.m. "Pretty sure."

Her head hits the pillow and she lets out a groan of frustration. "I have to go."

"You plan on hitting the lunch crowd? Sorry to say, but that might be a tough one. No one is liquored up enough to be careless."

"You do realize you're in New Orleans, right?" She turns to face me with a quirked brow. "There's always plenty of drunk people wandering around. But, no. I have to meet up with a friend." She sits up from the bed and scrubs her hand over her face. "I'm going to hop in the shower."

"Is this a guy friend?" Why am I asking questions that may have answers I can't care about? Nova has an entire life here that I'm not part of. And besides, I'm not the jealous type.

*Keep telling yourself that.*

"Kind of. More like a business associate." The shower turns on before Nova peeks her head out of the bathroom. "Jealous?" That little smirk she likes to wear around me is going to be the death of me.

"Nope. Just curious. I don't know much about your life here."

She smiles and ducks back into the bathroom. "Not much to know. I live here, and I work here. My roommate is a bartender at the bar where we first met."

I rise from the bed and head into the bathroom, spotting her naked form behind the fogged glass of the shower. "You meeting this guy as Charity or Nova?"

"Nova."

Opening the door to the shower, I step in behind her, and she turns to face me. "What are you doing? We don't have time for that." She pointedly looks at my half-hard cock then back to me.

I shrug and bend to give her a quick kiss on the lips before grabbing my shampoo. "Just ignore him. He'll go down."

"I doubt that," she mumbles as I rub the shampoo in my hands, working up a lather before bringing my palms to her head and massaging the suds into her hair. She lets out a small moan and brings her hands to my waist to steady herself with her eyes closed.

"So, business associate? I thought you were a one-woman operation."

"This is for another job. It's a big one, and I need some help."

"From this guy you're meeting with?"

"Yes, Cillian," she replies dryly. "From the guy who I'm going to find downtown."

"What's the job? Maybe I can help. Offer some advice."

Her eyes pop open and she stares into my gaze, mulling something over in her head. "Maybe you can."

"You going to tell me what it is?"

Nova tilts her head back to rinse the shampoo from her hair. I watch in fascination as the suds travel over her naked skin and down the drain. Fuck, I wish it were my tongue trailing over her body rather than the shampoo.

"In two days, there's a charity auction downtown. It'll be chock-full of richer-than-sin socialites. Several jewelry stores have donated to the auction. There's a lot of high-priced shit too, not just a few gold and silver bobbles."

"Sounds like the kind of thing people bring credit cards and checkbooks to, not cash."

"Which is why I'm not going to lift wallets and purses. I'm going to steal the jewels." Her smile is wide when she grabs a bottle of conditioner and squirts a small amount into her hand before rubbing it through the ends of her hair.

"Going from pickpocket to jewel thief isn't as easy as you think. How do you plan on getting in? How are you going to lift the jewelry without getting caught on camera? There are bound to be guards around. Even if you could get to a piece without being noticed, the second they realize something is missing, they'll shut the place down."

"Exactly. Which is why I need to talk to my friend. He's a wiz with computers, and I need him to hack into the security feed and erase any damning footage. Then I can grab a couple pieces and be out before anyone notices. A friend works at the Grand Dame, the hotel they're having the event at, and put me on the guest list. I have an invitation and everything. Figure I'll get in, figure out the big-ticket items, and find my opening."

I slowly shake my head from side to side. "Your plan

has more holes than Swiss cheese."

Nova looks at me with disappointment furrowing her brow. "Listen, I know it's not perfect, but I'm a quick thinker and even quicker on my feet. No one is going to expect a heist during a charity auction."

"Why are you risking it?"

Nova looks down and bites her lip before finding my gaze again. "I don't want to keep doing this, Cillian. I never set out to live some life of crime. Lifting wallets gives me enough to live on and a nice little nest egg, but if I'm ever going to get out of this life, I need something that will set me up somewhere else."

"When people get desperate, they tend to get caught."

"I'm not desperate, just ready to move on. This is my shot to do that."

"How are you going to unload the jewelry?"

"I know a few people who don't ask questions. Figure I'll hold onto them till the heat dies down then get rid of them."

"Well, that's smart, at least. Listen, I'm not saying it's not doable." I slide my fingers over her brow in an attempt to smooth the wrinkles there. "I just think we can come up with a better plan. This guy know you're wanting to meet with him?"

"No. I haven't said anything yet."

"So you don't even know if he's willing to help you?"

"I can be persuasive," she replies with a grin, and I don't like the sound of that one bit.

"You know, I'm good with computers myself. Hacking

into a security system would be no problem for me. Along with finding the building plans for all possible escape routes. And I look damn good in a suit if I do say so myself."

"Don't you have to get back to Boston to do your...I don't know...mob stuff?"

A chuckle rumbles in my chest. "It's not like I have a time card I punch. I can stay in New Orleans for a few extra days before Finn is going to need me back." *I hope.*

A wide smile stretches across Nova's damp face. "It *would* be awful to miss the opportunity to see you all dolled up."

I laugh and pull her warm, wet body against mine, my half-hard cock quickly turning into a full hard-on. "And you don't have to rush out of here to meet with some guy who couldn't possibly look half as good as me in a suit. Or be half as experienced with security footage."

"I just love how modest you are. Really, you should give yourself more credit," she says in a bone-dry tone.

"That mouth is going to get you in trouble," I tell her before pressing a languid kiss on her pink lips.

When her hand reaches down to take my cock in her fist, the kiss turns fierce and heated, just as it did every time our lips met last night. Her mouth leaves mine and she trails her tongue down my neck, licking and sucking as she continues her descent to my chest. When she lowers to her knees, my fingers brush the side of her cheek before she covers my length with her mouth.

"You don't have to do that just because I offered to

help."

Nova looks up and releases me from her mouth with an irritated scowl on her face that, for some reason, I find insanely sexy. "Are you going to stop trying to talk me out of blow jobs anytime soon? I'm starting to think you don't like them. Or is it just when I do them?"

"Trust me when I tell you there isn't a man alive that doesn't like blow jobs. And as far as you giving me one?" I cup both of her cheeks in my palms. "There's nothing I love more than feeling your lips wrapped around my cock. I just don't want you to feel obligated or something."

"If I have ever come across as the type of person who does anything out of obligation and not because she wants to, then I'm sorry for having given you the wrong impression." She strokes me from root to tip with a smile playing on her kiss-swollen lips. "Now, may I proceed?"

I lean back against the shower wall, properly put in my place. "By all means, please do."

# CHAPTER EIGHT
## CILLIAN

I'VE DECIDED THERE'S NO better head in the world than shower head. Especially if it's a tempting little vixen with dark hair and green eyes staring up at you while she throws you over the edge of ecstasy with her mouth.

"I need to go back to my place," Nova says as she brushes her teeth with the toothbrush I had the hotel concierge send to the room.

"Want me to come with you?"

"Nah. I'm just going to grab a change of clothes. Do a little laundry maybe."

"Are you coming back tonight?" Jesus, I sound like a whiny little bitch.

"I was planning on it. Unless you have a better offer somewhere else."

She rinses the toothpaste from her mouth, and I do the same. When I set my toothbrush on the counter next to hers, I step behind her, covering her back with my front. The only thing separating us is the towel she currently has knotted around her chest and the one around my waist. I pull her damp hair over one shoulder, and Nova tilts her head to the side, allowing me access to her long neck. My lips trail over her warm skin and the scent of my shampoo in her hair tugs at something in me.

"Well, we do have a lot of details to iron out." Kiss. "Plans to go over." Kiss. "Outfits to coordinate." Kiss.

"Outfits?" she asks in a breathy whisper.

"Since we're going to this event as guests, we need a story. I was thinking you could go as Charity, but instead of a grad student, you can play a newly engaged Southern belle, and I'll be your fiancé who just spontaneously proposed on our yearly vacation to NOLA. Since we were already coming to the event, we thought getting your ring here would be memorable and help out a charity at the same time. What's this thing for, anyways?"

Nova looks on with surprise and, dare I say, an impressive gaze. "Um, it's for meerkats or something."

"Meerkats?" I ask, confused as to why anyone would throw a multimillion-dollar gala for that. I mean, they're cute and all, but seriously?

"It's the South, and this is probably a pet project of the woman throwing it."

Nova walks from the bathroom into the darkened bedroom before heading into the living room. Her clothes are still lying on the floor—where they landed last night in my haste to get her naked. She finds her jeans, pulls them up her legs and turns to pick up her bra and shirt. Damn, those jeans really make her already fantastic ass look spectacular.

She turns and catches me staring with a smile tugging at the corner of my lips as she covers her tits with her bra and pulls the shirt over her head.

"Did you have that story already concocted in your head, or was it something you thought of on the fly?"

"You're not the only one who thinks fast on their feet." As the lieutenant of the Monaghan organization, I've had to do a lot of that. It's imperative for someone in my position to be able to walk into any room and take stock then adjust accordingly. Sometimes, I'm the stone-cold gun at Finn's side, and other times, I'm the businessman who is there to negotiate and cut a deal. And then there are times when I have to play the amiable, level-headed second when Finn plays the tough-as-nails head of the Irish mob. They've all become parts of me, and I've honed the skill to call on any of them at the drop of a hat.

"Well, color me impressed," Nova says, walking over to where I'm leaning against the doorframe leading into the bedroom. The very bedroom I'd like to take her in right now instead of having her leave.

"Told you I'm handy to have around." I loop my arm around her, pulling her against my chest.

"That you are. You're the best criminal mastermind I know," she replies, leaning up to kiss me before turning and escaping my hold to find her shoes.

Nova sits on the couch where I didn't have a chance to fuck her like I originally planned and pulls her phone from her purse before stuffing her underwear inside. She presses a few buttons then lays it next to her while she buckles her sandals.

"My car will be here in five minutes," she says.

"Just take mine," I offer.

"I can find my way, but thanks."

"Nova, I know you can, but I have a car that's just sitting in the parking garage. Better than having to pay for a ride."

I walk over to where I left my pants last night and fish the valet ticket from the pocket. When I step in front of Nova and hold it out for her, she crosses her arms.

"Do you know how to drive?"

"Of course I know how to drive. But I don't have a license."

"Why not? How do you get into bars and not have an ID?"

"I have an ID, but it's fake. If I got pulled over, it wouldn't be in their system and getting busted for a fake ID is not on my list of things to do."

"I'll fix that when you get back. In the meantime, don't get pulled over."

"What do you mean you'll fix that?"

"Told you I'm good with computers. Hacking the DMV is child's play."

"Seems you're a man of many talents."

The corner of my lip tips up in a smirk. "I am. Now hurry back so I can show you some of the talents I didn't get a chance to last night."

Nova groans but takes the ticket from my hand. "Dammit, I walked into that one. Again."

She stands and I grab her around the waist, pulling her against my naked chest. "I'll see you later." Then I kiss her deeply as though I'm going to miss her terribly. Which, to my surprise, I am. When I pull away, Nova sways a little on her feet, her eyes slightly dazed before she shakes her head and stands straight.

"Drive safe," I tell her and she shoots me a dirty look on her way out the door.

After getting dressed in a pair of black slacks and a dark-gray button-down shirt, I roll the sleeves and grab my computer, settling on the couch. I need to find the plans for the hotel where the event is being held. It's always a good idea to have a layout in my mind before I head into any situation. I pull them up and study the ballroom and all the exits, including the hallways surrounding the room. There looks to be two janitor closets just outside of the room itself on either side. There're a couple ways we could go about this little heist, neither of which include slipping a few necklaces into Nova's purse. If she wants my help, then I think we should be smarter about this and, at the same time, get a little more bang for our buck, if you will.

I pick up my phone and dial Finn's number. It's late afternoon, so hopefully he isn't on his way to the casino or in the gym.

"Hey, what's up? Are you back yet" he answers on the third ring.

I didn't tell Finn my plan to extend my stay yet. It wasn't something I necessarily planned for. Hell, there was no plan for any of this, which is completely out of character for me and strangely thrilling at the same time.

"No, I'm staying in New Orleans for a few extra days."

"Everything okay? Does Liam need to be informed of anything?"

"No, it has nothing to do with that. I have a friend, and I'm going to help her out with a few things before heading back to Boston." Though that wasn't my intention when I offered to change my flight last night so Nova and I could spend a little more time together, it's the truth now.

"Who's this friend?" Finn asks with amusement lacing his tone.

"A girl I met last time I was in New Orleans. She...she stole my wallet, and I caught up to her."

"Why is this the first time I'm hearing about her? And how on earth did she get *your* wallet?" Finn knows my past with lifting wallets and such. And he also knows how aware of my surroundings I always am. I don't want to tell him I was attempting to have a night on the town and acting like some regular Joe Schmoe instead of the ever-vigilant Cillian Doyle.

"She caught me in a distracted moment."

What I don't tell him is that I was distracted by her emerald-green eyes and the words falling from her pouty pink lips that turned out to be lies. I also don't tell him that when I caught up to her, I was ten times more enraptured with those eyes that held a glint of mischief. Or the way she volleyed every question I had for her back to me with the lips she painted red that were far more enticing than when I first met her as Charity.

There's a certain kinship amongst thieves that Finn doesn't understand. It's not like the mob where you're constantly looking over your shoulder, waiting for someone to screw you over. Especially when you decide to work together—like Nova and I will be in a couple days. The last thing you want in this life is gaining a reputation for screwing over the hand that's helping feed you.

"And what? Did she steal your car this time around?" Finn asks with a laugh.

"No, I gave her the keys willingly."

"You sure she's going to come back with it?"

The thought hadn't crossed my mind until just now, but it's not as though I couldn't find her if she did. "The rental agency has GPS on it if she doesn't." Plus, I have something she needs a lot more than a car, that is if she wants to make the biggest score of her career.

"You know, I noticed something different about you last time you came back from New Orleans. I couldn't put my finger on it, but I think I've figured it out."

"What are you going on about?"

"Sometimes I could tell you were somewhere else, a little distracted."

"Are you saying I'm not doing my job as your second?"

I ask, offense tainting my question. My commitment to the family and my job has never come into question.

"Hell no. Have you forgotten I've known you since we were fourteen? I could tell you had other things on your mind is all. I thought maybe it was this shit with Farina, but now I know what—or rather, *who*—is taking up valuable real estate in that big brain of yours."

"Fuck off. She's a friend in need of my particular skill set."

Finn lets out a contemplative hum that says he's not buying what I'm trying to sell, but he won't push me on it. Yet.

"Just be careful," he warns.

"When am I not?"

He laughs and I can picture him rolling his eyes. "True. I forgot who I was talking to."

Interesting, because when I'm with Nova, I forget I have to be acutely aware of everything around me and need to weigh out every possible consequence.

"I see you're a fucking comedian today," I reply, but there's no real heat behind my words.

Finn and I have always given each other a healthy amount of shit, regardless of our differences in rank. He's a brother to me. Even Eoghan is to some extent, but I have more fun threatening him with hard looks when he's on a roll. It brings me immense joy to see him flustered or annoyed that I won't take his bait. Serves the little shit right. But just like his brother, I would protect him with my life, and I know he'd do the same for me. "I'll be back in a couple days—four tops. We have that meeting with the Black Roses set up to discuss new trade routes."

"Sounds good. Let me know when you get back. Ronin's doing a good job with security at the casino. He sends me over a four-page report every night of everything he did and everyone who was in and out."

"Kid's thorough. I get the same reports."

"Maybe now that you have someone taking over a few of your responsibilities, you'll be spending more time in New Orleans?"

I haven't really thought about what happens next for Nova and me; instead, I've been living in the moment, not thinking too hard about the future. His suggestion does bring up some interesting questions, though. Especially after the night the two of us shared in this very hotel room.

"We'll see. It's not like I've been spending my off time twiddling my thumbs."

The work with Liam has kept me plenty busy when I haven't been working within the Monaghan organization.

"I know I've told you this a million times, but you need to take a break every once in a while, Cill. This life will burn you out, especially if you don't have someone to share the burden with. Isn't that what Dad always told us?"

"I'm not marrying the girl, Finn. And I do take breaks. What your parents have, or even you and your brother, it's not something I've ever looked for, and I'm not now."

I've seen relationships fall apart under the weight of this life. To some, it can be stifling and others don't like the danger associated with it. My commitment is to the family who took in a broke fourteen-year-old kid and his sick mom and treated them as one of their own. I'm not about to divide my time or loyalty, even if Finn thinks I should. What he found with his wife and what Cormac and Maeve have is one in a million.

There's no doubt in my mind that eventually this thing between Nova and I will fizzle out. I don't care what anyone says; when you burn as fucking hot as we do, there's no way it's sustainable—especially with thousands of miles between us on a normal basis.

"Whatever you say. I'll see you when you get home, then. Hey, maybe Alessia and I can take a trip down with you one of these days and have a double date."

"Goodbye, Finn."

I hang up the phone without waiting for a response and look at the building plans for the hotel again, thinking about my idea from earlier. If Nova wants a big score, I think I have the perfect plan to give it to her.

My phone dings with a text from Nova a couple hours after my conversation with Finn.

**Nova:** *I'm downstairs. Don't have a key card for the*

*elevator.*

I'm a jackass. I completely forgot since switching to the suite, a specific card is needed to get to this floor.

**Me:** *Be right down.*

I step into the elevator with a smile on my face, and when it opens to the lobby, my smile grows. Nova is in a short summer dress with a pair of beat-up high-tops, her hair wrapped in a bun on the top of her head as she stares at her phone. When her gaze finds mine, I catch the flare of desire in hers.

"Afraid I'd take off?" she asks, picking up her bag and walking to meet me beside the elevator.

"Thought didn't even cross my mind." I look down at the bag. "What's in there?"

"A couple changes of clothes so I won't have to run back to my place."

"We could just spend the next two days naked," I offer. "Save you from having to worry about laundry and all that."

"Good to know you care about my laundry habits, but I was thinking, since you're staying for a couple days, we could have a little fun in town. My roommate is working tonight. Thought we could grab a drink and see where the night takes us."

"I'm hoping it takes us to the same place it did last night." I grab the bag from Nova's hand and walk into the elevator, swiping the card to my floor.

"I'm a lady, I'll have you know," she says in her most prim and proper Southern accent. "I expect dinner first."

"I'm more than happy to wine and dine you. But first, I want to go over the plans for Saturday."

"You know what they say about all work and no play."

"Trust me, I'm perfectly aware. Do you know what I say about preparation and opportunity?"

Nova gives me a flat look then sticks her tongue out at me.

"I'm glad to see you're taking this seriously. This isn't just a little petty pickpocketing, Nova. We need to be prepared for what we're walking into."

"I think I'm seeing the serious side of you finally. Is this what you're like in Boston?"

"Yes, but people tend to listen to me a lot better there. Could be the gun I carry that scares them straight, though."

"Do you have said gun with you?"

"No. The FAA frowns upon firearms on airplanes."

"Mmm. Pity. I bet mob lieutenant Cillian is hot as fuck." The door opens, and we step out of the elevator and walk to my suite door. "And I do take this seriously. I'm just of the mind that you can do what needs to be done and have a good time while doing it."

"That's...not how I do things."

Nova's eyes widen in surprise, but I can tell it's fake. "Shocking."

A huff of laughter falls from my mouth as I open the door. After walking into the bedroom to put Nova's bag down, I find her on the couch in the living room of the suite, looking at my open laptop.

"Plans for the ballroom and hotel," I supply, sitting next to her. I point out the exits, then pull up the pictures the hotel has on the website. "The ballroom has cameras all over the place." I point to several that I found in pictures alone. There are probably more, but I won't know until I get in there. "I think we should rethink our strategy."

Nova's head whips in my direction with a scowl on her face. "If you don't think you can help me pull this off, tell me now. I have the invites and the dress. I just need someone to help with a few other things. If that isn't you, now's the time to tell me."

"Whoa, there. I said *rethink*, not *call it off*. I came up with a better plan."

She eyes me with suspicion for a few moments before I continue. I don't know who let this girl down and shattered her trust in men, but there's not a chance I'm going to be the one to do the same.

"I think we should have a romantic night in one of the hotel rooms, my little dumpling."

Her brows knit together as she shoots me a withering look. "Uh, excuse me? Dumpling?"

"I'm testing out nicknames for my future wife. You know, since we're playing a newly engaged couple."

"I'm going to nix that one right now. There's no way I'll be able to keep a straight face if you start calling me food items."

"Sunshine? Angel? My little mint julep? You know,

because you're from the South."

"No, no, and fuck no."

"How about my star? Kind of like a supernova."

The tinkling laughter that falls from her lips brings a wide smile to my face. I seem to do that a lot around her.

"Jokes on you. I was named after the car, not the death of a star."

"Really? Are your parents gearheads or something?"

"Not after they had me. Dad had to sell it with a second kid on the way. Get something more family friendly, I guess. Could have been worse. I could have been named after a tire, like my brother."

"I didn't know you have a brother."

"Had. He died."

Her eyes harden a fraction, and though it's a slight change, I feel the second she tenses up. Of course I'm curious about her life, but I know when to push, and now isn't the time.

"As I was saying, I've booked a suite at the hotel. We'll go to the gala, get wined and dined. Hell, I'll even bid on a ring. Chances are they'll be keeping the items in a separate secured location. If we're at the right place at the right time, we can swipe the key card and let ourselves in." I lean over and kiss her shoulder. "Why only grab a few pieces when you could have the whole kit and caboodle?"

Nova looks over at me with humor in her gaze. "You sound like an eighty-seven-year-old grandmother."

"I don't know where you come from, but I don't think my grandmother ever planned a jewel heist."

"Fair. Okay. How do we keep out of the eyes of the cameras?"

"I'm going to loop security footage after they make the drop but before you lift the key card."

"Wow. This is a lot more than I was expecting."

"I know. I'm a genius."

"And there's that modesty again." Her lips purse, but there's humor dancing in her eyes.

When her stomach lets out a loud rumble, I stand from my seat and hold out a hand. "Come on, let me take you to dinner."

Nova smiles when she takes my hand and stands. "There's the wining and dining I expect." She leans up and kisses me before pulling me toward the door. "Play your cards right, and you might get lucky."

"Might?"

When Nova looks back at me, her heated gaze sweeps over me. "Definitely."

# CHAPTER NINE
## NOVA

"NOT BAD," I SAY as I spin in the suite Cillian reserved for the night at the same hotel where the charity auction is going to be held later.

We've spent the last two days in Cillian's hotel suite across town, which is just as elegant but much more understated. The second night I stayed, Cillian did, in fact, take me out on the town. We met Harper at Geraldine's and she was nearly as smitten with the man as I am if the looks she kept shooting me were anything to go by. Harper has never needed to give me her stamp of approval, and honestly, I don't think she ever has. When she hugged me goodbye before we left the bar, she leaned in and whispered, "I like this one, Chevy. Don't fuck it up." I'm not sure what she thinks is going to come of this, but there isn't anything to fuck up. He has his life, and I have mine, but I'm having one hell of a good time in the moment, which is all I can ask for.

When we walked into this suite, there was a note on the ornate entryway table with a bottle of expensive champagne next to a vase of magnolias, thanking us for our stay. Considering this is one of four suites—and probably the most expensive—I'm more than happy to sip their champagne as I walk around the room, admiring the Renaissance-inspired paintings framed in thick gold.

The walls are covered with cream-and-gold baroque wallpaper, while the large windows overlook the courtyard of the hotel. The windows are layered with gauzy curtains, which give the room a hazy sort of feel, and pulled to the side are thick burgundy drapes that can be pulled closed to shut out the sun. The seating area in the living room is furnished with couches that look more stylish than comfortable, though I'm sure they're ridiculously expensive, with their floral velvet upholstery and intricately carved filigree on the arms and feet. Cillian walks to one side of the suite, opens the door, and disappears for a moment with our bags. He returns a few moments later, sans bag and suit jacket.

He decided it would be easier to hack the security systems from the comfort of a suite in the hotel rather than trying to hide somewhere after the gala. I was, of course, one hundred percent on board with the idea, especially since squeezing into a janitor's closet for an undetermined amount of time didn't strike me as particularly appealing.

Cillian checked us in under his fake persona: William Bentley. He's a finance guy in New York who met the ever-charming and dazzling Southern belle, Charity, during a business trip to New Orleans three years ago. She was here with a few girlfriends for a bachelorette party, and it was love at first sight. The two travel to New Orleans every year to commemorate the fortuitous meeting, and over a beautiful candlelit dinner, the need to ask her to be his wife was so strong that he spontaneously popped the question. It was all very last minute and romantic—*blah blah blah*—but that left him with a fiancée and no engagement ring. Rather than buy any old extravagant and expensive ring off the street, she wanted to find something at the charity event they were scheduled to attend. She loves meerkats, after all.

The story is pretty close to what I usually go off when I'm working a bar like the one I met Cillian in as Charity. He came up with the rest on his own, and honestly, I have to say I was quite impressed with his flair for storytelling. Who would have guessed a lieutenant for the Irish mob would come up with such a romantic backstory?

Cillian walks up behind me and wraps his arms around my waist. "You should see the bathroom. The tub is big enough for four." His lips trail the column of my neck as I tilt my head to the side, allowing him access to that sensitive spot he's found right under my ear.

"Work first, play later," I say regretfully, pulling myself away from him. I would love nothing more than to wrap myself up in Cillian right now, but there's plenty to do before the event tonight.

Cillian growls and nips the skin of my neck. A squeal

escapes me as I free myself from his hold.

"No love bites on my neck, mister. Think of the scandalous looks I'd get from all those very rich and very proper Southern women."

Thankfully, the gown I found at a secondhand shop in the Quarter covers the bite mark that is still faintly visible on my neck from the first night I spent with him in his hotel room.

"Party pooper," Cillian grumbles as he walks back into the bedroom and returns with his computer.

"You know, it's funny. You were getting on me about not taking this seriously enough, and now you're the one pouting about not having a roll in the sheets."

"First of all," he starts as he lays his laptop on the low coffee table in front of the couch in the living room and takes a seat. "I don't pout. Second, I want to fuck you in that huge bathtub—not the sheets."

A bark of laughter escapes me. "My, how the tables have turned."

"I heard the craziest thing the other day. It seems you can work and have fun at the same time. Shocking revelation really, but figured I'd give it a shot."

"Oh, yeah?" My brow arches as he looks up from his computer. "Who told you that? They sound brilliant."

"She is." His dark gray stare sweeps over me. "And one of the most beautiful and enticing women I've ever met."

I turn to study the painting I'm standing in front of, but I don't really notice anything except the heat of the blush creeping up my fevered cheeks. I take another sip of champagne, hoping the alcohol will help me get my nerves back under control. I've never been good at receiving compliments. Jokes are one thing, but when Cillian looks at me and says shit like that, it unnerves me. He sees past my bravado and smart mouth. Sometimes it's as though his gaze pierces into the deepest parts of me, and he likes what he finds there. It's not something I've ever shown anyone. I had no intention of ever showing him either, but like most things I've come to realize with the man, my walls don't matter to him. He finds a way to squeeze through no matter what. I don't know if I love it or hate it. Right now, it's a mix of both.

"And...I'm in," he says before I turn back around.

"That was fast."

"Told you I'm good with computers."

"Do you hack into a lot of security feeds in your work?"

"I've been known to. Bank accounts, county records, things like that."

"I had no idea the mob employed hackers."

"It's not all bullets and brawn. I discovered I had a knack for coding and figuring out ways into back channels. I used to hack into my school's system and change my attendance records."

"Not your grades?"

"I always had good grades, so no. I just had better things to do than go to school."

"Are you trying to tell me you're some sort of genius?"

"I was a smart kid who had more important things to do than go to class."

I have a sneaking suspicion he's downplaying things a bit, but I'm not going to push. It's not my business. If there's one thing I've learned in this life, if someone wants to stay quiet, you let them. We all have our baggage, and I've never been one to press any issue. Especially considering I'm rarely, if ever, willing to do the same.

I sit next to him on the velvet couch, watching as his hands fly over the keyboard and the images on the screen change at a rapid pace. He toggles between windows, his gaze laser-focused.

"Okay, I'm set to go in later tonight." Cillian sits back on the couch with his fingers linked behind his head, and a proud smile flashes on his face.

"Holy shit, that took hardly any time at all." It's been fifteen minutes at most.

"This shit is child's play for me. Now come here." He grabs me by the hips and jerks me onto his lap. "You said when we finished working, we could play."

His lips find my throat as his hands move under the back of my shirt, trailing his soft touch over my skin. My fingers thread through his thick, dark hair. The simple touch of his lips and fingers sends electric shocks straight to my core. Watching him work on his computer had me squirming in my seat next to him. There's something so damn sexy about a man confident in his abilities. The entire time Cillian was typing away, he absolutely oozed this sort of self-possession that I've come to attribute to him. He's assured in his abilities in a matter of pretty much everything, and it's something I find irresistible. It's not the cocky bravado that would have me rolling my eyes. It's a quiet sort of bold confidence that says he's a man who can talk the talk *and* walk the walk—or hack into a security system within a few minutes. Or say he's going to give me more orgasms than I can handle, then proceed to actually do it.

Yeah, I think I'll take a few of those right about now.

My hips move back and forth on his lap, rubbing myself over his hardening length. I lean forward and fuse my mouth to his, nibbling at his lips while my hands travel from his shoulders to the buckle of his belt.

Then, a loud alarm from my phone sounds throughout the suite, dousing the need and excitement.

"Shit," I breathe out and lean back. "It's time to get ready."

"I'll make it quick," Cillian says, his lips returning to my neck.

"What every girl longs to hear."

He pulls back with a challenging grin on his face. "You doubt me?"

"That you could make it quick? No. I've had plenty of experience with that."

"You're a wretched woman," he replies, narrowing his eyes.

"But Charity is sweet as sugar," I say, using an

exaggerated Southern accent. "And it takes time getting ready, so…" I pat his shoulder and lift myself from his lap, holding out my hand for him. "Come on, Billy, it's time to get into character."

"I prefer William. Billy Bentley sounds ridiculous."

"William it is, then. Do I have any nicknames for you?" I ask as I walk into the bedroom where Cillian put our bags earlier. This is the first time I'm seeing it, and hot damn, if I thought the living room was completely over the top, it has nothing on the bedroom. A massive armoire sits against one wall, its wood ornately carved like the living room furniture and painted in gold and light-blue accents. On the opposite wall, the bed is a monstrous four-poster frame, raised high with thick dark blue drapes pulled aside and tied to each post. It looks like something that will completely envelop a person the second you sink into the mattress. That, I can definitely get behind. Cillian set my bag on the gold velvet settee in front of the bed, the soft, plush fabric adding to the luxurious feel of the entire suite. I grab all of the things that transform me into the demure Southern belle and head into the bathroom. Lo and behold, Cillian was right about the bathtub. The giant marble jacuzzi tub could easily fit four people. Hell, probably six.

"We will definitely be making use of you later," I murmur, admiring the cream marble with gold veins. Jesus, this place spared no expense. The decor may not be up my alley, but I can certainly get behind living in the lap of luxury for a night. Setting my things on the marble counter that matches the bathtub, I unzip the large bag and pull out the blonde wig, my dress, a steamer—because Charity wouldn't be caught dead in wrinkled fabric—my makeup, and the heels I borrowed from Harper.

Cillian enters the bathroom as I'm plugging in my steamer. "I need to take a shower. Care to join me?" His burning gaze tells me he has more in mind than just getting clean.

"No time," I reply as I hang my dress on one of the gold hooks mounted on the bathroom wall.

Cillian shrugs as if my brush-off doesn't faze him in the least and begins unbuttoning his shirt, exposing every inch of his defined chest and the tattoos that run down his thick arms as he slips it off his shoulders. Next, he undoes his belt and pulls his pants down his toned legs, stepping out of them and tossing them to the side. His grinning face meets mine when he slips his boxers off.

Damn him. He knows exactly what he's doing, and if we didn't have somewhere to be within the next hour, it would most likely work. He steps into the shower before turning the nozzle on. When I catch a glimpse of his delicious backside, I amend my earlier thought. It would definitely work. I mean, people are fashionably late to these things all the time, right?

*Stop it, Nova. Don't get distracted by the very sexy, very naked man in the shower five feet from you. Head in the game.*

As I steam the dress in front of me, I glance at Cillian and the way he's soaping up every inch of skin. My mouth waters as the suds from his body wash are rinsed down the drain. Fuck, what I wouldn't give to be the one in there washing his back.

I shake my head and turn back to my task. "Focus," I whisper to myself.

"What was that?" Cillian asks as he turns the water off and opens the shower door to grab a towel.

"Huh? I didn't say anything."

His grin tells me he heard exactly what I said as if the redness of my face and neck don't already give it away.

When he steps out, he dries himself, and I turn toward the counter to lay out the makeup I need for Charity.

"No red lipstick?" Cillian asks when he sees the pale pink I usually wear as Charity.

"Charity is far too sweet for red."

"You're pretty sweet yourself, and you wear red."

"What about my personality screams sweet and demure? I must be doing something wrong if that's the impression you have of me."

He presses his damp front against my back and places a soft kiss to that spot between my shoulder and neck, sweeping his tongue out for a brief moment. "I wasn't talking about your personality."

When he backs away, Cillian hangs his towel on a hook and walks into the bedroom, his firm ass on display for my viewing pleasure.

Double damn him.

Instead of letting him distract me further, I shut the door to the bathroom and the view of him from my wandering gaze. His faint chuckle sounds through the wood.

Asshole.

It doesn't take too long to slip into my disguise—or work uniform, as I like to think of it. I've done this so many times it's like slipping into a second skin. After I've donned the wig and painted my lips the soft pink that's pretty but so not my style, I open the door and step into the bedroom. Cillian is sitting on the bed, reading something on his phone, before he looks up at me and smiles.

"I remember you. Charming girl with sticky hands."

"Hmm. Maybe keep that meet-cute to ourselves. At least for tonight."

"Trust me, no one would believe me if I told them."

I laugh and turn around. "Can you help me with my zipper?" The dress I'm wearing is a sleeveless, flowy little number adorned with a print that looks like pastel watercolor flowers. Very ladylike and pretty. But the zipper goes all the way up the halter-style neck, making it a bitch to get on by myself.

"Are you nervous about tonight?" I ask after he zips me up as I sit on the settee and slip into my heels.

"Not particularly. I have every faith in our ability to pull this off." Cillian grabs his jacket from a hanger and puts it on, giving me the full William Bentley effect. Instead of his hair loosely styled and swept to the side, he has it slicked back with gel, making him look like one of those finance douches in the movies.

"Did you even have to buy something for this thing?"

He looks absolutely delicious, but I have a feeling he lives in suits when he isn't in New Orleans. Not that he dresses down in a T-shirt and jeans, but he's usually without the jacket and tie.

"Nope. I had it in my suitcase. These I grabbed from the store down the street while you were getting ready." He pulls a pair of thick black-rimmed glasses from his pocket and slides them on his face.

"Nice touch. Very Clark Kent."

"That's what I was thinking." He holds out his arms, allowing me to loop mine through before brushing his lips lightly over mine. "Charity or Nova, you look absolutely stunning tonight."

I give him a small smile as I try my damndest not to melt in a puddle of goo at his feet. It's not so much the nerves of being in a room with a bunch of rich assholes for the evening or the heist that's getting to me. It's Cillian, wearing his dark suit and pale-blue silk tie that somehow matches the blue in my dress. It's how damn good he looks in a pair of glasses and a clean-shaven face. It's the idea of his stubble rubbing against the sensitive skin of my inner thighs later.

"Ready?"

"As I'll ever be," I respond, and we head out the door.

# CHAPTER TEN
## NOVA

"WHAT A ROMANTIC STORY," one of the older ladies who we've been making small talk with comments when Cillian—or William, as she knows him—finishes telling her the story of the proposal. He was so good at it, I could practically see us at that little table in the French restaurant two nights ago.

Cillian leans down and kisses the top of my head. Even with the four-inch heels, he still towers over me. "When you know it's right, a little thing like not having a ring isn't going to stop you. Isn't that right, dumpling?"

*This motherfucker.*

"So right," I reply, pinching the skin at his waist with the hand I have looped around him.

"So, did you see anything that caught your eye, Charity?" the woman asks.

I see a whole lot that's catching my eye.

"A few things, but I'm going to let Billy pick it out." I send him a saccharine smile using the name he hates. *Two can play at this game, asshole.*

"Don't worry. I'll find something befitting the princess you are, lovebug. Something big and sparkly."

I'm going to make him choke on these stupid fucking pet names.

"Ah, young love," the woman says. I swear she has hearts in her damn eyes before her attention is taken by someone else in the crowd. "Oh, I have to go talk to Mimsy Halfred. She's a complete bore but unbelievably rich." The woman winks before turning, and moments later, I hear her call, "Mimsy, it's been too long!"

I turn toward Cillian and use every ounce of self-control to not burst out laughing. "Mimsy?"

"Jesus Christ. Rich people are weird," Cillian says. "I mean, I'm used to being around people with money, but this is on a whole other level."

"They may be weird, but you have no problem charming them." We've talked to a few couples, most well over the age of sixty and dripping in diamonds. But give Cillian thirty seconds, and they're absolutely tittering with excitement. Can't say I blame them a bit.

"It's the Yankee charm."

"If only they knew what was under that makeup," I say, tracing my finger over his wrist.

Cillian covered up the tattoos that would have been visible on his wrists while I was getting ready. He said he was trying to look the part of a stuck-up financier. It made me realize how much I liked seeing the flashes of ink when his sleeves would ride up or when he rolled them to his elbows. There's something about a man with rolled-up sleeves, strong forearms, and tattoos on display. Don't ask me to explain it because I can't. It's sinfully enticing, and that's all there is to it.

"Let's have another turn around the table. I want to bid on something," he whispers into my neck.

"Why?"

"Because it sells our story."

He leads me to the front of the room where the items are being displayed. Sapphires, rubies, and diamonds cover the tables—making my heart beat that much faster as I think about all the money this is going to net me.

"This would look stunning on you," Cillian says in earshot of one of the attendants. "Can she try it on?"

The attendant nods, and Cillian picks up the diamond necklace, placing it around my neck.

"Starting bid is seventy-five thousand," the man says, and I nearly choke on my breath.

"That's a good deal," Cillian comments.

When the attendant hands me the mirror, I have to admit it is stunning. The necklace itself is made of diamonds that connect in the center, where a large, round emerald sits at the hollow of my throat.

"It brings out your eyes," Cillian says from behind me. Our gazes connect in the mirror, and there's a flash of something in his, but it's gone before I can decipher it. I lift my hair slightly, taking care of the fact that I'm wearing a wig, and Cillian removes the necklace, handing it back to the attendant. We walk along the table and a sparkly diamond ring catches my eye.

"Look at this one, Billy," I say, casting him a smile.

Cillian turns to the attendant again. "Can my dumpling try that one on as well?"

The smile I direct is syrupy sweet when the attendant hands him the ring. He places it on the third finger of my left hand, and I hold out my arm, examining the four-carat center stone with a diamond-encrusted band.

"It's perfect. I can't wait to be Mrs. Billy Bentley."

Cillian chuckles, enjoying the little game we're playing.

"Starting bid is fifty thousand," the attendant states.

"That's practically a steal," Cillian says. He writes his name and a number on a piece of paper before handing it to the man, who drops it in a gold bowl.

"Thank you, sir. The selections will be made tonight, and if you win, your items will be delivered to your place of residence tomorrow by courier."

Little does he know, no one is getting anything delivered tomorrow.

We wander away from the table and over to the bar where I order two more glasses of champagne.

"You know, you never told me what you want out of this little adventure," I tell Cillian, careful to keep my words as benign as possible. People love eavesdropping at these events, at least from what I've heard. Though, I doubt anyone can hear what I'm saying, considering how low my voice is.

"Consider this pro bono work." He leans down and kisses my cheek then moves his mouth to my ear. "I can think of plenty of inventive ways for you to pay me back if you feel the need to, though."

My head pulls back and I look him in the eye. "I was thinking along the lines of you getting a cut of the profits. No one does anything for free or other 'perks.'"

Cillian shrugs and sips his champagne. "I do."

That's the thing about Cillian. He has never reacted to a situation like I'd imagine. The first time we met, he didn't fly off the handle when he caught up to me after I lifted his wallet. Instead, we hung out and formed a strange camaraderie— the only kind you can really have among thieves. He didn't try to get in my bed that first night, either. I thought maybe he wasn't interested, but then the night he came back to New Orleans a few days ago, he made his intentions perfectly clear, and we've spent countless hours tangled together since. It's all very confusing, and I'm not entirely sure what to trust.

"So you aren't interested in a score?"

"I'm very interested. Just not that kind of score." His hand traces up my arm and over my shoulder, until he swipes back the hair covering my collarbone. "Listen, financially speaking, I don't need this. Trust me, I'm well compensated by my boss. But I like helping people."

I quirk a brow in skepticism.

"Okay, let me rephrase. You were going to do this with or without me, correct?"

I nod.

"You didn't have the best plan in place, and I'm sure you can admit that I came up with a better one..."

I nod again, although more reluctantly than before.

"And you can also admit I look much better in a suit than your friend who you were going to try to rope into your terrible plan originally?"

My head cocks to the side, and I shoot him an irritated scowl.

"You don't have to answer that last one," he says with a smirk. "I saw an opportunity to help you out, and I took it. I happened to be in the right place at the right time. That's all."

"How *did* you happen to be here?" Cillian and I have never discussed what business the Irish mob has in New Orleans.

"Business," is all he says.

"As in none of mine?" He doesn't react other than a small shrug. "I get it. And it's fine. Honestly, it's probably better I don't know. Wouldn't want to end up in the Gulf with cement shoes and all that."

Cillian chuckles and kisses me briefly. "It's been years since we used that as a means of disposal."

That...does not make me feel better. Before I can comment further, our emcee for the evening takes the small stage behind the display of jewelry in the front of the room.

"Ladies and gentlemen, thank you so much for coming here tonight." He proceeds to thank everyone for making the night possible and *blah, blah, blah.* Thank God this night is almost over. My damn feet are killing me in these heels.

"Now it's time to announce the winners of our auction. Thank you again to everyone who participated." The emcee goes down the list and when he gets to the ring Cillian bid on, the breath stalls in my chest. From what I could tell, there were a few slips of paper in the bowl, but wouldn't it be the worst luck for his name to be called? I doubt he has a credit card or checks with the name William Bentley on them. Or maybe he does. This is Cillian we're talking about.

"Edmund Bell," the emcee states.

Phew. One less thing to have to worry about.

After he's announced all the winners of the auction, the room begins to thin out, and we decide to head back to the suite so we can start phase two.

I change into another dress, this one a little less fancy-pants than the one before, but still as flowy and romantic. When it comes to disguises, I always pick something I normally wouldn't be caught dead in. Instead of a blonde wig, I change into a long golden-copper wig and swipe the pink lipstick off to replace it with a nude color. It takes all of five minutes before I step out of the bathroom and into the living room, where Cillian is watching the security cameras in the ballroom where the gala was held.

"There are a few stragglers getting hammered on the free booze," he says, staring at the screen. "It shouldn't be too much longer until they take the jewelry to whatever location they're keeping them safe in." He glances at me, then his eyes go back to the screen before he does a double take and lets out a low whistle.

"Who's this?" he asks, leaning back while his gaze sweeps over my new look.

"Ava," I reply, doing a little spin.

"How many different disguises do you have?"

"Just these two. You like?"

"I do. I've always been a sucker for a redhead," he says with a wink.

"Play your cards right and I'll keep the wig on later."

"Nah. When we're together I like you to be exactly who you truly are." He turns back to his computer as though those words didn't strike me like an arrow to the heart, nearly knocking the breath from my lungs.

"Here we go." Cillian leans closer to his laptop, readying himself.

I have a seat next to him and watch as three men begin packing everything up into black velvet cases and loading them onto a cart.

"Here, take this," Cillian says, handing me a small earpiece. "As soon as they're on the move, I'm going to direct you where to go. We don't know exactly where they're keeping everything, but I'll follow them on the cameras."

I put the device in my ear and Cillian puts one in his.

"Can you hear me?"

"Loud and clear," I reply.

Cillian hands me a card like the one on the belt of the guys packing everything away. "Here. I picked this up earlier today. It's not coded, but should be easy enough for you to switch it with the one on his belt loop when you run into him, yeah?"

"Easy peasy, lemon squeezy," I reply, and he looks at me from the corner of his eye, shaking his head.

"They're moving." Cillian switches between screens to map out exactly where they're headed then switches back to the camera that faces our door.

"Go time. I'll direct you through the earpiece. When I tell you to stop, you stop. I'll be looping footage as you go so you don't get caught on camera."

"Not that anyone would recognize me."

"True, but if it comes down to it, I don't want anyone being able to get a picture of you that matches a description, even with the getup." He presses a few buttons, but I don't see any change. "Okay, time to go."

Leaning in, I kiss him before standing. "See you down there."

I step out of the room and into the elevator.

"When you get downstairs, take a right," Cillian's voice comes through my earpiece.

The door opens, and I see the camera pointing in my direction. "You have that one covered, yeah?"

"Do you doubt me?"

"Never," I reply and mean it. I get to the end of the hall and Cillian directs me to take a left, another right, and two more lefts.

"Okay, wait there. I want to see where they go when they leave the room."

It's silent for a few moments—except for the loud

thumping of my heartbeat in my ears. Every part of me is tingling with anticipation and excitement. I can't wait to have those jewels in my hand and get the hell out of New Orleans. I haven't told Harper my plans, but I hope she's up for a relocation, too. I'm one step closer to that beach bar and finally being able to put the days of counting every last penny behind me.

"He's leaving the room," Cillian says into the earpiece. "Okay, Nova, he's walking in your direction. Three, two, one. Go."

I tilt my head to the phone in my hand, and as soon as the guy comes around the corner pulling the dolly, I run smack dab into him.

"Oh, my god," I say as I drop my phone and bend down, fumbling as I attempt to pick it up. The guy is totally caught off guard and bends to try to help me grab my phone, which only serves to have us getting tangled together. My hand goes to his waist as I try to steady myself, and within half a second, I've secured the new badge holder with the one in my other hand, slipping it into my pocket.

Dresses with pockets for the win.

"Are you okay, ma'am?"

"Oh, yes," I reply in a breathy voice. "I really need to pay attention to where I'm walking. I'm so sorry."

The hotel worker smiles and hands me my phone. "Here you go."

"Thank you. I'm so sorry."

"It's fine. It's fine. Have a good night, ma'am," he says,

continuing on his way.

"Very smooth, I'm sure. Okay, turn right. The door is the fourth on the left. I'll meet you in there."

"Are you going to have a secret knock?" I ask as I head to the doorway and swipe the card. "How will I know it's you?"

"Well, I figured if I knock and say let me in, you would figure it out."

"I don't like it. I still think we need a secret knock. And a password."

I open the door and slide in, shutting it firmly behind me.

"Fine. What do you suggest? Two quick knocks then two long?"

"And the password is kumquat."

"Kumquat?" he asks, his tone dry as the Sahara.

"Well it's not like anyone is going to accidentally let that slip and have me letting them in thinking it's you."

"If anyone gets in there, trust me when I tell you, we're in a lot more trouble than we anticipated."

"Are you going to pull a gun on them?" I know he doesn't have one on him, but I like to tease him in a tense situation.

"I told you, I don't have a gun with me. Besides, there're plenty of other ways I can incapacitate someone without firing a bullet."

"Well, aren't you a jack of all trades?"

"Do you always talk this much when you're nervous?"

"Who says I'm nervous?" I'm totally nervous but

mostly excited. I have every faith that Cillian has this handled on his end, and all I have to do is wait for him here. But damn, I wish he'd hurry.

"I do. You talked nonstop when I first met you and you had no clue what I was going to do with you, and you're jabber-jawing now."

"Good lord, are you sure you aren't an eighty-seven-year-old woman trapped in a hot thirty-something-year-old body?"

"And you're seriously going to tell me you aren't nervous?"

"Cool as a cucumber," I reply.

"Are you sure you aren't a 1940s jazz sax player trapped in a twenty-something-year-old body?"

"Well, we are in New Orleans. Phantom possessions are practically a regular occurrence around here."

"As long as he gives you back to me in the next ten seconds."

There's a knock at the door. Two short then two long.

"Kumquat," Cillian says from the other side of the door.

I unlock the door but don't open it all the way, allowing him to slip in. He silently closes it behind him and smiles when he sees me.

"You don't look possessed."

"Does anyone ever really *look* possessed?" I look at him like that idea is ridiculous.

"In the movies, you can always tell."

"That's Hollywood for you. They never get it right," I

say, waving my hand at him.

Cillian shakes his head with a grin on his face. "You're something else."

It's not the first time he's said that to me, but I have a strong feeling he likes my *something else.*

We look around the room, which is nothing more than a large supply closet, except for the two tall safes lining the back wall.

"You said you were good with computers. I hope that extends to safes," I tell Cillian.

"It pains me you didn't think I'd come prepared." Cillian sets the duffel bag on the table and pulls out his laptop, along with a small box and a computer cable. He hooks the cable from his computer to the box, then the box to the safe right above the keypad. After pressing a few buttons, Cillian smiles and enters the combination on the safe's keypad.

"Holy shit," I breathe out. "I need one of those."

"I don't suggest adding B and E to your bag of tricks."

"Where did you learn all this stuff? And where did you get that fancy box of yours? Is that your business in New Orleans?"

"Cormac Monaghan is my boss's dad—the head of the Monaghan family when I came on board. He was a bit of a traditionalist. Before Finn took over, he made sure that we had a well-rounded criminal education. His philosophy is you may never need to use it, but it's a bitch if you do and don't have it. So, there are three things I never leave home without. My computer, this little black box"—he nods to the contraption on the safe—"and a lock pick set."

"Cormac sounds like a smart man."

Cillian opens the safe and inside is case after velvet case stacked in the safe. "He is."

A wide smile stretches across my face when I kneel next to Cillian and begin filling the bag he brought with him with the cases. Once the safes have been emptied, he sets his computer and the black box on top and zips it closed, grabbing the handle as we both stand.

"All set?" he asks, closing the safe door with his foot.

"Let's go."

# CHAPTER ELEVEN
## NOVA

WALKING TO OUR SUITE is a true test in patience. I want to run, jump, and scream that we did it. I want to dance down the hallways as we make our way back. Cillian looped in footage for the stairwell so we wouldn't have to go through the lobby and run into anyone. Though we're still in disguise, the fewer people who see us, the better. The urge to yell in the stairwell is nearly too much to resist, but I contain myself.

As soon as Cillian and I walk into the suite and he shuts the door behind him, I jump into his arms and let out the squeal I was holding back.

"We did it," I exclaim, peppering kisses all over his face and neck.

The large duffel bag he was carrying drops to the floor, and he laughs, holding me tightly against his chest. He lifts me off the floor before walking us both to the bar in the living room. He sets me down and looks me straight in the eye.

"You were amazing. *Are* amazing." His palms cup both of my cheeks before he shakes his head and releases a little chuckle. "Don't get me wrong. I had every faith we'd pull this off, but damn, I have to admit it feels fucking good."

Cillian releases me and walks around behind the bar to retrieve a bottle of whiskey and two glasses, pouring a healthy splash in each before handing me one.

"To us." He holds up his glass and clinks it against mine. The whiskey burns as it goes down. I don't think I'll ever be used to drinking it straight like Cillian does.

"Aren't we supposed to cheers with an expensive bottle of champagne or something?"

Cillian smiles and grabs a soda from the fridge, adding a little to my glass. I take another sip. Ah, much better.

"Not if you're Irish. We toast with whiskey for just about everything."

"Have you ever tried a whiskey 7?"

Cillian scoffs. "I was taught that's sacrilege."

"By whom?"

"The boss of the Irish mob. Both of them actually."

I take another sip of my drink and hum in appreciation. "Well, you don't know what you're missing."

"I'll have a taste."

I hand him my glass, but he shakes his head. Instead, he grabs me by the back of my neck and pulls me partway over the bar to meet his mouth before plunging his tongue inside. His twirls and teases mine with deep strokes as though he has all the time in the world to explore my mouth. When he breaks the kiss, his tongue dances across my lips before pulling back, but only slightly, still keeping my neck in his grasp. I love this demanding side of Cillian that comes out to play every so often. I've been on my own for so long, always having to be strong and in control. Sometimes it's nice to turn a bit of that over to the man in front of me. Even if it's just for a little while—until he gets back to his life and I start my new one.

"You're right," he whispers against my wet lips. "Delicious. But I still prefer it straight."

Cillian releases my neck, and I fall back onto my heels as he casually walks around the bar to stand in front of me. The hungry look in his eyes sends flutters through my chest, to my belly, and then shoots down my legs. I'm still high from scoring the biggest single take I ever have, but the way Cillian looks like he's ready to devour me is making it near impossible to form any other thoughts, to have any other wants except letting him fulfill every decadent promise he holds in his steely-gray gaze.

His hand reaches for the front of the red wig I'm wearing, and he pulls it off along with the cap that's under to keep my real hair in place. His fingers tousle the long, dark strands that spill out.

Cillian leans in and gently brushes his lips against mine. "There she is," he whispers before slamming his mouth to mine again.

His hands move to my shoulders and he roughly pulls the straps of my dress down, causing the top to fall, exposing my breasts to him. Cillian nibbles his way down my neck, nipping at the skin of my collarbone before trailing his tongue down. His tongue circles my nipple, then he pulls it into his mouth, sucking hard. My hands tangle in his dark hair, and the bar digs into my back as I arch into his touch. A hiss escapes through my teeth when Cillian bites down. He runs his tongue over the stinging flesh, then gently blows on it to relieve the twinge of pain.

He stands to his full height and takes a small step back before looking over my shoulder and grabbing something behind me.

"Time for another shot," he says, a sly grin lifting the corner of his mouth.

He tilts the bottle of whiskey and pours a small amount over my breast before his head dips and he licks and sucks the whiskey from my nipple.

"Mmm. Tastes good straight. Especially from your gorgeous fucking tits."

My hands grab the bar behind me to keep myself upright as he repeats the action over my other nipple, and a deep groan of satisfaction rumbles from his throat.

"My dress is going to smell like a distillery," I say, feeling the wet fabric against my waist.

"Can't have that." Cillian steps away and pulls the dress from my hips, allowing the soft fabric to fall in a puddle around my feet. His hand begins rubbing my center through the damp fabric of my panties as his tongue licks the remaining whiskey from my skin.

Cillian's fingers are taking me to the brink of orgasm, even with the barrier of lace between his touch and my pussy, but I want more.

"Fuck. Stop teasing me," I groan, yanking on his hair.

He lifts his head from my breast, and he has that damn smirk on his face again.

"You need to learn patience, Nova. I haven't finished my drink yet."

Cillian grabs my waist and sets me on the bar, spreading my knees apart as he stares at the damp spot at my center before his teeth scrape over his bottom lip. My panties are a little wet from the alcohol, but mostly from how fucking turned on I am right now.

"Lean back," he says before he grabs the bottle and pours a shot between my breasts. He watches the liquid spill down my center and over my pussy before he meets my gaze and bends down, moving my panties to the side, then licking the whiskey from my center.

"Fuck," I cry out when his tongue meets my clit. He swirls it round and round before sucking it into his mouth. I have to lock my elbows, so I don't fall backward. What this man does with his mouth is unlike anything I've ever felt before. He eats at me with ferocity and hunger, like I'm his favorite meal on the planet and he can't get enough. He growls against my skin, and I feel the orgasm building, tingles rushing to the tips of my toes. I move one hand to the back of his head and grab a fistful of hair, anchoring myself against his face.

"Fuck. I'm going to come," I pant out.

Cillian slides two fingers into my trembling channel, and that's all it takes for me to detonate. I scream into the hotel room, chanting a string of obscenities over and over as the orgasm rushes through me. Cillian continues pumping his fingers inside me, licking my clit as his groans send delicious vibrations through me. He stands straight and takes my mouth in a brutal kiss, his fingers still inside of me, slowly pumping in and out.

The taste of whiskey mixed with my arousal on his tongue invades my mouth. The erotic flavor of my release combined with his drink of choice is a heady combination.

When Cillian lifts me from the bar top, my legs wrap around his waist, the bulge behind his zipper rubbing against my core with each step he takes. He walks us to the bedroom while my mouth tastes his neck, the same way he likes to taste mine with his lips, tongue, and little bites here and there. Cillian lets out one of his panty-dropping groans, and his fingers dig into my ass before he throws me on the giant bed.

"Fuck, I need to be inside you," he says, unbuttoning his shirt.

"Finally," I reply, slipping my drenched panties off and throwing them at him.

He catches the material, shoves them into his bag sitting on the settee, and pulls out a condom, tossing it on the bed. "Those are mine now."

"Oh, my God. Are you a panty thief? Do you go around

stealing women's underwear?"

"You threw them at me. I get to keep them. Fair and square." He shrugs out of his shirt and unfastens his pants, pulling down his zipper and letting them fall to the floor. "Now, spread your legs and play with your clit."

"Demanding."

"You have a problem with it?"

"Not at all," I tell him, doing as instructed and bending my knees before letting them fall open. I run my hand over my pussy before circling my clit with my middle finger. My back arches and my other hand instinctively goes to my breast, pinching and twisting my nipple as I pleasure myself in front of Cillian.

"Goddamn, you look so good. Is that what you did when you thought about me last month? Would you run your hand over your cunt and fuck your fingers, wishing it was my cock?"

I let out a whimper and a jerky nod. God, this feels so good.

"Slide a finger inside yourself. Feel how wet and tight you are. But don't make yourself come. I'll be the one who gets that honor."

When I slide one finger, then two, inside of myself, my hips buck off the bed. Having him standing there, watching me fuck myself with my fingers and the heel of my palm rubbing deliciously against my clit, it's making it nearly impossible not to come.

Cillian pulls his boxers down his long legs and fists his

cock, running it through his hand in long, slow strokes.

He walks closer to the bed and runs his palm over the inside of my thigh, staring at my hand and the wetness dripping from my center onto the sheets.

"I thought about you like this. The weeks I was away. I wished I'd kissed you that night. The second I got on that plane back to Boston, I wanted to turn right around and fly back down here, knock on your door and devour every inch of you."

"You should have," I pant, closing in on the orgasm he told me not to give myself.

"Then I wouldn't have had a chance to plan all the ways I was going to make you come once I saw you again."

"You're a smart guy; I'm sure you would have improvised."

"Mmm. That mouth of yours..." His voice trails off as his eyes stay transfixed on my center while he kneels on the bed between my thighs. "Give me your hand."

When I pull my fingers from my core, he grabs them and immediately sucks them into his mouth.

"I can't get enough of the way you taste, Nova. Fuck. I want to eat you out every day and hear you scream my name over and over again when I make you come."

I've never had a man say half the things Cillian says or make me feel half as desired as he makes me feel. It's doing all kinds of things to my heart that I'm in no position to look at, so I don't.

Cillian leans over and grabs the condom from where

it's sitting on the mattress and tears the wrapper open with his teeth. Once he's sheathed himself, he prowls up my body, looking like a starving lion ready to devour his prey.

My legs wrap around his waist, ready for him to finally sink inside me, but he flips us, him landing on his back with a cocky grin on his face.

"Take what you want from me while I watch you bounce on my cock."

I lift myself and stare down at the sexy-as-sin man beneath me, staring with heated anticipation. Goddamn, is he a sight.

As I sink down onto him, his thick erection stretches me deliciously. My head tips back. "God, you feel so good like this," I whimper as I begin to slowly move up and down, leaning back and resting my hands on his thighs for support.

"Fuck, you should see how beautifully your tight pussy takes me." When I look at Cillian, his jaw is set in a firm line as his gaze stays laser-focused on where we're connected. "You're so fucking wet. That pretty pussy is drenching my cock."

His words spur me on, ratcheting up my desire, my fierce need to come just like this. My pace quickens, and Cillian lets out a hiss.

"God. I'm going to come too fast if you keep that up."

A smile graces my lips, and I double my efforts.

"That's how you want to play it? Fine by me," Cillian says, his own challenging gaze meeting mine.

When his hands grasp my hips, he slams me even harder onto his cock. I didn't think he could get any deeper than he was, but the man does enjoy proving to me he can achieve the unthinkable. His own hips leave the mattress as he pumps up in me, taking control of my movements and fucking me from the bottom.

And holy shit. Cillian is a man possessed. And he's apparently trying to kill me by fucking me to death, but what a fantastic way to go.

The orgasm comes on hard and fast, and I scream out as Cillian continues to piston into me, his gaze never leaving mine. When he slams me onto him again one last time, his grip tightens on my hips—sure to leave little bruises where his fingertips dig into me.

"Fuuuck," he bellows, and his cock jerks inside me, his body practically shaking with each twitch. He releases my hips and rubs his hands back and forth on my thighs as we're both still panting hard and trying to catch our breaths. A bead of sweat trails down my spine, eliciting a shiver along with the aftershocks of my orgasm.

"Fuck, baby, keep that up and I'll be fucking you again in about five seconds."

I giggle softly and pull myself off of him with a groan. "I think I need a couple minutes to recover."

"Isn't that supposed to be the guy's line?"

Cillian's arm wraps around me when I settle next to him, my fingertips trailing over his sweat-slicked chest as his glide over my waist in slow, languid movements.

"I think you broke me."

"Hmm," he replies with a quizzical look in his eyes. "Let's see." He rolls to his side, facing me as he brings his fingers to the apex of my thighs, gently rubbing me before slipping past my lower lips. When my breath hitches with the exquisite sensation of him grazing my clit with the tip of his finger, he lets out a soft growl. "I think she still works perfectly well. In fact, I don't think she even needs five minutes." He continues his ministrations, and I feel wetness flooding my core once again.

"Jesus Christ, what are you doing to me?" I ask as my hips begin moving on their own accord.

"Testing your theory," he whispers before licking my lips. My mouth opens, and his tongue slides in, twirling lazily with mine and matching the motion of his finger. "It seems you were wrong, but I think it needs further investigation. We should probably test it in that giant bathtub I've been wanting to fuck you in all night."

So we do. And wouldn't you know...

He was right.

"Pretty sure that was the most comfortable bed I've ever slept in," I say the next morning as I zip my last bag. I've donned my blonde wig again as we get ready to check out of the hotel, deciding that leaving as Charity and William would be the smart move for appearance's sake.

"Considering we didn't get much sleeping done in it, I'd have to say it was one of the most comfortable places I've ever fucked you in."

Cillian grabs my bag and his own before leaning down and placing a sweet kiss on my lips that contradicts his filthy words—and my even filthier thoughts.

"Come on. Let's get out of here and get some breakfast." He heads out of the bedroom, and I follow, giving the giant bed one more longing look.

It's still early, not even eight a.m., but we decide to head out of the hotel before the couriers are scheduled to get here to pick up the jewels that are no longer in the hotel safe.

As we ride down to the lobby, I can't keep the wide grin from my face.

"I still can't believe we pulled it off," I whisper, even though we're the only ones in here. "I mean, I *can* believe it, but it doesn't feel real yet."

"I think this ridiculously heavy bag in my hand is proof that it's as real as it gets." Cillian smiles and leans in for a light kiss. For a big, bad mob guy, the fact he's so tactile comes as a surprise to me, like most things with Cillian.

When the door opens, he takes my hand and walks to the reception desk.

"How was your stay, Mr. Bentley?" the woman at the front desk asks as she takes Cillian's key card.

"Wonderful. My fiancée especially liked the bathtub." Cillian sends me a little wink.

"Oh yes, it was absolutely divine." The orgasm Cillian gave me in it wasn't half bad either.

"You're all set, Mr. Bentley. Have a safe trip home."

"Thank you."

As we turn toward the doors, I see a frantic woman rush from the hall leading to the room with the safe and approach one of the hotel managers, according to his name badge. She whispers something in his ear, and his face loses all color. When he leans back, he gapes at her in surprise, and together, they hurry down the hallway.

"Hmm, wonder what that could be about," I say to Cillian as we walk out of the automatic doors into the bright morning sun.

Cillian hands his ticket to the valet and shrugs. "I'll give you three guesses and the first two don't count."

We share a conspiratorial grin and my hand loops around his arm as I lean my head against his shoulder.

"I'm so damn tired, I think I could sleep for three days," I say as the valet pulls up to the curb with Cillian's car.

Cillian opens the door for me, and when the valet offers to help him with his bags, Cillian declines and walks to the trunk, opening it and placing the bags in himself. When he gets in the driver's side and pulls away from the curb, a grin matching my own stretches across his face.

"There it is." My fingertip pokes the side of his check. He turns his head, snaps his jaw like he's going to bite my finger, and a loud laugh bursts from me. "I was beginning to think this was just another day in the life for you," I say as he drives farther away from the hotel.

"There's nothing 'just' about any day with you, trust me on that."

And there he goes being all sweet again.

"I'm starving and you promised me breakfast. Turn right at the light." And here I go, not knowing how to handle it and changing the subject.

After giving him directions to a local favorite breakfast spot with no hour-and-a-half wait like the touristy places, we're sitting on an outdoor patio, coffee in hand.

"So, what are you going to do with the money?" he asks.

"Probably get out of New Orleans. I've got a couple ideas. Maybe open up my own little bar somewhere." Call it superstition from living here for so long, but I'm afraid to talk too much about what I have planned for the money. What's the saying? Don't count your chickens before they're hatched, or would this be considered a don't put all your eggs in one basket situation? I'm not sure, but it's something to do with poultry. "It's going to take a minute before I can start selling them off anyways. And I probably won't be doing it in New Orleans. This is sure to be the talk of the town for a hot minute."

"I know some people up north that can help with it."

I shrug noncommittally and sip my coffee. It's not that I'm opposed to seeing Cillian again, and the sex has been out of this world fantastic, but the more I invite him into my life, the more I'm going to depend on him or start having expectations of more than a good time. Our lives are going in opposite directions, and I'm not sure I want that to change. But I'm also not sure I don't. Scratch that. I'm pretty certain I don't, and that's what scares me.

When the waitress drops off our plates, I dig into my food. "I was so nervous last night, I could barely eat. Consider this making up for lost time. Or meals, I should say."

Cillian looks at me with amusement in his gaze. "I wasn't saying anything," he says, taking normal bites of his food as opposed to the way I'm shoveling mine in my face.

"I saw the look," I reply, pointing my fork at him.

"If there was any look, it was only one of being impressed at the amount of food you can fit in your mouth."

"Well, I'm starving and exhausted. I want to go back to your suite and strip down so I can crawl between cold sheets and sleep for at least four hours."

"Sounds like a good plan to me."

We finish our plates and head back to his hotel. Cillian undresses, and when he lies down, his arm stretches out, inviting me to curl up into him. I could say I'm too tired to question why that little space between his shoulder and his chest looks like the most inviting place to rest my head, and maybe I am. But I also know there aren't going to be many more opportunities for me to curl into him and let myself feel...I don't know...taken care of? Maybe even cherished a little? Instead of thinking too hard on the matter, I allow myself the indulgence. Just before sleep overtakes me, the last thought that runs through my mind is how fucking good this feels.

# Chapter Twelve

## Cillian

I WAKE FROM MY nap and turn my head—and inhale a mouthful of Nova's dark hair. She hasn't moved from the little spot right beneath my shoulder. Her light snores sound throughout the otherwise silent bedroom of my suite, making me smile. Since when does snoring make me smile? Hell, since when has half the things this woman does ever made me feel like this? Never would be the correct answer.

Though the room isn't as glamorous and over the top as the one we stayed in last night, this rather modern suite will always be special to me. Which is another anomaly altogether. I've slept with women. They've been to my place, and I've been to theirs, but never had there been a place that always seemed like "ours," or an entire city for that matter. New Orleans will always be Nova to me.

When she walked out of the bathroom as Charity last night, I was stunned speechless for a few moments. I fucking loved that under her disguise, I still saw Nova. Not the woman who I was planning a heist with, not the pickpocket I met only a few weeks ago, but the real her.

She somehow has the power to stun me stupid at every turn. And I fucking love it. Her wit, her charm, hell, everything about her has been completely unexpected. I find myself falling under her spell, falling for her more and more every moment we spend together. I could fight against it, but Nova is a force. It doesn't matter what I've told myself or Finn about not wanting what he has with his wife; I can't help but think I was a fool for thinking I could resist this stunning creature lying in bed next to me.

I have no idea if there's a future for us, but I hope to God there is. If there's one thing I've come to realize about Nova, it's that you can't rush her or push her into talking about something she isn't ready for. Good thing I've learned to play the long game in my line of work. When she talked about taking her money and getting out of New Orleans, she didn't give me the impression she considered Boston as a viable option. Nova was quick to shrug off the idea of me helping her unload the haul from last night. I'm beginning to think she has something against the city or something.

"Are you staring at me while I sleep?" Nova asks in a raspy voice as she peeks at me through the hair covering her face.

"Busted." I gently swipe the hair from her face. "Your damn hair nearly choked me to death."

"That's what you get for being creepy." She rolls off my shoulder and onto her back, scrubbing a hand over her face. "What time is it?"

I reach over and grab my phone, turning the screen on so I can check the time. "Almost four."

"Jesus Christ, we've been sleeping all day."

"We had an eventful night," I say, smiling as I remember just how eventful it was when we got back to the suite.

Nova looks at me and groans when she sees the grin on my lips. "You're a sex fiend, aren't you?"

"I'm a *you* fiend," I reply and grab her waist, hauling her over me. Nova lets out a squeal but doesn't try to get away when my arms wrap around her, holding her tight to my chest.

Then I hear what has to be the loudest stomach rumble come from Nova.

She laughs and buries her head in my chest. "I'm a little hungry. Again," she says, though it's muffled with her face smashed against me.

"Alright. Let's get you some dinner."

"Ugh, it's so early for dinner." She pops her head up and rests her chin on my chest. "I'm going to feel like an old fogey or something."

"Fine. Call it a late lunch."

"What are we going to have for dinner then?"

"Are you trying to be difficult?"

"It's an honest question. If this is lunch, then what's for dinner?"

"A spanking if you don't be quiet."

"If that's supposed to be a threat, you're missing the mark by a long shot."

"So you ask absurd questions to get spanked? Good to know."

Her stomach rumbles, and I tap her bare ass. "Alright, up and at 'em. The early bird special waits for no man."

"I hope that's not your version of a spanking. It's weak as shit."

She rolls to get off me, and as soon as she stands, my palm connects with her ass—hard.

Nova lets out a yelp and turns her head to face me, her brow quirked with an otherwise flat expression on her face. I smile triumphantly at her before leaning over and pressing a kiss to the cheek that now bears a red handprint.

"I'll kiss it and make it better after we get you some food."

Nova walks into the bathroom completely naked, and I lie back, looking on with satisfaction at the pink handprint. It's a good look on her.

When the light flips on, she turns to me. "Or, you could kiss it and make it better now," she says before disappearing into the bathroom and turning on the shower.

Well, with an invitation like that...

The good thing about having dinner at five o'clock in the afternoon is there's no wait at the little French restaurant I take Nova to. After sharing a bottle of wine and a three-course meal where she polishes her plate with every course, we each lean back in our chairs with glasses of wine, enjoying the little patio and late afternoon sun.

"You pull off that Southern belle accent pretty well," I say after the waiter has cleared our plates. "Are you from New Orleans?"

Considering the amount of time Nova and I have spent together over the last few days, we really don't know that much about each other. Sure, I've figured out all sorts of ways to make her come, I know how she makes *me* feel, but I don't know her history or her life before she came to New Orleans. Throughout the last few days, I've gotten a strong feeling she likes to keep it that way. I've never felt the same sort of intense infatuation toward another woman as I have with her, especially with so little knowledge about her life outside of the handful of days we've spent together.

"Close. My hometown is a few hours from here. I moved down here when I was seventeen."

"What made you decide to come to New Orleans?"

Nova chuckles to herself and shakes her head. "I was *in love*," she answers before sipping her wine. "It was your typical high school romance. He wanted to get out of the little town we lived in and thought New Orleans would be where he could make his dreams come true or some shit."

"I take it that it ended badly?"

Nova inhales a deep breath and lets it out in a long huff. "Would you consider walking in and catching him having sex with his merch girl badly?"

My eyes widen. "I...yeah, I'd consider that to be bad." Who in their right mind would be stupid enough to destroy something with this gorgeous woman? His loss is my gain, I suppose.

"We were living here for about a year," she continues. "He had a friend who swore it was easier to have their band discovered down here rather than moving to Nashville or LA. His friend's cousin was a musician and was signed after playing local bars for six months or something, so he convinced my boyfriend this was where they needed to be, and I was all too happy to follow. My brother was fucking pissed when I dropped out of high school to follow him."

This is the first time Nova has mentioned her brother since she told me he'd died. She didn't open up to me about him when she first brought him up, and I certainly wasn't going to pry. But if I'm going to convince her that she can trust me with her story and her heart, I have to nudge a little here and there.

"Were you and your brother close?"

"Yeah." She wears a wistful smile on her face as she sips her wine and falls silent for a few moments. I recognize that look. It's one I've worn many times when someone brings up my mom. It's as though she's reliving a memory, a fond one if her smile is any indication. "It was pretty much just the two of us growing up. Our dad was in and out of jail when we were kids, and my mom...well, she was in and out of relationships after they got divorced."

"Where are your parents now?"

Nova shrugs. "Probably doing the same shit they were when I left. They didn't care enough about me and my brother to get their lives together, so I don't care enough to talk to them."

"What about when your brother passed? You didn't talk to them then?"

"I called my mom when I found out he'd died, but I doubt she remembers. Or maybe she does, but she hasn't called me since. She was wasted off her ass and bitching about how my dad was in jail again and she didn't have any money, *blah, blah, blah*. I guess my brother's friend had called her and told her what happened and she inquired about life insurance or some shit. Like Cooper's line of work offered a benefits package."

There's a darkness that falls over her face, which is also one I recognize. It's the same one I had when my mind would carry me back to that day my stepdad walked out on us after my mom's cancer diagnosis. I remember the way she cried as she sat on the couch—not knowing if she was about to die and leave me alone in the world. It's the devastation and pain of realizing that sometimes the people who are supposed to love us are selfish assholes—people we've entangled our lives with, only to be burned so harshly by them.

"So how did you end up doing what you do?" I ask to change the subject and hopefully see those clouds move out of her eyes.

"Being a thief?"

I nod and Nova laughs.

"It was a dare, actually."

"What? What kind of person dares you to steal wallets?"

Nova raises her brows, and I remember the first night we met and our little competition.

"That was different," I say. "It was already established what we've both done to make money."

"Fair." She sips her wine and smiles. "Harper and I were at a bar drunk off our asses—"

"As all good origin stories begin," I interject and Nova smiles.

"Anyways, we were hanging out with a group of locals and not all of them were on the up-and-up, if you know what I mean."

"I'm familiar."

"Some of them had inventive ways to make money, and one of them was a pickpocket. Said it beat waitressing, which is what I was doing at the time. He dared me to try it, and I did. Best high in the world. I walked away with three hundred dollars from one bar. The rest of it, with the disguises and knowing where to target, were things I worked out on my own. And he was right. I make a lot more than I ever did waitressing."

"And Harper? She bartends, right?"

"Yeah. She's not exactly cut out for a life of crime, but doesn't judge me for what I do."

I raise my glass for a toast, and Nova mirrors my movement. "To drunken dares. If I could, I'd shake that guy's hand." We clink glasses and down the last of our wine.

"Why?" she asks as she sets her glass on the table.

"Because if it wasn't for his nefarious influence, I wouldn't be sitting across from you tonight."

Nova smiles but doesn't comment. One of many things I've noticed about Nova is she's uncomfortable with any sort of compliment or sweet words. Can't say as I blame her. It's hard to trust people mean what they say—especially because it seems as though she hasn't heard very many nice things in her life. It sounds like she only really had her brother when she was growing up, and now that he's gone, she's only had herself to rely on. People can say all the pretty words they want, but are they actually going to stick around when the going gets tough? I can say, with the utmost certainty, that the family in my life will always be there, but can she say the same apart from Harper? I doubt it.

"Let's head back to the hotel, yeah?" I say, throwing a couple hundred dollars into the check presenter the waiter dropped off.

"Sounds good."

The ride back to the hotel is quiet. Me thinking about having to leave tomorrow and Nova thinking...well, I don't know what she's thinking about; the woman isn't exactly an open book. But if I had to guess, her thoughts are probably somewhere with her brother. There's a certain mood one feels when they've lost someone they love, and I'm feeling it in the small space of my car.

"Want to grab a drink in the bar?" I ask when we enter the hotel lobby.

For all the times I've stayed in this hotel, I've never stepped foot in the bar. Usually I take care of whatever business I have and maybe sleep a night or two here then fly back to Boston—like I have to do tomorrow afternoon. The thought brings a twinge of pain to my chest. I've never *not* wanted to leave New Orleans. I'm always ready to get back to Boston. To my apartment. To my family. To my life. But being here the last few days has done something to that part of me that was solely focused on the family business. Hell, since the night when I helped Liam take out the buyers at the little house in the middle of nowhere, New York. There was a certain restlessness I'd been feeling before then, though. I thought working with Liam would fill something inside me that I couldn't put a name to. And it did. Until I met Nova a month ago, and that pit seemed to open back up. I'm not unhappy with my position inside the organization, but there's an incessant little voice that keeps telling me there's more to life. And it's been quiet for the first time since I saw Nova at that bar a few days ago.

"Oh...sure," she replies, probably confused about why I'm not rushing her back to the room so I can spend the rest of the night buried inside of her. I'm a little perplexed myself, to be honest. But I want to have a real conversation with her about where she sees this going. Jesus Christ, who am I right now? I've never had "the conversation" with any woman, let alone one I barely know. But I can't escape this damn feeling in my chest, and I'm done denying it's there. A few days with Nova simply aren't enough.

Only a few patrons are in here as we have a seat at the bar. The bartender takes our drink order and when he returns, Nova raises her glass.

"*Sláinte.*"

"*Sláinte,*" I reply, smiling at her use of the Irish term. I take a sip of my whiskey and set it next to her drink on the bar top. "I'm impressed."

"That I can use Google?"

"That you thought to."

Nova shrugs one shoulder. "Seemed appropriate with your line of work and all."

"Speaking of work," I begin. "I have to get back to Boston."

"I figured you'd be on your way out at some point." She looks at her glass on the bar then back to me. "When do you leave?"

"Tomorrow afternoon."

Nova blows out a long breath but doesn't say anything. Though I never want to see this woman sad, I have to admit it gives me hope that she's come to the same conclusion as I have.

"You know, just because I'm leaving doesn't mean—" My phone vibrates against the bar, and I look down, seeing Finn's name flash on the screen. "Shit. I have to take this."

I pick up the phone and hit accept. "Yeah," I say in an irritated tone. Leave it to fucking Finn to interrupt me.

"Is that any way to greet your boss?"

"Shut the hell up. What's going on?"

"Do you want me to shut up or tell you why I called? I'm confused."

"No, you're an asshole who calls at the worst possible time."

Finn's laugh sounds through the phone, and I roll my eyes.

"Just making sure you were going to be here for the meeting with Ozzy. And that you weren't sitting in a jail cell because of whatever you've been getting up to down there."

"Nope. No jail cell. I'll be flying back to Boston tomorrow, so I'll be there the next morning for our meeting with Ozzy. Anything else? I'd like to enjoy my last evening here."

I look at Nova and notice her shoulders have tightened. There's some sort of emotion in her green eyes that wasn't there moments ago. I guess the reality of my impending departure is sinking in. The last thing I want to do is sit on the phone with Finn when my girl looks like the weight of the world is on her shoulders right now.

Finn chuckles. "I just bet you do. Alright, talk tomorrow."

"Bye." I disconnect the call and toss my phone back on the bar. The last thing either of us needs is another reminder that it's my last night with Nova and we have so much still unsettled.

"That was a little bit of a reality check, huh?" Nova says, looking at me as I take a sip of my drink. There's an uncharacteristic tension in her tone now. Maybe she hates the idea that real life is knocking, or maybe that's just wishful thinking.

"Yeah. I have to be back for a meeting with an MC we do work with." My entire body turns toward Nova, and I take in her long dark hair and green eyes. There's no way I can leave town and not tell her I want more than the weekend we just had. It makes no sense with the distance between us, but fuck, the idea of never seeing her again sits like a lead weight on my chest. Sure, she could shoot me down, and I'd have to live with it, but if I don't try, I'll always wonder *what if*, and I'm not the kind of man who is willing to live with regrets or *what-ifs*.

"Listen, I want to talk to you about me coming back or—"

"Oh, shit. You know what? I think I left my phone upstairs. Harper was talking about wanting us all to get together for drinks with her boyfriend tonight and is supposed to text me."

"Do you want to get out of here and go back to the suite?"

"No, I'll just run up real quick and grab it. Order us another round, yeah?"

I like the idea of Nova making plans with her best friend and including me. Like we're already a real couple who does shit like that.

"Sure," I say, reaching into my pocket to pull out the key card.

"I'll be back." Nova scoots off her stool and grabs her purse, rushing out of the bar to the elevators.

I order us another round and wait for her to get back.

And wait.

And wait.

What could possibly be taking so long? I try calling her phone, but it goes straight to voicemail. So I wait some more. It's been about thirty minutes, and she still hasn't come back down.

"Charge these to my room," I tell the bartender and throw some cash on the bar for a tip.

Heading over to the reception desk, the attendant smiles at me when I approach.

"How can I help you, sir?"

"I think I left my key in my room. Would you mind making me another?"

"Of course."

I give the woman my room number, and she hands me another key card to my suite. My jaw tics with apprehension that's nearly ready to explode from my body. There's a sinking feeling that when I walk into that suite, I'm not going to like what I find, or rather, what

I don't find. Do I have a reason to think Nova bolted? No. Call it a gut instinct, though. There was something about the way her mood shifted when I was on the phone with Finn. Through my years as Finn's lieutenant, I've become adept at reading a room, and there was something in her entire demeanor that was off when she said she needed to run up to the room, but like a dumbass, I ignored it.

I unlock the door to the suite and walk in. The first thing I notice is how fucking quiet it is. We could have just missed each other. Maybe she took the other elevator, and she's down there wondering where I ran off to.

Walking into the bedroom of the suite, any hope I hold is quickly dashed. Her bag is no longer sitting in the corner of the room. I check the closet. Her dresses are gone. I walk into the bathroom, and every bit of makeup has vanished from the counter. Lastly, I open the bottom drawer of the armoire where I'd stashed the bag that contained our haul from last night—including my computer.

The bag is gone. But the computer is sitting in the drawer.

Well, at least she left me that.

I stand in the middle of the room while thoughts race through my mind. It's not as though Nova running isn't on brand for her. Thieves aren't exactly known for their trustworthiness. But I thought this was different. I wasn't a mark. I was her partner. Though, it's not like she screwed me out of anything. I told her I didn't expect or want anything beyond helping her with her harebrained idea. We never made promises to each other or defined anything further than what it was in the moment. Logically, I have no reason to be angry.

And yet...

Fuck this.

Storming out of my room, I head down to the lobby and to the valet. When I hand him my ticket, he looks confused.

"What?" I snap.

"Um, sir, your girlfriend has your car. She came down about a half hour ago. Said she left the ticket upstairs. She said she didn't want to run back up because you were sleeping and didn't want to disturb you."

I look at him, my mouth opening and closing without words coming out. I want to scream at him, but knowing how convincing Nova can be, I can hardly blame the kid.

"Oh, right," I grit out, trying to reign in my anger. It's not the kid's fault he's been had like I so obviously was, and I have at least fifteen years on the boy. "I forgot she said she was going to run some errands. I'll call a service."

The kid lets out a relieved breath, sure that he was about to get in trouble for handing my keys to someone who didn't have a ticket. He probably should be, but fuck, getting a teenager fired isn't on my to-do list at the moment. No, finding the thief who stole the damn thing in the first place is priority number one. I could call the rental company and have the car located through GPS, but I have a feeling I know where she went, and if I'm wrong, guess I'll be scouring New Orleans to get the damn thing back.

When the car from the rideshare app parks in front of Nova and Harper's little bungalow, the first thing I notice is my car parked in front of her house. Well, at least I know I'm on the right track.

I hand the driver a cash tip and get out, probably slamming the car door a bit more forcefully than necessary. I walk to the car, noticing how quiet the street is, particularly the house. Call it gut instinct, but I don't get the impression anyone is home. I open the driver's side door and find my keys sitting on the seat. Grabbing the keys, I close the door and head up her front steps. My fist connects with the front door three times. No answer. I attempt to peek in the window on her porch, but there's no movement inside the house.

Walking to the side yard, I come across a low chain-link fence. It doesn't take much to haul myself over, and I walk to her back door. I knock again and again, but there's no answer. Unfortunately, I don't have my lockpick set on me at the moment. I scan the yard and move a couple flower plants, hoping to find a key or something else I can use to pick the lock.

Nothing.

Alright, if she's playing dirty then I suppose I have to as well. Grabbing a larger rock that lines the cement walkway to her back porch, I smash the window before putting my hand through the broken glass to unlock the door. I step into the small kitchen and walk through to the rest of the house. The pale-yellow kitchen opens into a hallway, and on the other side is a small living room with a worn red couch and a couple deep blue chairs in front of the window that faces the street. I listen for any movement in the house but I'm met with only silence.

The front door is to the right, and to the left, the hallway continues to the back of the house with two rooms to the left and one to the right. I make my way down the hall, stopping at the first closed door. Opening it, I can tell it's a woman's room. It's distinctly feminine with the white eyelet quilt and gauzy curtains, but the scent is all wrong. Still, I walk in and take a look around. When I open the closet, I can tell at first glance it isn't Nova's. Everything has a much more girly and sweet feeling rather than the edgier tanks and dark clothes I've always seen Nova in, except for when she's playing one of her roles. Then, an unnerving thought crosses my mind. What if *Nova* was a role to begin with? Was this whole thing one giant scam? But to what end? I shake my head, determined to find the girl and get some fucking answers.

Stepping back into the hallway, I pass the open door of the bathroom and keep walking, coming upon another closed door. This time, as soon as I open that door, Nova's scent hits me in the face. It's a rich sandalwood and mint that belongs to the tempting fucking thief I'm searching for.

I walk into her room, and it looks like a damn tornado tore through it.

*Fitting.*

Her closet is nearly empty, but I notice the more demure dresses she owns are still on the hangers. So she didn't take her "work" clothes. Her drawers are open and empty as though she was in a hurry to disappear. She knew I would eventually come looking, and she didn't want to waste even the second it would take to close her drawers. On her bed is a note and a pile of cash with only one word written on the paper.

*Kumquat.*

I grit my teeth as I read the word over and over. That was *our* word. A stupid word that I thought had no meaning. I suppose nothing between Nova and I ever had any real meaning—not to her, anyways. It was a different story for me. And doesn't that just fucking figure.

I head out the back door and get in my car, slamming the door behind me as I sit in the driver's seat and contemplate my next move. She stole my car and left me in a fucking hotel bar. How goddamn cliché is that? No goodbye—not even a *fuck you.* She just disappeared.

Starting the car, I pull away from her house and find myself at Geraldine's about twenty minutes later. Harper wasn't home, so I'm assuming she's here. I park on the street and walk into the busy bar, spotting Harper by herself behind the bar. My gaze surveys the room, hoping to catch a flash of black hair and red lips, but no one stands out. When I sit at the end of the bar, Harper notices me right away and looks behind me as though she expects to see Nova. Her brow furrows as she makes her way to where I'm waiting and stewing.

"Hey. Where's Nova?"

"I was hoping you could tell me."

The lines between her eyebrows deepen with confusion. "I'm not following."

"She took off. Left me waiting, and when I went to check, she was gone along with all of her things. Stopped by your place and all her shit is gone."

Harper is still looking at me, but now her entire demeanor has become stiff.

"She left you a note," I say. "Kumquat mean anything to you?"

Harper's jaw works back and forth for a few moments before she answers. "She isn't coming back."

"Yeah, I figured as much when she left me with my dick in my hand. Any idea where she went?"

"Nope."

"Would you tell me if you did?"

Harper doesn't answer, just holds my stare.

I pull out my wallet and throw several hundred dollar bills on the bar.

"What's that for?" Harper asks, glancing from the cash back to me.

I stand from the stool. "You're going to need your back door replaced."

Turning away from the bar, I head to the front door.

Fuck Nova.

And fuck New Orleans.

# Chapter Thirteen

## Nova

### One Month Later

"Nova, order up," my uncle calls from the kitchen of the dive bar he and my aunt own in a little town in Texas.

I walk over to grab the basket of food from the kitchen window and smile at my Uncle Hollis before turning and walking over to one of the guys sitting at the bar with his friends.

"Cheeseburger and fries for you," I say, setting the basket of grease in front of the man who looks like he should be watching his cholesterol rather than scarfing down an order of fries. "Need anything else?"

"Your number."

I don't even attempt to hide my eye roll. "Give it up, Dale. You're old enough to be my dad."

"You can call me Daddy," he replies with a half smile that's partially hidden by his unkempt mustache.

"And you can go—"

"Dale, you better watch your mouth before my niece shoves that burger down your throat. Or before I call Shelly and tell her you're hitting on my bartender. Again. I don't think your old lady would take too kindly to you sexually harassing Nova," my Aunt Trina calls from the other side of the building. I swear that woman has the hearing of a bat.

Dale suddenly has a nervous look on his face. "Sorry, Trina," he calls back to her.

No apology for me though.

This asshole is only sorry he got caught, not that he's a fucking pig with the manners of a feral tomcat.

I walk back to the other side of the bar and feel Dale's eyes on my ass the entire time.

*Gross.*

When I left New Orleans almost a month ago, I showed up on my aunt and uncle's doorstep, and my aunt welcomed me with open arms and one of her hugs. You know, the kind that suffocates you but makes you feel safe and loved at the same time. The kind that makes the noise from the rest of the world fade into the background. Although, I suppose that could be caused by the lack of oxygen to the brain.

Aunt Trina is the kindest woman I've ever known. Unless you get on her bad side, then watch out. She's a Texas tornado wrapped in a five-three body. Trina is my dad's sister, so she knows all about the bullshit Cooper and I had to deal with growing up—my dad in and out of jail and my mom floating from one asshole boyfriend to the next. Cooper and I didn't have a stable home environment after my dad started hitting the bottle when he was laid off from work. Especially when my mom ran off with the first in a long life of loser boyfriends. She'd always come back and beg my dad to let her come home and be a family, then six months later, she'd run off again. The only person I had to depend on was Cooper, and that fucking MC in Massachusetts took him from me.

The one Cillian apparently does business with.

My aunt and uncle didn't ask questions about what brought me to Texas. Aunt Trina saw the exhaustion written all over me and ushered me into the house, feeding me and sending me to bed. When I finally rose from sleep the next morning, they offered to let me work in their bar until I figured out my next move. I had a nice little nest egg, even after leaving half of it for Harper when I bailed on her, but money goes quick these days. Once I can unload the jewelry Cillian and I made off with, I'll leave here, find some quiet little town, and open up my own beach bar. A place where guys like Dale will get a swift kick to the balls if they harass me or any of my employees. But it's going to be awhile before I step foot back in New Orleans. Unfortunately, that's where all my contacts are who can get me the best price for things that may or may not have been acquired by less than honest means.

After I cash out Dale and his buddies and they leave me a whopping seven dollars on their sixty-dollar tab, Trina flips the open sign around and starts sweeping the floor.

"Closing early tonight?" I ask.

"It's been a long day. I don't think closing a little

early on a painfully slow night is going to make any difference."

That's the nice part of her owning a bar in a small town. She can say screw it and shut it down whenever she pleases. And considering my tip jar only has about forty dollars in it, I'm inclined to agree. I make a fraction of the money here that I would if I were still in New Orleans. But at least there's no threat of Cillian finding me after I ditched him in the hotel bar, took the jewels and his car back to my place, then cabbed it to a town about an hour outside of the city before hopping on a train to Texas.

When he said the name that's become synonymous with the worst day of my entire life, I thought I was going to pass out. I fucking hate Ozzy and that club. I hate Cash for coming down to New Orleans to visit and convincing Cooper that he could set us up for life in Massachusetts. Who the fuck wants to live there anyways? It's winter like seven months out of the year or some shit. But Cooper wanted to make a go of it since he really didn't have anything going on where we were, and he always looked up to Cash. Cooper liked the idea of being part of a family who had your back when shit went south.

Well, where the hell were they when he was shot and killed? They had him out there by himself, protecting some chick from her crazy family, and look what happened to him. He shouldn't have been there. He should've been with me, safe and sound, where none of that shit would have touched him.

"You look like you're chewing on something tough over there, girl," my aunt says when she walks up to me as I'm wiping down the beer taps behind the bar.

"Got a lot on my mind."

Trina sits at one of the stools and taps the bar. "Pour me a shot of whiskey and one for yourself. Let's have a chat."

Though I groan inwardly, I don't dare let it show. I'm not about to slap her in the face for her hospitality, family or not. Pouring us each a shot—mine tequila, because I can't even stand the smell of whiskey anymore, let alone the taste—I walk around the bar and sit next to her. Trina sips the drink and lets out a long exhale before my uncle peeks his head from the kitchen window.

"I take it I'm driving you two lushes home?"

"Mind your mouth and get back to cleaning that damn kitchen, Hollis."

My uncle blows my aunt a kiss and ducks back into the kitchen.

"So, my sweet niece. You gonna tell me what brought you to my doorstep, or are you planning on living in my guest room for the rest of your days?"

"Sorry if I'm an imposition," I grumble while staring at the tequila in front of me.

"Those words never left my mouth, Nova Reed. If you're running, I think I deserve to know from what."

Though Trina and Hollis don't judge me, and they

never judged Cooper for what we did with our lives, I've never exactly told them how I survived in New Orleans. I hadn't thought about what I was going to say when I finally unloaded what was still inside the black duffel under the twin bed in their spare room.

"I thought I could trust someone and, as it turned out, I couldn't. He has...connections...that I don't want any part of."

The question that plagued me from the second I heard Ozzy's name was, did Cillian respond to me because he knew I was Cooper's sister? Was he sent to keep an eye on me by his buddy Ozzy?

On more than one occasion, Ozzy tried to reach out and send me money. I had to change my phone number—because *fuck him*. He doesn't get to ease his conscience with blood money. He and his club are the reason my brother was taken away from me. I can chalk up Cillian and me meeting in New Orleans that first time as a coincidence. I doubt he expected to get pickpocketed at a bar. But he said he was there on business both times he came to New Orleans and was never forthcoming with what that business entailed. Could I have been that business? Maybe getting me to trust him was a way for Ozzy to get to me. If Ozzy thinks he can make it right by handing me a wad of cash, he has another thing coming. I don't know what it would take, but that sure as shit isn't it.

"Is this person dangerous?" my aunt asks.

"He can be, I suppose." I never thought Cillian was

dangerous to me. At least not physically. Emotionally? Well, that's another story. When he told me he had to leave the next day, I could barely feel anything past the lump in my throat from the idea of not sleeping next to him. It was crazy and fast, but I thought the connection we had was real. It was so easy to fall for him. And now, looking back, maybe he made it a little too easy.

"Are you safe?"

"Yes, I'm safe." I don't believe Cillian would hurt me.

"Is your heart safe?"

Isn't that the million-dollar question?

I let out a long breath and take the tequila shot in front of me, wincing as the burn travels down my throat. "I thought it was. But I'm beginning to think I was an idiot."

Before that phone call I overheard, Cillian was gearing up to talk to me about what the future entailed between us. I could tell he wanted to continue what we'd started. And though I hate the idea of being anywhere near Shine, Massachusetts, I would have thought about it. Maybe I would've even given it a shot if things worked out that way. But then his damn phone rang...

"We're all idiots when it comes to matters of the heart, sweet pea. But if whoever you ran from is worth it, doesn't it beg the question, what if you misunderstood the situation?" Trina smiles as she sips the whiskey in front of her. "I've known you your entire life, and one thing I've always loved about you is your fierce heart. But at the same time, I've always worried about your tendency to act first and ask questions later. You feel things to the extreme, sweet pea, on both sides of that pendulum swing."

When it comes to Ozzy and the Black Roses, I have a long-standing hatred of him and the club. First, Cash convinced Cooper to leave everything behind and follow him to Massachusetts with the promise of family, yet he left me in Louisiana. Granted, I wasn't ready to pack it up and move up north, but still. Then, when they got my brother killed, Ozzy wanted to give me some cash as though that was going to make up for losing Cooper. And to top it off, Cillian works with them and probably knew exactly who I was—if not at first, definitely by his second time in New Orleans.

At the time, the idea that this was just an unhappy coincidence was a little out of reach. After all these weeks, I honestly don't know if I overreacted—like Trina says I have a tendency to do. I'm still pissed—once again—I trusted a man who very well could have been lying to me. The last time I trusted a man with my heart, he was caught fucking another girl on the couch I paid for. I never wore my pain like armor. I simply walked away. But this time feels different. This feels like a betrayal that cuts deeper than some asshole cheating on me. The pain in my heart is just as present and piercing as the day I left New Orleans. And when I'm hurt, I run. But now, I'm sitting next to my aunt, wondering if I misread the situation. The second that thought crosses my mind, I think about what it felt like to hear Ozzy's name fall from Cillian's lips and the blinding anger returns. That damn pendulum is swinging hard.

Trina correctly reads the obvious apprehension and lack of assuredness I had when I walked into her house a month ago. "Don't be too hard on yourself. We all make mistakes, especially when emotions are running high. And if it isn't perfectly clear, I'm happy you decided to land here so you could catch your breath and sort it out. Your uncle and I love you and only want what's best for you."

"I know, Aunt Trina."

She sends me a warm smile and squeezes my arm before standing from the stool. "Alright. I'm going to finish up here and take Hollis home. No matter what he says, driving after dark is hard on his old eyes."

"I heard that," Uncle Hollis calls from the kitchen.

"I wasn't trying to be quiet," Trina yells back then turns to me. "You can go ahead and get out of here if you want."

Since coming to Texas, I've been using my aunt's old truck. The thing is a beast, but it's reliable, which is more than I can say for a lot of other shit in my life.

"I'm going to take a drive. I'll see you at home."

Trina's eyes are soft when I stand to leave. She knows she hit the nail on the head, and I need some time to think about what she said. Time to face what could have been a horrible misunderstanding that I made worse by bolting. Honestly though, I don't think I would have been able to have a rational conversation at the time. I'm not even sure I can make sense of it now, but if I have any chance of moving forward, I need to untangle all this shit.

My drive takes me out to a little lake Cooper and I used to swim in when we were kids and would come visit my aunt and uncle during the summer. So many good memories flood my mind when I get out and have a seat on the hood of the truck. The moon is reflecting off the still water as my eyes fill up with tears.

"Why did you have to leave with him?" Talking out loud to my brother, who isn't here, feels strange, but these questions have been bottled for so long. "You should have stayed. Why wasn't I enough of a reason for you to stay?"

A tear falls down my cheek. Though it's not the first I've shed when thinking about my brother, it's the first time they're followed by a deep sense of anger and betrayal.

"You left me alone to find a new family. I didn't want you to go. I asked you not to. Why wasn't staying enough for you?"

The tears are falling faster now as I look toward the dark sky. "Fuck you, Cooper. You should have stayed, you selfish asshole. And fuck you, Ozzy, for not protecting him. And fuck you, Cillian, for making me fall for you and lying to me!" I yell into the ether, and then press my head against my knees and let myself just fucking sob. There's no one here to try to make me feel better, no one to rub my back and tell me it's okay, and no one to judge the absolutely unhinged shit spewing from my mouth. "Fuck you all!"

The vibration of the phone ringing next to me startles me out of my mini breakdown. Raising my head to look at my phone, I see Harper's name on the screen.

"Hey, Harper."

"Nova," she says in a frantic whisper. "I think I'm in trouble, and I'm really fucking scared."

My back immediately goes ramrod straight. "What's going on?"

"I'm not sure. I heard Tony talking on the phone, and he was telling someone he'll have me at the dock tomorrow night. Said something about there being a full cargo for the buyers in Russia. Me and seven other girls."

"What are you talking about?" I ask. "Tony, your boyfriend?"

"Yes," she hisses into the phone. "He thought I was asleep in my room, and he was on the phone with someone. I heard him say, 'Massimo promised the Russian buyers a full stable.' What does that mean?"

What in the actual hell?

"Harper, get out of there. He's talking about shipping girls to Russia. That's what a stable is."

"What the fuck?"

"Do you know who Massimo is?" I ask.

"It's his boss. I've heard Tony talk about him a couple of times with his friends."

I remember Harper saying that Tony is from somewhere up north, but he would come down for business all the time. That's how they met. He was here on a business trip with a few colleagues, and they came into Geraldine's a few months ago. Harper thought his East Coast accent was sexy.

"Where is Tony right now?"

"He's outside having a cigarette."

"You need to get out of there, Harper. Tell him you got called into work or something."

"He's going to want to come. He likes hanging out when I'm there."

I'll just bet he does.

"Tell him you've been getting shit for him hanging around or something and get somewhere public. Text me when you get there so I know you're safe."

"Okay."

"I'm going to meet you at Geraldine's, okay?"

"Okay. Shit, I gotta go. I heard the door."

# Chapter Fourteen
## Nova

H ARPER HANGS UP BEFORE I can say anything else.

I hop in the truck and haul ass back to my aunt and uncle's house. When I walk in the front door, the house is still dark and my uncle's car isn't in the drive. They must still be at the bar.

Opening the front door, I run into the room I've been staying in, grab a duffel bag from the closet, and begin throwing clothes from the hangers and the drawers in the bag. I kneel to the floor in front of the bed and pull out the bag of jewels and cash. It crosses my mind to take the entire bag with me, but I plan on hauling ass to New Orleans. If I get pulled over and they were to search the truck...yeah, I'd never make it to New Orleans. I shove the cash I have in my duffel and zip it closed. It'll be enough to get us away from New Orleans when I find Harper. I have no idea what I'm going to do about her piece-of-shit boyfriend, but a few ideas are running through my mind. I'm not ready to face any of them, but I don't give a shit. I'll knock on the door of the devil himself if it'll save my best friend.

After shoving the bag back in its spot, I stand and

throw the duffel over my shoulder. I walk into the kitchen and find a pen and paper, scribbling a quick note to my aunt and uncle to tell them I have a friend who needs me and I'll be back. I hate leaving them like this, but I don't have time to wait for them to explain the situation, and I also don't want to worry them.

It takes me all of four minutes inside the house before I'm flying down the I-10 back to New Orleans and whatever I find there. I'm a nervous wreck. My mind keeps replaying what Harper said. Is there something I could be misconstruing? It's not as though I ever got a bad feeling from him before, but that doesn't mean he isn't an expert in hiding his true nature.

It's not as though I haven't been fooled before.

I end up making the five-hour drive in four and still haven't heard anything from Harper. When I pull up to Geraldine's, I park across the street and hop out. Heading into the bar, I scan the inside for any sign of Harper or her boyfriend if he did indeed follow her here. When I come up empty, I make my way over to the bar, where Damon is talking to a few customers. He looks my way then does a double take before walking over to me.

"I thought you skipped town."

"Took a vacation. Have you seen Harper or Tony?"

At the mention of Harper's boyfriend, a scowl forms on Damon's mouth. "Nope."

Fuck.

I turn to leave before Damon calls after me.

"Everything okay?"

My answer is a wave as I head out the door and walk to my car. Okay, so they're not here. I start the truck and do a U-turn to head to the house. I try calling her again, but her phone goes directly to voicemail. When I pull up to the house, there's no sign that anyone's home. Harper's car sits in the driveway, but not Tony's. Maybe he left, but why wouldn't Harper have left like I told her?

I park my aunt's truck behind Harper's and head around to the back before grabbing my house keys from my pocket. When I slide the key into the back door, I notice though the key fits, the door is brand new. It even still has the manufacturer's sticker on it. Well, at least she didn't change the lock.

The house is still as I quietly shut the door behind me. There's a block of kitchen knives to the right of me on the counter. Slowly and silently, I pull one of the biggest knives from the block and head through the kitchen and into the living room, choosing to forgo turning on the lights.

The moon shines through the front window, illuminating the empty living room. I turn left down the hallway and find Harper's bedroom door open. Again, empty. Then I head to my room, silently open the door, and my eyes sweep over the space. Empty.

No one is home.

Heading back to Harper's room, I kneel at the head of her bed and reach under the frame, pulling out a lockbox. Harper insisted on having a form of home protection, so last year, she started taking lessons at the shooting range and bought a gun she keeps under her bed. When I enter the combination, the gun is still there. I pull it from the box—along with a couple magazines—and head out of her room. Having spent summers in Texas with my aunt and uncle, I'm not new to handling a firearm, but I've never owned one myself.

I slide into my truck and rack my brain, trying to figure out where Harper could be. Admittedly, I don't know much about her boyfriend, only that he came to town a couple times a month and would stay at various hotels, but I couldn't tell you which ones. They would often go have drinks with his friends when Harper wasn't working, and I'd occasionally tag along. I point the truck in that direction and take off, careful to obey the speed limit, considering I have a 9mm and two extra magazines shoved under my seat.

I head to the first bar. It's a little dive frequented mostly by locals since it's off the beaten path of Bourbon Street. When I walk in, three people are sitting at the bar, and a couple people are playing pool off to the left. No Tony or Harper in sight.

The second bar I head to is within walking distance from Geraldine's, which makes it a great spot to have a drink after work without having to sit with the people you just spent the last several hours serving. I walk in and notice a group of three guys sitting off to the right in the corner with several bottles and shot glasses in front of them. Tony raises his for a toast, and the three men clink glasses before tipping them back.

*Deep breaths, Nova.*

"Hey, guys," I say, walking up to them with a wide smile on my face. "Long time."

One of the men to Tony's left shoots me a lecherous smile. I pretend that the look on his face doesn't make my skin crawl and return the smile.

"Nova. I thought you went to visit your sick aunt or something," Tony says, looking me up and down.

"She's doing much better, thanks for asking." Even though he didn't. "Have you seen Harper?"

Tony shakes his head and shrugs. "She said she was going out with a few friends and she'd call me later. Did you try calling her?"

"Yeah, it went to voicemail," I say as though it's no big deal. "It probably died. She's notorious for never charging it."

"Well, how about I buy you a drink and when she calls Tony, she can meet up with us. Make a party out of it," one of the guys says.

"Sure." I sit at the table. "What are you guys drinking?"

"Whiskey."

Of course.

"Sounds good to me," I reply.

The guy who invited me to stay, Emile, signals to the bartender for another round.

"Anyone want to play a game of pool?" I suggest. The last thing I want is to hang out with any of these assholes, but I need them distracted.

"Sure. Just let me hit the head first." Tony stands and slides his phone into his pocket before heading to the bathrooms while the rest of us walk over to the pool tables.

"I'm actually going to use the restroom as well," I say while Emile and Aldo, the other guy he's with, select their pool cues hanging from the wall.

"Hurry back," Emile says with that disgusting grin on his face.

I smile and head to the back of the bar, where the hallway leading to the restrooms is located. I stop at the end of the hallway for a moment before the door to the men's room opens. Quickly, I look down at my phone and begin walking toward Tony, who just stepped out.

"Oh, shit. Sorry," I say, colliding with him. I drop my phone, and as we both bend down to pick it up, I slip his wallet from his back pocket and quickly slide it into mine before either of us stands back up. Tony hands me my phone with a smile on his face.

"There you go, sweetheart," he says and I offer him an appreciative smile.

"Sorry, I should watch where I'm going."

I step around him and lock myself inside the women's bathroom before pulling his wallet from my own pocket.

"Let's see what you've been up to, asshole."

There's so much you can glean about a person from the contents of their wallet. Take Tony's for instance. His driver's license was issued in Massachusetts. That's where Cillian is from...Oh, my God. Do they know each other? Are they working together? Again, Cillian never told me why he was in New Orleans, just that he was here on business. What if they work together to traffic women? Cillian works for the Irish mob. Is Massimo an Irish name?

I sift through every memory of my time spent with Cillian and try to remember if he ever mentioned a Massimo or Tony, but come up blank. Fuck, but that's a pretty fucking big coincidence that they're both from Massachusetts.

*Focus, Nova.* If Cillian is involved in what Tony is doing, then fuck him. It doesn't change the fact that I need to find Harper and get the hell out of New Orleans.

He has a few hundred dollar bills and some smaller ones as well, a couple credit cards, and a key card for the St. Augustine, a mid-range hotel not too far from here. At least now I know where he'll probably be spending the night, though I don't know if Harper is there or not.

I put everything back in the wallet and walk out, ignoring the knot of fear that Cillian is involved and head back to the pool tables.

"Hey, this was on the floor in the hallway," I say and hand Tony back his wallet. "Guess I'm not the only clumsy one."

"Shit. Thanks," he replies and hands me a pool cue. "Ladies first."

We play a couple rounds of pool, and I buy us all another round of drinks. No way do I trust any of these guys with my drink. After about an hour, I'm sick to death of these guys, their stupid jokes, and all-around machismo attitudes.

"Sorry guys, but I have to call it a night. I'm going to head home." I turn to Tony. "When you hear from Harper, let her know where I am, yeah?"

"Of course. See you later, Nova."

I smile and wave as I walk out the door and get into my truck. I pull down a side street and park so I'm facing the bar and keep an eye on the front door. After about thirty minutes, the three douchebags exit the bar and get into a black sedan with tinted windows. When they pull away, I start the truck and follow them, making sure to keep several cars between us. Five minutes later, they pull into the parking garage for St. Augustine. I drive past the garage then loop back around, find the exit and park once again. I seriously doubt they have Harper—or any girls—stashed in a hotel in the middle of the city. Way too many things could go wrong with that, but until they leave to wherever they're keeping them, I have nothing to go on or to even tell the cops. As a criminal, I have a strong aversion to law enforcement, but what choice do I really have? I can't exactly walk into a precinct and say, *Hey, my best friend thinks she overheard some shady shit, and now I can't find her.* They'd laugh at me on my way out. Now, if I can figure out where they're holding her or catch them with her or the other girls, I can report a kidnapping and give them a location.

So, wait it out it is.

Sitting in silence with nothing to entertain me but my racing thoughts is nothing if not the most anxiety-inducing way to spend two hours of my life. Where's Harper? Is Cillian involved? What can I do instead of sitting here and waiting? Absolutely nothing is the answer to the last question. The first two? I still don't know. But I'm certainly going to find out.

The gates to the parking garage open and out drives Tony in the same car he drove in. It looks like he's alone. Considering it's about three in the morning, I have no idea where he could be heading, but it might offer me some insight as to where Harper is. I turn the truck on and follow him at a fairly far distance. Seeing as we're in New Orleans, it's not as though the streets are empty, but they aren't as crowded as usual. Tony drives out of the city, and I can only pray that he doesn't notice someone is tailing him. When he turns down what looks like a deserted road, I drive past, turn off my headlights, and make a quick U-turn before backtracking and taking the same road he did. I barely make out the taillights of his car, but that means he won't notice the truck following him either. There are no other houses down this stretch of road—and no street lights either. When his lights illuminate a house to the right, I pull over behind a thicket of trees and kill the engine before he steps out of the car. It's pitch black outside, which makes the light coming from inside the house look bright as day.

Tony walks up the stairs and opens the front door, stepping inside without ever looking around. Good. That means he doesn't suspect anyone was following him.

I get out of the truck and cross the street, keeping myself hidden within the trees lining the road on the other side. An owl hoots in the distance, and the sound of bullfrogs echo around me. It's a stark reminder that many creatures go bump in the night this far out of the city. It's not that I'm a city girl by any stretch of the imagination, but when there's no light and no one around...? No thanks. Who knows what kind of animals I'm sharing the ground with?

*Stop it, Nova. Your mind is working overtime.*

Making my way to the edge of the trees before it clears around where the house sits, I turn right and walk to the back of the house. There's light coming from one of the rooms inside, but the window is covered with curtains or something because I can't see inside. I stand still for a few minutes to make sure no one is outside, then jog over to the window, stop again, duck low, and wait. No sounds aside from the bullfrogs meet my ears.

There's a small gap between the brown paper window covering and the corner of the frame. I peer inside, and what I see stalls the breath in my chest.

Girls handcuffed to a metal pipe line one of the walls.

I can't see Harper, but there's no doubt this is where Tony is keeping her. She might be in another room or something, but having a room full of girls who are obviously being held against their will is enough to go to the police with. I duck back down and turn to run back to the tree line. But when I turn, I'm met with the barrel of a gun aimed at my forehead.

"Well, look who came to join the party."

# Chapter Fifteen
## Cillian

I STEP OUT OF the airport terminal into the humid New Orleans afternoon. *Fuck, I hate this city.* There are too many memories of the last time I was here, and I've decided all of New Orleans can go to hell. Especially one person in particular.

I spent these last four weeks wondering what I could have possibly said to Nova to make her run. Did she think I was going to ask for a cut of the money? Did she think I was going to ask her to come back to Boston with me? The questions swirled in my head over and over—as did every emotion under the sun. But they all landed back at anger until settling into indifference.

Or so I thought.

Then Sampson called and said he's been seeing those same Italian fucks around the docks, and the ship from Russia is scheduled to go out tonight. I called Liam and hopped on a plane, and now I'm back in this god-forsaken city. And my anger is back in full force along with me.

Finn was more than happy to see me off on this trip. He's been privy to more than a couple of my angry outbursts over the last few weeks. But so what if I'm a little short-tempered these days? It's not like he has much room to talk. Anyone looks at his wife wrong and he's liable to shoot them in the kneecap, especially now that Alessia is expecting. Suddenly, when I punch a guy in the face for making a joke about New Orleans working some voodoo magic and making me a grumpy bastard, it's an issue. I mean, fine, it was his brother, but still. Sometimes the kid gets on my nerves and needs to be put in his place every once in a while. Eoghan is the annoying little brother I never had and never wanted, and it's not the first time I've hit the little asshole. I got him an ice pack for the split lip, for Chrissake. What more did he expect from me?

I didn't have to tell Finn shit went south with Nova; he read it on my face clear as day when I met him the next day for our meeting with Ozzy. I barely said more than two words, and Ozzy kept shooting me confused looks. I'm not exactly the chatty one of the family, but that day I was particularly quiet, seeing as I'd just had my car stolen and been fucking ghosted the day before. As soon as the meeting was over, Finn made me spill all the gory details about how I'd essentially been had by a con artist who I thought was just a simple pickpocket. *Oh no.* Nova got me fucking good, and I had no clue.

There's sure as shit no way her little story about wanting to hit that charity auction with some guy who she thought could help her out was true. No, I think her plan solidified when I told her I was in town. She knew exactly what she wanted from me the second I texted her about wanting to see her. She had the perfect opportunity to have a professional help her, so she did whatever she thought was necessary to secure that help. She fucked me for three days, then fucked me over. What other reason did she have to run? She got what she fucking wanted then decided she was over keeping up the charade, so she bolted.

And I'm the one who fell for it—hook, line, and motherfucking sinker.

The drive to the little hotel Liam and his team are staying at takes me about thirty minutes. Nothing but disgust rolls through me at the sight of the city I'd happily never step foot in again. And hopefully after tonight, I never will. Once this shit with Farina's men is figured out, I'll make damn sure everyone knows the port of NOLA is off-limits for any of this human trafficking bullshit. God, I hope they put up a fight. I'm in the mood to wipe some pieces of shit from the earth tonight.

I pull up to the roadside motel outside of the city and knock on room 7. Liam opens the door with a wide smile on his face that quickly disappears when he gets a good look at me.

"Jesus, mate. Who pissed in your Cheerios?"

I roll my eyes behind my sunglasses—so I doubt he notices—and shoulder past him. The room is sparse, with beige walls, a bed, and a dresser with an old TV sitting on top. The window facing the street has a small round table in front of it, which is where Sawyer is set up with his laptop.

"We're good to go. Abel has everything set up down there," Sawyer tells us.

I walk behind him to take a look at his screen. There are several small windows displayed, each with a different view of the docks. There are a couple different views at the entrance gate where freight vehicles pass through, and a few cameras pointing at the freight carrier scheduled to go out tonight.

"How'd he get in?" I ask. Sampson never called me to tell me anyone else was snooping around, and I'm pretty sure he wouldn't have missed Abel.

"Facility maintenance. You'd be surprised how easily that works in most situations, especially places like this where unfamiliar faces aren't out of the ordinary," Sawyer answers.

"Come take a look at this," Liam says, leading me into the adjoining room.

Laid out on the bed is everything we're going to need tonight. Vests, comms, guns, extra magazines, and a few knives. Even some brass knuckles, a few pairs of handcuffs, and several bundles of nylon rope.

"Judging by"—Liam waves his hand up and down in front of me—"everything, I'm going to go out on a limb and guess you're in no mood for prisoners, but I'm going to ask you leave at least one of them alive," Liam says.

I send him a smirk and pick up one of the .45 pistols. "I'm not making any promises."

The ride to the port is silent. We decided to take two black Sprinter vans—one loaded with all the weapons, along with Liam, Sawyer, Abel, Hendrix, and myself. Kingston is driving the other that contains medical equipment and plenty of room for the women who these scumbags plan on shipping. When we pull up to the gate, I show my paperwork to the lone guard, who barely glances at it before waving us through.

"Top-notch security they have here," Hendrix comments as we make our way through the gate.

"It works in our favor. Hopefully the same can be said once we find the container," Liam comments.

I drive slowly, with Kingston following behind. I know where I'm going, seeing as Sampson and I were out here a month ago. But now is not the time to think about that trip and everything that happened following our meeting. The last thing I need is to be distracted by thoughts of a deceitful, dark-haired thief.

I pass the row of containers and some heavy machinery used to load the huge containers onto a ship until I find a break in the row. Pulling into the small area that's just wide enough for one car to drive through, Kingston follows, and we get out of the vans.

"Load up, boys. Who knows when these assholes are going to show."

Kingston joins us at our van, and we open the false floor of the interior before opening the cases that contain everything we would possibly need. Each of us don a vest and several handguns with extra magazines strapped to our sides. I slide a knife at each side and double check each of the guns before putting them in the holsters.

"Like Columbia?" Sawyer asks, and Liam nods.

"You know, I really wish you would explain what the hell that means. Not all of us have been working together for the last ten years," I grumble as we get back into the van, and Abel shuts the doors behind us.

Liam smirks at my obvious irritation then proceeds to explain what we're in for. These guys have an organized system in place, and I respect that. Once he finishes with his explanation, he leans back against the wall of the van. "But you know it could all go tits up, so be on your toes."

"That's reassuring," I tell him, and the group has a nice little chuckle at my expense.

"That's life," Liam replies with a casual shrug.

Sawyer's eyes are locked to his computer screen when he says, "Incoming." He expands the view of one camera, which is pointed at the containers less than a hundred feet from where we're parked. A large white van stops in front of one container and parks before two men jump from the front. The first thing I notice is the nice clothes they have on, not jeans or coveralls you would expect from any run-of-the-mill delivery service. The next thing I notice is the shoulder holsters. Definitely *not* delivery men, then.

One of the men walks to the container and opens the heavy metal door, while the other heads to the back of the van and opens the door. Two more guys jump out before Sawyer switches the view on his computer screen to the opening of the back of the van.

What I see next makes my blood run fucking cold.

Nova's best friend, Harper, is being dragged from the back—and she's followed by the bane of my existence herself. *What the actual fuck?* The terror on their faces is plain as day through the computer screen, even in the dead of night. The other girls that are being hauled out after Harper and Nova wear similar expressions. Every muscle in my body aches to charge out of the Sprinter van doors and get Nova and Harper away from here as fast as humanly possible.

"I know both of those girls," I say through a clenched jaw.

Liam's head whips toward me. "Keep it cool, Cillian. We stick to the plan and everyone makes it out."

My head jerks in a nod as my eyes stay glued to the screen.

"Sawyer, how many girls?" Liam asks. There's an urgency in his voice, either from the adrenaline coursing through all our bloodstreams or because he can tell I'm about three seconds from jumping out of this van and killing every last one of these motherfuckers.

"It looks like six more, but I don't have the best angle. I'm not sure if anyone else is in the van with them."

"I'm not waiting," I grit out.

Liam nods. "Alright. Let's try not to have another Argentina, yeah?"

I roll my eyes as Abel opens the doors, and the six of us hop out on silent feet. We crouch low, each of us with a weapon in our hand, and make a right at the end of the row, heading toward the storage container. The four assholes are too preoccupied with keeping the squirming girls under control, so they don't notice us quickly approaching them, ready to make them wish they'd stayed the fuck out of this business.

"Tony!" one of the guys calls and immediately reaches for the gun in his holster. Before he pulls it out, the sound of a suppressed gunshot comes from behind me and the man falls to the ground with a bullet between his eyes. Three of us duck behind one huge forklift while the other three dive behind a mobile crane for cover. When I peek my head around the corner, I spy Tony looking to his dead friend and then to where we're hidden. He grabs Nova and dives to the other side of the van. Another man grabs Harper to use as a human shield, but she stumbles when he tries to drag her back into the van, giving me the opportunity I need. I expertly aim my gun, and the bullet hits the piece of shit in the chest before he crumples to the ground and blood pools around him. Two down. One of the men is inside the container, taking shots at us from behind the heavy door. Each shot goes wide since he's only reaching his arm out and firing. Fucking amateur.

"I'll kill every last one of these girls if you don't let us leave," Tony calls from the other side of the van. "Let us go and you can have them. No bitch is worth this."

"Farina know you're willing to trade his money for your life?" I call to the man holding Nova at gunpoint behind that fucking white van.

I don't socialize with the Italians other than Alessia's family, but I'd be an idiot if I didn't know exactly who Tony Castalenti is. He's made a name for himself within the organization as being a fucking ruthless psychopath. He was making his way up to a capo when his predecessor met an untimely demise under suspicious circumstances. Of course, that isn't something to be looked at too closely in the Farina organization. The old man made it to the top by stepping over a few dead bodies himself.

Tony peeks his head from around the van then quickly hides himself again.

"Cillian Doyle. You're a long way from Boston."

"I could say the same about you."

I hear Tony curse. "Goddamn it, you stupid bitch. Try that again and I'll shoot you in the head."

"Cillian!" Nova yells.

"Well, would you look at that? Seems the girl knows you, Cillian."

*Goddamn it, Nova.*

"Let them go, Tony. That's the only way you and

what's left of your crew won't leave here in body bags," I call.

I feel Liam's eyes boring into me from where he's standing behind me. Hey, I said I'd *try* to leave at least one alive, not that it was a guarantee. But if this fucker hurts Nova, all bets are off.

"Yeah, I don't think so." Tony walks around the back of the van with Nova in front of him—a gun pointed at her head. "I think you know exactly how this is going to go. You're going to let me get inside the van, and I'm going to take off. Or I'm going to put a bullet in your girlfriend's skull and see where the chips fall."

Nova's gaze meets mine, and a million thoughts run through my head. Tony is perfectly capable of killing every last girl here and sleeping like a baby. Me? I don't care how fucking pissed I was about her bailing. If she no longer walked this earth, I would feel the loss in the very depths of my soul. And isn't that just the mindfuck I don't need right now?

Tony has to know there's no way he's getting out of this alive. It's all bravado, right? But am I willing to take the chance?

"Okay, Tony. Leave the girl, and I'll let you go."

Tony smirks. "Actually, I changed my mind. This one comes with me. I like her fight." He runs his nose along the side of her cheek, and bile threatens to erupt from me.

Nova winces and looks at me for a split second before she pulls her feet off the ground and drops to her knees.

Before Tony can latch on to her again, she punches him square in the dick and he doubles over in pain, losing his gun as he falls over. Nova grabs the gun and points it at the man behind the container door, then fires three times in quick succession. The girls are screaming, and Nova freezes in fear. Tony stumbles to his feet, and I point my gun at him, but before I fire off a shot, he's slithered behind his van. As I'm running to where Nova is sitting on the ground, stunned as she stares into the container at the man she shot, I hear the van start and see Tony in the driver's seat. He ducks low as he peels away from the scene. Son of a bitch. I fire into the van, but I have no way of telling if anything hit him as I watch the taillights disappear around another row of storage containers.

"Let him go," Liam says. "We'll catch up to him later. You can trust me on that. We need to help these girls and get out of here."

Nova is still crouched on the ground. She's pointing the gun at the still body she shot before I made it over.

"He killed one of the girls right in front of us last night. Or maybe it was this morning." Her stare is focused on the man, but I'm not entirely sure she's seeing him or reliving her experience.

Hendrix jogs over and bends where the man is lying in a pool of blood.

"He's still alive."

"You didn't kill him, Nova. You can hand me the gun. You're safe."

She finally looks at me, her eyes clear for the moment. "No offense, Cillian, but I don't know the meaning of that word anymore. I'll hold on to this if it's all the same."

My jaw clenches, but I nod. If that's what she needs to feel safe, then fine. This team of guys and I *only* saved her life for Chrissake.

Harper comes running over to Nova with tears streaming down her cheeks, and for the first time tonight, I see something other than terror on Nova's face.

"Shh, I've got you," Nova coos in her best friend's ear when Harper practically falls into Nova. "It's over."

God, how I wish that were true. Unfortunately, with Tony recognizing me and then getting away, this shitstorm is far from done.

# CHAPTER SIXTEEN
## NOVA

I HOLD HARPER AS she cries in my arms. I'm not sure the fact that this is over has registered for Harper. Christ, it's barely registered for me. The other six girls I spent last night and today locked in a dingy room with still sit on the ground with us. Some are quiet, and some are holding each other, much like Harper and I, as we all try to wrap our heads around what the fuck just happened.

When Tony found me outside the window yesterday, there was no doubt in my mind that I was done for. Harper and I were going to be shipped off to Russia, and no one would know where we had disappeared to. When he threw me in that room, Harper started crying and didn't stop the entire night, apologizing over and over for involving me in the hell she was facing. Though I tried to reassure her, there wasn't much I could say. There were two men in the house with several guns, and they had no qualms with using them—as witnessed when one of the guys pistol-whipped a girl in the head for crying too loudly, then pulled the trigger when she cried from that. He was the piece of shit hiding behind the heavy container door whom I shot. Too bad it didn't kill him, but I have a feeling Cillian or the other guys with him will make him wish I had.

"We need to get this cleaned up," a guy with Cillian says. "Kingston and Hendrix, you two grab the vans and help the girls get settled in one. Abel and Cillian, you two load these assholes into the other van, and we'll drive them out."

"What about the one who's still alive?" the man, who I'm assuming is Abel, asks.

"He can take a little trip with his dead friends in the back. Grab the rope and tie him up."

Two of the men nod and jog off to where I'm guessing their vans are parked.

"Where are we going?" I ask.

The man doling out orders answers, "Back to our hotel. From there, we can figure out what to do with everyone."

"I'm sorry, but why should we trust you? I don't even know your name," I reply.

The man lets out a deep breath. "Sorry about that, love." He may think his English accent is charming or soothing, but he'd be wrong on both counts. "I'm Liam Ashcroft. This is my team. Sawyer and Abel"—he gestures to two of the men—"as well as Kingston and Hendrix, who will be right back so we can get you all out of here. And I believe you already know Cillian."

The two men who I've never seen before today nod in my direction.

"And who exactly *are* you?"

"I run a private security firm out of Philadelphia and also dabble in breaking human trafficking rings, which is what you and the rest of the girls were about to be sold into."

"Dabble?" I ask, quirking my brow.

"Well, it doesn't exactly pay the bills, so I can't say it's my full-time job."

"I've been working with Liam and his team for a few months. That's what I've been doing in New Orleans," Cillian interjects.

"How does this tie into you being...well, what you are?" I'm not sure how open he is with his current career as a mob lieutenant if, for all accounts and purposes, these are the good guys. Though, I suppose that term is relative.

"Finn's lieutenant?" Liam asks, looking between the two of us. "It's no secret, love. That's how we met actually. My brother's MC and his organization go way back. Me and my guys aren't exactly delicate little flowers who let the law have all the fun, are we?"

Sawyer and Abel laugh and shake their heads as they step around us when Hendrix and Kingston park the two Sprinter vans on either side of the open container, probably trying to hide the dead bodies that are still lying on the ground.

Jesus, this is fun for them?

"Listen, as much as I'd love to stand here and play the get-to-know-you game, we need to get out of here,"

Liam says. "I'd rather not have to explain two dead bodies, a shitload of guns, and a van full of scared women to port security or the police."

I look around to the girls on the ground with me. They aren't saying anything, but they look hopeful, like maybe they're desperate to believe these guys really are here to save them.

"I'll be honest, I don't know the rest of these guys, but I know this one." I point to Cillian. "And when it comes to making sure we get out of here safely, I trust him. If he's working with the English rose over here"—I point my thumb toward Liam and he smirks—"I trust him, too."

"You've got your work cut out for you with that one, mate," Liam says to Cillian as he pats him on the shoulder and walks over to Abel to help him clean up the shell casings.

The girls look between me and Cillian and begin standing one by one from the ground. Sawyer, the less intimidating one of the group, comes over with a small, gentle smile on his face.

"Ladies, we're going to take you back to the hotel. You can shower, and we'll get you some food. Does anyone need medical attention?" They all shake their heads no. "Okay. We'll get you back to your families right away." I watch a few of the girl's faces fall, and Sawyer notices it too. "Don't worry. If you don't have anywhere to go, we have homes set up for women who were in similar situations. Follow me." He nods to one of the vans, and Harper and I also start to walk in that direction.

"Not so fast, you two," Cillian says.

"What?" He'd better not try to hash out my sudden departure last month right now. I'm fucking tired, dirty, and hungry. Not to mention the fact that I'm still carrying the gun I just used to shoot a man. Now is *not* the time.

"Tony knows who you are. Both of you." He looks between Harper and me. "And if there's one thing I know about that asshole, it's he's going to hold a grudge like you've never seen against both of you. Especially because he knows that we're...acquainted."

"What do you mean? What do you suggest, then?" I ask.

"I'm taking you back to Boston with me. You need protection until we take out Farina."

"We'll be fine. We can go stay with my aunt and uncle or something. No need to bother." I attempt to move past him, but he steps in my way. Again.

"You want to put your aunt and uncle in the crosshairs of the Italian Mafia?" he asks.

"No, I don't, but I'm not sure if I can trust you."

He looks at me with surprise. "You just told those girls they could."

"It's not my safety or any of the others that I question. When I heard your voice, any doubts I had about you working with Tony were squashed." It's the fact that I hate depending on anyone, especially someone who I was starting to have serious feelings for and who has ties to an MC I've been actively avoiding. I haven't asked him if his connection to them has anything to do with him helping me because, quite frankly, I'm afraid of his answer. I don't trust my heart not to break if I'm right, and if the reason he was so keen on meeting up with me last month was that he was doing it as some sort of favor to Ozzy, that's exactly what will happen. I'd rather deal with Ozzy, even after all these months of avoiding him and his entire club, than have my heart shattered by the man standing in front of me.

"You thought I was working with that piece of shit?" The look of disgust on his face is impossible to ignore and makes me feel like a shit person for even considering it.

"I didn't know what was going on, but when I looked in his wallet and saw he was from Massachusetts, well... I assumed the criminal world up there can't be that big. So, yeah. The thought crossed my mind." It's an asshole thing to admit after everything that went down, but it's the truth. I may be a thief, but I own my shit.

Cillian shakes his head and looks away from me as his jaw clenches.

"It's not as though you ever told me what 'business' you had in New Orleans. How was I supposed to know for sure you weren't here to help him?"

"Jesus, Nova. Just...stop talking. The fact that we spent as much time together as we did should have clued you in on the fact that I'm nothing like that waste of human life."

"Well, Tony did a fantastic job of hiding who he was

for the last few months. It's not like I'm so off base knowing you don't exactly make your money legally." I have no idea why I'm defending my assumption, considering I've never been more happy to be wrong in my entire life.

"Neither do you, but that's one hell of a leap." He looks to Liam and the other guys who have finished cleaning up the scene. At least it looks better than it did a few minutes ago. "We need to go."

"We'll come with you tonight, but like I said, we're going it alone after that."

"The fuck you are. If you can think of somewhere other than a place where you put more people in danger, then I'll take you there. You aren't going to your aunt and uncle's, and you aren't going with the other girls and putting them back in Tony's crosshairs. So, for now, you're coming with me."

He turns on his heel, effectively cutting off any other argument I would have on my tongue.

"Let's just go with him for now. We'll figure something else out," Harper says. "But if Tony is as dangerous as he says, then going to your aunt and uncle's definitely isn't the right move."

"I know," I reply even though it pains me to admit Cillian is right. While we swalk to the van, I think about the shitstorm I've found myself in. Going with Liam to where he's taking the girls who have no other safe place is out of the question. Having Harper and I there could potentially put them in danger all over again if what Cillian says is right, and I have no interest in that. We can't go back to our place for obvious reasons. We probably should get out of New Orleans altogether. A thought crosses my mind. It's something I would only consider since Harper is with me, and there's no way I'm leaving her until all this is flushed out. I hate the idea to my very marrow, but I love my best friend more than I hate the person who owes me something big.

"There's a place I think we can go." He's going to shit his pants when I call him expecting his help. "Fuck, I don't have my phone."

"I'm sure you can use Cillian's if you know the number."

"Oh, I guarantee Cillian already has it."

When we get back to the hotel, Liam's team makes sure all the women have showered and eaten before loading them back into a van. He doesn't want to waste time getting the girls to a safer location and urges Cillian to do the same.

The profound sense of relief I felt when I heard Cillian's voice was like something out of a dream—or a nightmare, considering the situation I was in. He came to save me in a situation where I was sure we were all doomed. I'll never forget it. But now that relief has given way to all the questions, suspicion, and anger

I've held toward him for the last month. It's the kind of feeling you can only have toward someone who you were so close to giving your heart to, only to find out they betrayed you.

"You did good today, mate," Liam tells Cillian as they stand in front of the hotel room. It's an out-of-the-way roadside motel off one of the highways leading out of New Orleans. I may or may not be eavesdropping on the other side of the door, but if they wanted their conversation private, they should have picked somewhere else to stand.

"So you're taking the girls back with you?" Liam asks.

"I don't know where else to put them. At least I can hide them in Finn's penthouse until all this is taken care of. Where's Hendrix?"

The man in question left in a van with the dead bodies and the guy I shot about an hour ago.

"We have a little place not too far from here. I have some questions for the asshole your girl put a couple bullets in. I'll be meeting him there as soon as I get the other women situated."

"Not my girl."

I peek around the curtain and catch sight of Liam's expression that screams *Yeah, right,* even though he keeps his mouth shut. I don't know why on earth Liam would think anything differently than what Cillian just told him. We aren't together, and I have a sneaking suspicion Cillian will want to keep it that way.

"Alright then, I'll be in touch when I get the info we

need," Liam says.

"What are you going to do with him when you're finished?"

"What I did to his buddy back at the port."

Cillian nods, but I can't see his expression seeing as I'm staring at the back of his head.

When he turns to open the door, I jump on the bed next to Harper's. She's sound asleep in hers, probably like I should be, but the reality of where I'm taking us is sitting in my gut like a lead weight. I keep reminding myself I'm doing this so she'll be safe. Because if I know one thing about the Black Roses, it's that they protect women at all costs, even to the possible loss of their lives.

Cillian walks into the room and looks at me, then Harper, before nodding toward the door, signaling for me to follow. When we get outside, I close the door so we don't wake my best friend, who desperately needs some rest.

"You decide where I'm taking you?"

"Yup."

We stare at each other with so much anger between us. He's obviously still pissed that I ran out on him, and I'm none too happy with the idea that he lied to me about knowing Ozzy.

"You care to clue me in?"

"I need your phone to make a call. Considering you know the person, I'm sure you have his number."

Cillian stares at me in confusion. "Who's number

could I possibly have?"

"Ozzy's."

His head rears back while his brows furrow even deeper than a moment ago. "Ozzy, the president of the Black Roses, Ozzy?"

"That would be the one."

"How do you know the president of a one-percenter motorcycle club? Actually"—he holds his hand up to stop me from answering—"nothing about you would surprise me."

"Oh, that's really fucking rich coming from you."

"Why the hell are you so fucking mad at me? You're the one who took off a month ago and left me waiting for you like a fucking idiot in a bar. And you stole my fucking car because you were so desperate to get away from me." He's attempting to keep his voice down but every word is enunciated clear as day through clenched teeth.

"Well, let's ask your friend Ozzy, shall we? I'm sure he can shed some light on why I hate him and his club."

"If you hate them so much, why do you want to call him? And what could Ozzy possibly tell me about you that would explain why you apparently hate me now or why you ran from me in the first place?"

"Dial him up and ask him." I wave my hand to Cillian's pocket, where I see the outline of his phone.

"I'm surprised you didn't lift it and make the call yourself," he mumbles while he pulls the device from his pants.

"Phones these days are fingerprint protected at the very least. Unless you're suggesting I take your finger, too."

Cillian rolls his eyes like a twelve-year-old girl and presses the screen before bringing the phone to his ear.

"Hey, Ozzy. Sorry to bother you so late. I have a girl here that says she knows you." He's silent for a few moments. "Nova." Ozzy must tell him exactly who I am because when his gaze collides with mine again, his eyes widen and there's a look of pity that I fucking hate in them. "Yeah." He hands me the phone, and I keep my gaze locked with his.

"Hello," I say to the man I've never actually spoken to.

"Nova, is everything okay? What are you doing with Cillian Doyle?"

My spine bristles. Does he seriously think he has the right to question anything I'm doing—or be concerned for me at all?

"Long story, but my best friend and I got mixed up in a fucked-up situation and Cillian wants us somewhere safe. Since you owe me, I figured you'd be inclined to help."

"Of course. Anything you need. We take care of our own."

"I'm not yours, Ozzy, and the only reason I'm reaching out is because my best friend's life is on the line."

Ozzy is silent for a few moments before I hear him exhale a lengthy breath. "Okay, Nova. I get it."

"I need to ask you something, and I need you to be

one-hundred-percent honest with me."

"I've never been in the habit of lying, and I don't intend to start now. If I can answer any questions you have, I will."

I'm not sure that makes me feel any better. What would be considered a question he *couldn't* answer?

"Did you send Cillian to New Orleans to keep an eye on me?"

"Nova, until about two minutes ago, I had no idea Cillian was in New Orleans. Our club does business with the Irish, and we've helped each other out when our interests are aligned, but we don't exactly call each other and chitchat about our business. I have never asked Cillian to track you down or keep an eye on you. If I thought you needed safekeeping, I would have sent one of our guys, not the Irish."

I stare at Cillian, who doesn't look any less angry than he did a few minutes ago.

"Okay. I'm coming to Shine with my best friend, and we need a place to hide out until Cillian takes care of some business. This isn't going to make us even though, Ozzy. But Cooper told me your club protects people who need it."

"I'll make damn sure no one hurts you under our watch, Nova. That's the least I owe to Cooper."

I don't rage at him for daring to speak my brother's name to me. Like I said before, I'm doing this for Harper. I don't need to like the man or his club if it gets her the protection she needs. At least staying with them doesn't have the potential of destroying my heart like staying with Cillian would.

So he didn't know about me when he came back to New Orleans. At least he isn't the liar I pegged him as. But if the last twenty-four hours have proven anything, it's that I need out of this life, and he is firmly entrenched in it. I want a life filled with sunshine and a little place to call my own. I don't want to deal with MCs, the Mafia, or mob lieutenants who look at me like I've betrayed them.

"I'll see you in a few days then, Ozzy."

I hand the phone back to Cillian before giving Ozzy a chance to respond.

"Hey. Yeah, we'll be flying out tomorrow. Thanks for clearing that up." He's silent for a few more moments. "Loud and clear. Goodbye."

He disconnects the call and looks at me. "Satisfied?"

Hardly. "Yeah. What did you hear loud and clear?"

"Ozzy warning me to keep my hands to myself."

"Little late for that."

"He doesn't have anything to worry about."

Fucking *ouch*.

"It seems you and I need to have a very candid discussion," Cillian says with that *don't you dare argue with me* look on his face.

"Seems so."

Fuck. Admitting I'm wrong sucks.

# CHAPTER SEVENTEEN

## CILLIAN

She's Cooper Reed's little sister. That was not something I was expecting when she told me she knew Ozzy. Shit, never in my life did I expect her to know the man—period. What are the chances she would've had any clue who the Black Roses were or that she was connected in any way, shape, or form?

The fear I felt when her terrified face came into view of the camera was like nothing I'd ever dealt with before. And I pray to whatever God is out there, I never feel it again. The energy running through me was screaming for me to get to her and protect her. Now that the dust has settled, the energy is screaming to get answers to why she would rather break my heart than talk to me about a stupid fucking misunderstanding. As much as I'm relieved beyond belief that she's safe, I'm still unbelievably pissed that she chose to run away over choosing us.

"Let's have this conversation in my room so we're not standing out in the open," I suggest, and Nova nods.

"Let me leave a note for Harper in case she wakes up. I'll meet you over there."

"I'll wait right here."

"You're literally right next door," she says, waving her hand in the direction of my room.

"And you have a habit of running instead of talking things out."

Nova rolls her eyes and lets out a huff of annoyance, but nonetheless, I stand in front of her door with my arms crossed over my chest, still wearing the dark clothes I had on at the port, minus the vest. Though, with the way she's looking at me and the fact she has a gun in her room, I'm questioning if that's the brightest move.

"Fine." Nova walks inside and leaves the door cracked. She moves out of my view and returns moments later, laying a sheet of motel paper next to her friend. She bends down and kisses Harper's forehead before she turns and catches me spying on her through the crack in the door. And then, of course, she rolls her eyes again.

When she steps out of the room, Nova closes the door gently and locks it from the outside; since this motel is so old, it still has actual keys rather than key cards.

I hold out my arm, indicating for her to walk in front of me to the door next to hers and Harper's. When I step in behind her and shut the door, she's standing with her arms crossed like mine were. We're both on the defensive, but there's a charge in the air that seems to be between us every time we're in a room together. Especially when we're alone.

"Okay, Cillian, I'm here. What do you want to know?"

*Everything.*

"Let's start easy. What's your last name?"

"Reed."

"Where were you for the last month?"

"With my aunt and uncle."

I let out an annoyed breath. "Which is where?"

"Texas."

I quirk a brow, and she tilts her head, staring at me before letting her arms hang loose at her side. "Fine. A little town on the border of Texas and Louisiana. Lenore."

"Was that so hard?"

"Yes," she says with a straight face, but a moment later, the corner of her mouth twitches slightly as though she's trying to contain a smile.

"How about a drink?" Lord fucking knows I could use one.

"God yes," she groans, and I'd be lying if I said the sound didn't send a zap of longing through me. Nova stands in the middle of my room in a pair of cotton shorts and an oversized T-shirt with no makeup and wet hair. She just endured a terrible ordeal that I couldn't even fathom. Being taken and almost sold off like cattle to men whose sole purpose is to use and abuse them. Then, having to save her life by nearly taking the life of another person. I've become accustomed to the violence, but she hasn't. It's a lot to go through in one night, hell, any night, and I'm over here feeling my dick twitch when I hear that throaty sound come from her.

I walk over to the minibar in the room and grab a couple bottles of whiskey, two glasses and a soda from the fridge.

"Shit, I don't have ice." I tend to drink it straight, but this isn't exactly the high-class stuff I enjoy.

"I'll grab some. The ice machine is right down the way," she offers.

"No. Sit down and relax," I say, grabbing the ice bucket. "I'll be right back."

I need a few seconds to clear my head. We need to have a discussion, not get swept up in some wave of attraction. I don't even want to feel this way about her. She fucking bolted on me for no reason. She stole my car for Chrissake, then completely ghosted me without a word. Yet, being this close to her in a hotel room is bringing back memories of the nights we spent tangled in each other. Even though I'm still fucking pissed at her, and I can't trust her not to run again, there's this thing that's been between us since the first time we met. Nova has this way about her that's unlike anything I've ever experienced—and it still has the same effect on me. I loved the way she made it so easy for me to live in the now and not care about anything happening in the outside world. I was so wrapped up in her and that feeling of living for myself and the moment that none of the details of our lives mattered. Now, though...those details matter a lot more than they did a month ago. With every second we spend together, my anger—my only armor against her—is giving way to the feelings I've kept suppressed for the last month.

I get back to my room and open the door to see Nova lying on the bed with the old TV remote in her hand. She's laughing at something on the television and looks over to me. The sight reminds me of the time we spent lying in the same position over the days before the charity gala. That's when I learned about her distaste for thirty-minute sitcoms and that she thought horror movies were hilarious. Especially the old ones, with the cheesy special effects and the blood spray that inevitably looked like ketchup. That's when she also told me that fake blood will never dry brown like real blood, so it's unrealistic when people are running around wearing the same white shirt with red blood for days. As though that's what makes the scenario unbelievable.

When I don't move from my spot in the doorway, she arches a brow. "Are you stunned stupid that I didn't take off or something? Come in before you let in all the bugs."

That's another thing I learned about the gorgeous thief in my bed. She absolutely hates bugs of all types. A tiny beetle found its way into my room at the hotel, and from the way she screamed, I was certain hotel security would come knocking on my door.

And why am I thinking about her as being gorgeous? I'm still mad at her. Fuck, this is what she does to me. Muddles shit up for me. I thought her mouth was her superpower for getting out of trouble, but I'm beginning to suspect she really does have those witchy powers that I teased her about when we were in New Orleans.

I shake myself from my errant thoughts and shut the door behind me before setting the ice bucket on the dresser next to the TV. After making each of us a drink, I hand her a whiskey 7 and take my whiskey on the rocks to the chair next to the little table in front of the window that looks out to the parking lot.

Nova sips her cocktail and scrunches her nose in disgust. "God, since you introduced me to good bourbon, nothing else tastes right."

Yeah, I know the feeling. Since meeting Nova and then having her take off on me, nothing has felt right. Not by a long shot.

I sip mine and relish in the distinct burn of cheap whiskey. It helps me focus my thoughts and not get swept away in everything that is Nova Reed.

"So your brother was the prospect who died saving one of the Black Roses' old ladies."

Nova nods and takes a long swig from her glass. "And Ozzy tried to give me money after Cooper died. I didn't want anything from him or his club. And I certainly didn't want to hear how sorry he was for me losing the one person in my life I loved more than anything—aside from Harper."

"I would have thought you'd be fine with taking the money."

As soon as I see her face fall, I feel like a complete

asshole. As I should. That was an asshole comment. And that's always been my problem. Piss me off or hurt me, and I'll bite back ten times harder. That's how men in this world handle business. But I need to remember she's not a man in this world. She's a girl who's been through a horrible ordeal, not just tonight but throughout her entire life. There was no one other than her brother she could count on. No matter how it happened, the fact remains he was ripped from her, and nothing can erase that pain.

"I don't take blood money, Cillian. No matter what you think about me. And, for that matter, do you really have room to judge?"

"I'm not judging you. But don't sit there and pretend you're some innocent little girl who lives by the letter of the law. And to be fair, it's not like I know you *oh so well* to begin with. Let's not forget how we parted ways, Nova." Should I be picking a fight with her after my comment? No. Am I anyways because I'm hurt and can't seem to keep my damn mouth shut? One hundred percent yes.

"When I heard you say Ozzy's name, I didn't know what to think." Her voice is rising, right alongside the angry flush covering her cheeks. "There was no way it was just some weird coincidence that you happened to know the man I'd been avoiding for the last year. A million thoughts ran through my head. Most falling back to you being with me for those few days because you were doing a favor for Ozzy and keeping an eye on me or something."

"Ozzy didn't even know where I was!" I yell back. "And you could have asked. You could have done a million things other than run out on me, steal my car, then go MIA for weeks, Nova. So yeah, I'm fucking pissed that you left me with my dick in my hand in some hotel bar when we could have easily cleared it up."

Nova finishes her drink, slams it on the nightstand next to the bed, and stands as she shoots daggers at me. "Thanks for the drink, but I'm not in the mood to be yelled at. Yes, I fucked up. Yes, there are a million ways I could have handled it better. I'm willing to admit that. But it's not like our weekend wasn't going to end and you weren't going to go back to Boston at some point. It's not as though this"—she waves her hand between us—"wasn't going to end."

"Bullshit," I spit out at her. "It didn't have to end, and sure as shit, not like that. You could have talked to me. Instead you ran, and I had no idea why. I thought you'd gotten what you wanted and bolted. I never would have done that to you, regardless of whether or not this thing between us had any chance of living past that day. We fucking had something. You know it just as well as I do. It fucking broke me when I found you gone. I was falling in lo—"

Nova moves to walk past me before I can finish, but I stand and grab her arm before she makes it to the door. The second my hand connects with her skin, a hot wave of lust washes over me. One that I wasn't prepared for, especially when her angry gaze bores into me. We stand like that for a few moments, both of us panting. I see the warring emotions in her eyes, just as I'm sure she sees the same in mine. One thing Nova and I have in spades is this insane chemistry I've never been able to explain. It was there the first night we met, and it exploded the night I met her in that bar while we were dancing. Just like it's about to now.

Nova's eyes fixate on my lips one second, and the next, she's crashing her mouth to mine. This kiss is like all the other times when it was as though we couldn't stand not to be touching for a second longer, but there's something else here that never was before. Anger. I'm still beyond pissed, and from the violence of her hands yanking on the strands of my hair as I lift her and wrap her legs around my waist, so is she. But this won't be contained, no matter how we feel about each other at the moment. We've been explosive from the first kiss. And that's the mindfuck of this thing between Nova and me.

I walk over to the bed and lay her on her back without unwrapping her from my waist. My weight presses her into the mattress, but if she's uncomfortable with me lying on top of her, she doesn't let it show. The only noises I hear are our combined moans and grunts as our tongues and teeth duel for dominance.

Pulling away, I sit back on my knees and look down at her swollen red lips and feel a sort of satisfaction that no matter what happens after this, she's going to bear the marks of our frenzied and brutal moment when she leaves this room. I rip the shirt from my body, and her nails score down the naked planes of my chest and tight abdomen until she reaches for my belt and begins trying to undo the buckle. Her hands fumble, shaking with aggravation. I slap them away and finish what she started, ripping the belt from the loops. After I undo the button of my pants and pull the zipper down, I pull out my hard cock and stroke it in front of her as I keep her trapped beneath me.

"I shouldn't give this to you," I say, relishing the way her eyes dart hungrily to my fist that's squeezing the head of my cock.

Nova's hand finds the bottom of her shirt and she pulls the material over her head. She isn't wearing a bra, so her pert tits and rosy nipples are on full display for my eyes to feast on. Her hand cups one of her breasts, her thumb and forefinger twisting the tightened bud while her other runs up the length of my thigh to my cock, and she swipes her thumb over the head, collecting the precum from the tip. She brings her thumb to her mouth and sucks, all the while keeping her gaze locked with mine. I let out an animalistic growl at the sight, and the hand that is around my cock moves to her throat as her head tips up before I slam my mouth to hers in another brutal kiss. Her legs are still around my waist and she tightens her grip, pressing her pussy into my hard length as she writhes beneath me, making it impossible not to feel her wet heat through the thin shorts she's wearing.

When I tear my mouth from hers, she looks at me with confusion and frustration in her green eyes. "If you stop now, I'm liable to go back to my room and grab that fucking gun, Cillian."

My mouth tips up in a smirk at her threat. "Such a violent little thing because I'm not inside you making you come on my cock."

"Damn straight." She rolls her hips beneath me again. "You need this as badly as I do."

Shit, she's fucking right about that. The only thing I can think about is being buried so deep in her wet pussy that every other thought and feeling is washed away. All that matters is her coming on my cock over and over. I release her throat from my grasp and stand from the bed, shucking my pants and boxers off my legs. Then I pull Nova into a sitting position at the end of the bed before pumping my cock. I take a step toward her, and she bites her bottom lip while rubbing her thighs together, anticipation and excitement rolling off her in waves..

"Suck," I command, and she parts her lips. When I slide into the wet heat of her mouth, my eyes nearly roll back in my head. I pump myself in and out and Nova groans, the vibration shooting straight to my balls.

"That's a good fucking girl," I praise before I reach for her arm and grab her hand, placing it at the base of my cock. "Show me that you deserve to be fucked."

Nova doesn't disappoint. Her grip tightens around my

length as she bobs her head back and forth, her hand reaching to where her mouth can't. I grab the back of her hair and push deeper into her, hitting the back of her throat and holding myself there. She chokes and her pretty eyes water, but she doesn't make an attempt to pull away. I draw back and out, allowing her to catch her breath.

"Turn over."

She does as I command, and before having to be told, she positions herself on all fours and props her ass in the air. I rip the shorts down her thighs, leaving them around her knees, then step back for a moment and admire the view in front of me. Nova's hair hangs over her left side, and I see her glistening pussy begging to be filled. She turns her head and looks at me through hooded lids. My finger glides over her center, spreading her wetness around and through her hot cunt.

"Fuck," she breathes out as I continue rubbing, moving my fingers from her opening to her clit, back and forth, but never entering her or providing enough pressure to make her come. And she's damn close. Her head hangs, and every time my fingers graze against where I want to sink into, she pushes back, trying to fill herself up, but that's not what I have in mind.

I remove my hand and grasp her hip, then twist her hair in my fist, pulling her head back before slamming into her from behind. Nova yells out in pleasure as I pound into her over and over, going as deep as possible with each thrust. Incoherent words fall from her lips as

I clench my teeth and stare at the way she takes me in so fucking good. This isn't soft or gentle or anywhere near sweet. It's an exorcism of my anger as I pump relentlessly into the body she's offering me.

Sweat beads at my brow, and I feel the impending release hover just out of reach. As soon as the walls of Nova's pussy begin to pulsate and flutter around me, my hand reaches around to her clit, and I rub furiously over the bud.

"Oh fuck, I'm coming," she shouts and her pussy clamps around me, sucking me deeper, then setting off my own orgasm. I pull out at the last possible second, gritting my teeth and pumping my cock as hot spurts of my release paint her back. When I finish, the relief knocks me back a step, and I have to grab her hip to keep myself steady.

"You okay?" she asks, turning her head to face me.

"Yeah." I swipe a hand over my damp face. "I'll be right back."

I walk into the bathroom and grab a washcloth before running it under the water. My gaze zeros in on the angry red scratches over my shoulders. Then my mind drifts to the first night we were together and the bite mark I left on Nova's shoulder. Then to the day she left me sitting at a bar, waiting for her to return. The anger I felt that day—and all the days after—comes flooding back. This shouldn't have happened. I was supposed to make sure she made it to Shine safely, then put her in my rearview. I wasn't supposed to give her some confession of love...and she was ready to bolt the second the words were about to leave my lips. That should tell me everything I need to know. But like all the other times I've spent with her, Nova has completely derailed my common *fucking* sense.

When I walk back into the room, she's sprawled on her stomach with her eyes closed. I wipe the mess from her back, and she tenses.

"That's cold."

"Would you rather be sticky or cold?" I grunt before finishing and walking back into the bathroom, throwing the cloth on the tile floor. I don't look at her as I stride over to the minibar and grab another little bottle of whiskey then over to the table where my glass was sitting, the ice now mostly melted. I pour the contents of the bottle into the glass and tip it back into my mouth, emptying it in three long swallows, but it does nothing to quell the utter disappointment and hurt I feel. I hear movement behind me and turn to see that Nova has risen from the bed and pulled her shorts up to her waist. She bends and picks up her shirt, pulling it over her head with jerky movements.

"What a surprise. You aren't sticking around."

"Obviously it isn't a surprise to you at all. That's what I do, right? Leave you hanging?"

Her gaze darts to my soft dick while I stand completely naked in front of her, not giving a single fuck.

A huff of sarcastic laughter tumbles from my throat.

"We leave in the morning. Be ready at six."

"How are you planning on getting us back to Boston?"

"I booked plane tickets since Liam's guys took the private jet he borrowed." I'd love to know what kinds of friends that man has. Who lets someone borrow their private fucking plane?

"No can do. Harper and I don't have IDs on us. Unless you think it's safe to go back to our house."

Fuck. I didn't think of that. I consider our little issue for a few moments as I grab my boxers and pull them back in place. Tony is probably long gone, but so are Liam and his guys. I have no interest in finding myself alone in a shitstorm of who knows what if he's watching the house for the girls' return.

But Liam did leave a car for me to take to the airport. Even though the last thing I want to do is spend the next two days in a car with Nova, it doesn't look like we have much of a choice.

"Driving it is, then. You still need to be ready at six," I say, walking around her and making myself comfortable on the bed.

Flipping on the TV, I feel her glare bore into the side of my face, but I don't give her the satisfaction of acknowledging whatever she may be feeling.

"Fuck you, Cillian." Nova storms to the door and wrenches it open before slamming it behind her. I listen for her as she slams the door to the room she's sharing with Harper.

"You sure fucking did," I mumble into an empty room

before turning the television off and rolling over.

Like I'm going to get any fucking sleep tonight.

# CHAPTER EIGHTEEN
## NOVA

THE LOUD BANGING ON my door wakes me from what feels like the shortest sleep of my life. I walk over and peer through the peephole, only to find myself staring directly at Cillian's stern face. I don't see his eyes since he's wearing sunglasses, but I hope to hell they're as red and bloodshot as I'm sure mine are. *Fucking asshole.*

Wrenching the door open, I stand in the doorway, refusing to say good morning or any other pleasantry that most civilized human beings start their day with. Fuck him and his almost declaration of love, then treating me like utter trash before I could even wrap my head around the last two days.

"Be ready in twenty minutes. We need to get on the road."

"Fine."

"Great. And here." He shoves two cups of coffee and what looks to be some sort of Danish wrapped in a napkin. "The hotel had breakfast out."

I grab both. "Thanks." Then promptly slam the door in his face.

If he has some idea that offering me shitty hotel coffee and some stale Danish is going to soften me up after last night, he's sadly mistaken. He could have given me a second to breathe, but he didn't. Instead, after fucking me, he came out of the bathroom even angrier than he was before. He's the one who was so fucking pissed that I ran without talking to him, but what would he call that? Hypocritical is the word that comes to mind.

"It's nice to see you two working out your problems," Harper says as she sits up and stretches her arms over her head. She sinks back into the pillows, scrubbing her hands over her face.

"No problems to work out. He's being an asshole, and I'm not going to put up with it."

"It sounded like you were putting up with it just fine last night."

"Oh shit, you heard us?" Embarrassment that Harper heard us, hell, embarrassment that I let it happen in the first place, washes over me.

"Honey, I'm pretty sure if anyone else was staying in this fleabag motel, they would have heard you, too."

I sit in the chair at the table in front of the window and take a sip of coffee. "Sorry if we woke you up. I went over there to explain what happened, and he was being a prick about the entire thing, and I don't know, I got up to walk out and he stopped me and...well, you heard the rest." I unwrap a Danish and start picking at the flaky crust, popping a piece into my mouth. Okay, not terrible. "Then, after we...finished, he was back to being a complete dick."

"I mean, you can't blame the guy too much." I look at her with indignation in my gaze, and she throws her hands in the air. "Whoa there, sister. If you hate him, then I'll hate him right along with you. United front, remember?" she says, waving her finger between the two of us. "But it's not like it's out of the realm of possibilities that the guy would be a little more than miffed with the way you left things. And don't get me wrong, if he was in New Orleans because your brother's prez wanted him to keep an eye on you,  then that's fucked up."

"Apparently, Ozzy had no idea Cillian was in New Orleans or that he'd met me at all."

Harper shoots me a knowing look. "Now do you think it may have been smarter to talk to him instead of running off?" It's not the first time she's brought it up, but this time, we have all the information.

"Is that your way of saying I told you so?"

Harper smiles sweetly in my direction and innocently bats her blue eyes. "Only in the most loving way possible."

She swings her legs from the bed and stands. We're both wearing the same outfit, a loose T-shirt and shorts provided by Liam since neither of us could stand to be in the grimy clothes from last night. I suggested we burn them, but she shot that idea down.

"I'm going to take a quick shower. Sounds like he

wants to get out of here, and I'm not particularly inclined to stick around here with Tony out there." Harper lets out a breath and turns toward the bathroom.

"You okay, Harpy?"

Harper stops at the doorway to the bathroom with her back toward me. "Not really, but I will be." She turns her head in my direction. "We both will." Then she steps into the bathroom and shuts the door.

God, I wish I had her confidence.

Cillian was none too happy when I told him I wanted to stop by my aunt and uncle's to get my bag. I have no money, no way of accessing any funds, and I'm going to be days away from the safety net that is the contents of that bag. There is absolutely no way I'm going up to Shine without it.

"Fuck. Fine," he finally relents after we've been sitting in the car for the last ten minutes arguing about it. Maybe he doesn't want to waste more time when it's clear as day I'm about to get out of this car and make my own way to Shine if I have to. Or maybe he understands my need to not be completely without anything to fall back on if I decide I need to skip town in a hurry. Either way, I get my way. The urge to stick out my tongue at him is strong, but I remind myself I'm an adult and, unfortunately, at his mercy for the next couple of days.

My aunt and uncle aren't at the house when we stop there, so after Harper and I change into some of my clothes that are still there, I make Cillian take us to the bar.

It's almost funny watching him walk into a little highway dive bar in his perfectly pressed black suit. You would think he'd be getting all kinds of strange looks from the few regulars that are here this time of day, but when we walk in and the three old guys take a look at us, they quickly divert their gazes. There's something about Cillian that screams predator. Especially since he's in the same foul mood he's been in for the entire drive.

My aunt walks from the back and sees Harper and me with a man she doesn't recognize, but she isn't one to shrink away from a man like Cillian. Or anyone, for that matter. She walks straight up to me and wraps her arms around me.

"You had us worried, girl," Trina says when she pulls away. She keeps a firm grip on my arms and looks me up and down. "You okay?"

"I'm fine, Aunt Trina. Just needed to grab a few things from the house and didn't want to leave without saying goodbye." I offer her a casual smile, but there's no doubt she knows I'm keeping something from her. The woman has always been able to read me and my brother like an open book.

She looks over to Harper and releases me, opening her arms to my best friend. "Harper, it's so good to see you. I think the last time I saw you was when I came up for the weekend last year, wasn't it?"

"Hi Trina. I've missed you. We need to have another girls' weekend soon," she says, letting my aunt pull her into a tight embrace. "Although next time, I refuse to match you shot for shot. It took a week to recover."

Trina laughs and Cillian watches on with aloof interest. My aunt steps back and looks Cillian up and down, taking his measure and probably deciding if she's going to allow Harper and me out of this bar with him.

"Trina, this is Cillian," I introduce, and he holds out his hand. Trina looks at the offered hand, then back to his face, finally sliding her smaller palm into his.

"Are you the reason my niece came running to her uncle and me?"

Cillian's eyes widen a fraction before he schools his features. My aunt's bluntness can be a little off-putting if you aren't prepared. He looks to me then back to Trina. "Yes."

She turns back to me. "Looks like you made your choice then."

It's not exactly like we have time to go into all the details of why I trust Cillian now, at least with my physical safety. My heart is a whole other story, and that shit is locked up tight like Fort Knox at the moment. So, instead, I offer her a smile and another hug.

"We have to go. I love you. Thank you for letting me crash with you."

"Anytime, sweet pea." She pulls back and looks Cillian

square in the eye. "You keep these girls safe."

"Yes, ma'am." Well, at least he doesn't forget his manners, despite being a broody asshole all day.

When we get back in the car and drive away, I watch that little bar get smaller in my side mirror. I hope to get back here sooner rather than later, but I suppose that all depends on what waits for us in Shine.

*Two days.* Two days of silent treatment and convenience store food. We only stopped once so Cillian could get some rest for a few hours at another little roadside motel. This time I did not wander into his room for any sort of conversation. We were only there for about five hours before Cillian banged on our door and told us we needed to get on the road again.

It's nearing six o'clock at night when we pull into the gravel lot of the Black Roses clubhouse. The prospect at the gate allows us in, and I wonder if that used to be my brother's job. When I would talk to him, he'd tell me they didn't have him doing anything dangerous; he was just around to clean up and do whatever grunt work Ozzy needed. Seems like guarding a gate would fall under that. I imagine his smile, the easy way he had with people. I remember the day he left New Orleans and the hug he gave me, telling me as soon as he was settled, he expected his little sister to come visit him. I remember the phone call from Cash telling me we lost him.

My throat is thick and my heart feels as though it's about to pound out of my chest when Cillian parks the car. Harper gets out first, stretches, then walks to my door. She doesn't open it or try to hurry me. She knows I need a few moments to compose myself. I've spent the last year believing this place, these people, were responsible for the death of my brother. I honestly didn't think it was going to be this hard, and at the time, it was a better alternative to being stuck with Cillian and dealing with all that shit. But I'm beginning to think I jumped out of the frying pan and straight into the fire I've been avoiding since Cooper died.

The door to the clubhouse opens, and a tall man with a beard and dark hair walks out, followed by a familiar face. Cash walks to the car with that Southern boy swagger he's always had. If I hadn't known him since I was a kid, and if he hadn't used to pull my hair and tease the hell out of me alongside Cooper, I probably would have had a crush on the man. He was always someone we looked up to as an older brother, and the thought of anything else gives me the heebie-jeebies. But that was then, and this is now. The only thing I feel seeing him again is anger. And the longer I sit here, the more I think this may have been a really bad idea.

*You're doing this so Harper can be safe and you don't have to rely on a man who hate-fucked you two days ago.*

"Hey, Nova," he says when I open the door.

I don't smile, don't jump into his arms like I used to when I was a little girl. It's not just Ozzy I blame for what happened to Cooper.

"Hello, Cash."

The look of disappointment is clear on his face. Maybe he thought that my coming here meant I forgave him for the part he played in my brother leaving New Orleans. Maybe he thought our reunion would be like old times. Either way, he's dead fucking wrong.

The tall man who was the first to step out walks over and stands in front of our moody driver.

"Cillian. Good to see you," he says, holding out his hand.

Cillian clasps his palm to the man's. "Ozzy. Thanks for doing this."

*So this is Ozzy.*

I never made it up to Shine before Cooper died, so I've never had the chance to meet the man standing on the other side of the car. The man who I blamed all these past months for taking one of the few people I would have laid down my life for. And the reason I'm here is to keep the other person I love more than anything from being hunted and killed by the man who tried to sell us.

Ozzy looks over at me, and I stare right back at him. I have to remind myself again that I'm doing this for Harper, and he's doing this for Cooper. It would be a poor decision on my part to attack the MC president in his own clubhouse, even though that's the scenario that played in my head over and over for the last year.

When he walks around to the other side of the car where Cash, Harper, and I still stand, he holds out his hand to me.

"I'm Ozzy Lewis."

I look at his hand, then back to him, reluctantly taking it. "Nova Reed. This is Harper." I promptly drop his hand as though it's on fire.

Ozzy smiles at my best friend, and she returns it, but hers is tight. That's Harper. When she says she'll hate someone because I do, she means it.

"Let's get your stuff inside," Cash offers, obviously sensing the thick tension in the fall air.

Cillian pops the trunk, and Ozzy reaches in to grab both bags.

"I'll take this one," I say, grabbing the bag of jewels. Cillian knows exactly what's in this bag. It's the same bag we stuffed the jewelry into in the first place.

Ozzy grabs the other one with all my clothes that Harper and I will be sharing for the foreseeable future. I'm not sure what the rules are for being under the protection of an MC, but I'm guessing trips to the closest clothing store are out of the question.

When I walk into the clubhouse, I'm taken aback by how *not* trashed the place is. I always thought there would be a plethora of naked women and dirty bikers everywhere—and ashtrays and beer bottles littering every surface. But this place is tidy and doesn't smell like three-day-old trash, so that's a good sign.

The bar runs along the back wall, and there's a hallway

leading to rooms beyond my view. To the right is a swinging door with a few small round dining tables and chairs set up close to it. To the left are several leather couches with a giant TV hanging on the wall, and beyond that is a pool table. All in all, a typical man cave, just on a much bigger scale. One thing I also wasn't expecting but probably should have is that every cye in the clubhouse is on me. They aren't ogling with their mouths hanging open like I've seen a million times in the various bars I've worked at. These are looks of reverence and respect. Looks that contain warmth and sympathy.

Another tall man who looks to be about the same age as Ozzy walks up to us and shakes Cillian's hand before turning to me. I read the patch on his cut. *Vice President.*

"I'm Knox, the club's VP. Your brother was a good man."

"I know. He was my brother." I suddenly feel possessive over Cooper in a way I never have before. I don't want anyone in this room telling me what a great guy my brother was. I fucking know.

Damn, that fire I jumped in is getting hotter by the second.

I notice a couple of the smen's eyes dart between Knox and me nervously. What do they think he's going to do? Smack me or something? Regardless of the fact Cillian is basically dumping me here, granted, by my request, I doubt anyone in this room would have the balls to try any bullshit with him around.

Knox nods and steps aside, clearly allowing me my space.

Well...okay then.

"Where can I set my things?" I ask Cash.

"I'll show you two to your rooms. We set you up right next to each other."

Cash takes the bag from Ozzy and leads the way to the hallway. Before we head down the hall, I look at the wall between the entrance to the hallway and the bar. My brother's smiling face—along with a cut—is mounted on the wall with a black band around the corner of the frame. I stop, and from the corner of my eye, I see Harper pause next to me and raise her head. She must see what I'm looking at because her hand finds mine and she squeezes. I'm not going to break down in this room in front of all these strangers, but when we get behind closed doors, that's another story entirely. My eyes close for a brief moment before we follow Cash down the hall and to our rooms.

"You okay?" Harper asks as I put the last of our things in the dresser in my room.

"I feel like we're asking each other that question a lot lately, and I'm *really* not a fan."

Her answering laugh is hollow and sad as she sits on the queen-size mattress in the otherwise sparse room. A bed, dresser, nightstand, and a lamp. That's it. Although, I suppose most of the people who travel through here aren't too concerned with anything other than a bed to sleep or do other things in. God, I sound like a spoiled princess looking down my nose at the people who are taking me and Harper in and protecting us. Anger aside, I'm above being a judgy bitch.

"Seeing Cooper's picture was…"

"Yeah."

"It seems like he had a lot of people who cared about him here. I wasn't expecting that. By the way they looked at you when you walked in, it was like they were about to get on their knees and bow their heads as a sign of respect or something."

"Leave it to you to exaggerate." I close the drawer and turn to face Harper before leaning against the weathered dresser.

"Maybe a tad. But seriously, Nova, I don't think any one of those men out there would let anyone get close to hurting you."

"So they aren't out to get women killed. Great."

Harper presses her lips together as her jaw works back and forth like she's chewing on something. "Nova, remember how I said I would hate anyone on principle right along with you?"

"Yeah…" My arms cross over my chest. It's one of those instinctual reactions, like I somehow need to protect myself from whatever she's about to tell me.

"I'm also going to tell you when you aren't seeing things as clearly as you could be." She raises her hand, stopping me from speaking when I open my mouth. "And before you argue with me, think about why you ditched Cillian and how it was a giant misunderstanding."

"This is different, Harper."

"I'm not saying you don't have the right to feel how you choose to feel about your brother's death. But how would you feel if, heaven forbid, one of these guys dies before all this is through and they have a sister who spends the rest of their life blaming you?"

My breath stalls in my chest before I let it out slowly through my nose. "I'd probably say they made their choice."

"Just like Cooper did. He made the choice to come here. He made the choice to protect that girl."

"He was a kid who wanted to be part of a family. They took advantage of that and put his life in danger."

"And *I'm* your family. Did I take advantage when I called you, scared out of my mind, needing you?"

I rear back. "Of course not. I love you."

"And he loved his club. He would have done anything for them. Just like he would have done anything for you. Just like you would do anything for me. You spend a lot of time blaming Ozzy and the Black Roses. But do you ever blame Cooper? Do you put the blame where it really belongs? On the man who killed him?"

"Of course I'm mad at Cooper! He broke my heart when he left and found another family." I throw my hands to the side as hot, angry tears run down my face. "He came to Shine and got himself killed instead of staying with me!"

Harper stares, her own eyes misty. She has never been one to let me cry alone. "Maybe the real problem was leaving and finding something with a group of people without including you. Babe, it sucks that he bolted like that. I hate that he left you. But that wasn't the club's fault or Ozzy's. That was his."

An angry tear tracks down my face and I bat it away, hating the fact that she's making sense.

"Anger has gotten you through the last year, Nova. Blaming everyone except your brother for abandoning you has kept your heart safe. But it might be time to consider it's misplaced. And it might be time to consider you aren't the only one who grieved his death."

I hang my head and let out a shuddering breath. "You might be onto something."

And dammit if it's not a kick to the gut.

# Chapter Nineteen

## Cillian

T HAT WAS THE LONGEST two days of my life. I couldn't wait to get Nova and Harper to Shine. The entire way here, stewing in anger and regret while stuck in the car with her and her warm sandalwood scent, was torture. I wanted to apologize. I was a complete dick the other night. But as soon as I had a second to catch my breath, all the anger and hurt came flooding back in. I didn't realize I could have such explosive sex with someone I was so pissed at, but I proved it was entirely possible and entirely wrong. Unfortunately, I'm too much of a hardheaded asshole to admit that I was...well, an asshole.

We stopped for a night so I could get some sleep, but it was a useless endeavor. I tossed and turned for a few hours, then decided *fuck it* and woke up the girls to finish the journey. As soon as we drove past the *Welcome to Shine, Massachusetts* sign, the tension in the car cranked up several notches. When I caught a glimpse of Nova, her jaw was tense—just like the rest of her. I wanted to ask her if she was okay, tell her if she wanted me to turn the car toward Boston, I'd gladly take her there and keep her safe in my apartment or Finn's penthouse. But the plan was laid before us, and I was too damn chickenshit to have her shoot me down. Ozzy and the rest of the Black Roses are perfectly capable of keeping her safe, and she obviously doesn't want to depend on me for anything. Hell, the only reason she's tolerating my presence is because I'm the one with the car.

It took everything in me not to walk around the car and wrap my arms around Nova when Ozzy introduced himself. It was obvious she was incredibly uncomfortable, but she wasn't going to lose her shit in the middle of a parking lot, no matter how much she may have wanted to. And even after everything, I wanted to comfort her, to share my strength with her. Though my anger toward Nova has waned a bit the last couple of days, hers has not, and I'd rather not get kneed in the balls in front of a group of bikers.

Then, when we walked in and Knox introduced himself, her ire toward the rather large man was anything but shocking, especially when he mentioned her brother. I get it, though. There's a certain possessiveness she has toward the memory of her brother that only someone who lost someone they loved can see. I saw her notice Cooper's picture hanging on the wall. If she would have looked back at me, or if I would have gotten any sort of hint that she needed a strong arm to hold her, I would have left the little group that I was standing in and rushed to her. But she didn't.

Harper was right there next to her, and Nova was able to gather the strength she needed from her friend. As it should be. As soon as all of this is over, I'll go my way and she'll go hers. Exactly how she wants it.

"Need a cup of coffee? Maybe a little something extra in there?" Ozzy asks, scanning my face.

I'm fucking exhausted and have been tangled in knots the last two days. Even longer than that, if I think about it.

"Yeah, that sounds good."

We head over to the bar and Ozzy walks behind it, grabbing a mug and pouring a generous amount of whiskey into it before topping it with coffee from the pot behind him then sliding it toward me.

"I didn't think MC presidents usually bartended."

"Seems there're a lot of misconceptions about me going around."

I hold my coffee cup up to him. "Touché."

Ozzy gives me a half smile and leans his forearms on the bar. "How the hell did you get tangled up with Cooper's younger sister, man?"

I chuckle and wonder if I should tell him the truth about our first meeting.

Fuck it.

"She stole my wallet."

His brows raise to his hairline as he blinks at me a few times. "That's definitely...different."

"You have no idea. When I caught up with her, she had this disarming charm I was not prepared for. I don't know. We talked, had a friendly little competition on who could score the most wallets on Bourbon then grabbed a drink and caught a band together. It was the complete opposite of how I saw my night going, and I liked it. A lot. Nothing happened the first night we met, but I gave her my phone number in case she found herself in a situation she couldn't get out of, and she texted me about a month later when I was in New Orleans on business for Liam."

"Yeah, I heard about you working with him for his side project."

"That's how I found out Farina was selling women. One of Liam's guys caught some chatter about Port NOLA being used for Russian trading, and I have contacts down there."

"Sampson?"

I nod.

"He's a good guy. How's he been?"

When we didn't have control of the Boston ports, the Black Roses assisted us with transportation of our weapons regularly, and one of the ports we used was NOLA, so he became well acquainted with Sampson.

"He's good. Expecting another kid."

Ozzy nods. "This shit is happening too close to home for my liking. I thought with Cataldi gone, the other families didn't have the same connections, or at the very least would have thought twice about this shit."

"It was only a matter of time before someone picked up where Carlo left off. With Petrov putting a stop to it in his organization in New York and the rest of the Cataldi organization answering to the Monaghan family now, there's a gap that someone was going to fill. Farina is nothing if not a slimy opportunist."

Finn's wife, Alessia, dated the man's son several years ago, and let's just say the relationship did not end well—meaning he nearly beat her to death and she left. When her brother found out and confronted Orlando, he was killed under "suspicious" circumstances. There was bad blood between Farina and the Amattos after that, but nothing could be proven. Alessia's father didn't want to start a war based on a gut feeling and potentially leave his wife a widow and his daughter without a father, so he sat back and bided his time.

When Finn and Alessia married, Carlo didn't take too kindly to the partnership between the Amattos and the Monaghans, knowing he was going to lose the ports and his power. With Orlando's help, Carlo tried to take Alessia from her home. Bad move on his part because when we caught up to him, a side of Finn came out to play that I'd never known.

I've seen him merciless and uncaring plenty of times. I've seen him take a man's life for all sorts of reasons, but this was different. When he had Orlando in his clutches, he was far from uncaring. He made the man suffer because Orlando had threatened someone precious to Finn, and that brought out a brutality in the man I'd never seen before, but have some understanding of what that felt like.

When Tony had Nova in his hands and was threatening to take her...let's just say I've imagined more ways I'm going to make that piece of shit suffer in the last forty-eight hours than any reasonably sane person should. Guess that says plenty about me where Nova's concerned.

Starting a war with Farina wasn't on my to-do list, but there's no way Finn is going to stand for this shit happening in his backyard. None of us are.

My phone buzzes in my pocket, and I pull it out to look at the screen, seeing a message from Finn.

"Finn will be here in about twenty minutes. Eoghan's coming with him."

I called him last night and told him about Nova needing a ride to Shine, and we had some developments that needed to be discussed with the Black Roses.

"I'll grab the good stuff then," Ozzy quips, pulling another bottle of whiskey from the shelf.

"The way I see it, Farina is done," Finn says about thirty minutes later while we're sitting in Ozzy's office.

Ozzy sits behind his desk while Finn and I have taken seats across from him. Eoghan and Jude, Liam's brother and the club's enforcer, are on the couch and Knox is propped against the door.

"We may not play on the right side of the law, but

we have principles, and the one thing I think we can all agree on is that selling women won't be tolerated. This shit was supposed to die with Cataldi, and I made it more than clear I won't tolerate it in my city or with any other families who do business through it. What Farina is doing is a slap in the face."

"Liam is working one of the guys Tony had with him." The one Nova shot, I recall with a touch of pride.

"Has he gotten anything?" Ozzy asks.

"No more than what we already know. I don't think he was high up on the chain. Just some guy on Tony's crew. He doesn't seem to have any information or details on the buyers," I reply.

Liam couldn't give two shits about a Mafia war, but he does want information on who's buying girls.

Finn sips his whiskey, and before he opens his mouth, I already know what his plan is going to be. Guess that comes with the territory of being the man's second for as long as I have.

"Listen, I've never been good at this espionage bullshit that Liam's involved with. I don't have the fucking patience. Tony knows Cillian was involved in what went down at the port. The way I see it, whether Liam likes it or not, the Monaghans are part of this now, which means I'm not waiting around for Farina to bring his bullshit to my doorstep like his son did. We go in soon and we go in hard, then we can finally be done with that slimy asshole once and for all."

Ozzy sits back in his chair and observes Finn before

speaking. "We'll help any way you need."

Ozzy and his old lady had their own run-in with Cataldi when he threatened to sell Ozzy's fiancée in the skin trade. Ozzy was there when we took out Cataldi. Even had a little fun with him before Finn's cousin put a bullet in his head. This is just as personal to him as it is to any of us in this room.

"I'll let Liam know." I turn to Finn. "What about Mario?" Alessia's father is still very much the don of the Amatto family—even though we've struck an alliance with him. And if anyone has the right to be there when Massimo takes his last breath, it's the father of the man Massimo's son killed.

"Mario has been waiting for this day for the last decade. He'll be more than happy to be a part of this."

"So we need a plan," Knox says.

"I like Finn's idea. Go in hard and fast. We did it in New York. What's the difference if we do the same at Farina's compound?" Jude asks.

"It will be a lot more guarded, for one," Eoghan says.

Jude shrugs as though that's the least of his concerns. "Between us, you lot, my brother's team, and Amatto, we'll have it covered, wouldn't you say?"

Eoghan tilts his head from side to side then nods. "Sounds solid." Eoghan has never been one to shy away from the most violent of plans. He can be a little shit, but he's one of the men I know we can always count on to have our backs.

"And Farina won't be expecting it," Finn says. "We'll

need to head back to Boston for supplies. Let's regroup here tomorrow afternoon since your compound is closest. We go in after nightfall." He looks to Ozzy for confirmation.

"Like I said, anything you need," Ozzy replies. "I'll call my guy and let him know his pigs are going to be fed well tomorrow night."

When we walk out to the main room of the clubhouse after our meeting, I look around the space for any sign of Nova or Harper but only find a few bikers playing pool and a couple of them sitting at the bar with beers in their hand.

Jude's woman, Lucy, is at the dartboard trying to teach Linc's old lady how to properly throw a dart while Linc looks on with amusement.

"God, I think you're worse at this than you are at pool," Lucy says to her friend as she pulls a dart from the wall next to the board.

"Missed you in there," I say to Linc, pointing at the hallway.

"View's better out here," he replies, and his woman, Charlie, turns and blows him a kiss. "Ozzy and Jude know I'll be down for whatever they decide to do with that asshole."

It wasn't too long ago Charlie was almost sold into a

human trafficking ring herself. It was at the hands of Cataldi, but we showed up and got her out before the deal went down, and we took out some of Cataldi's men in the process while Linc was holed up in the hospital. I have a feeling this will be some sort of cathartic retribution for Linc.

"Have you seen the two girls I came with?"

"As far as I know, they haven't left their room," Lucy answers. "I was going to go check on them, but I have a feeling I'm the last person Cooper's sister wants to see at the moment."

Considering she was the woman he was protecting when he died, I'm inclined to agree.

"Let me know if she's a problem for you, and I'll talk to her about going back to Boston with me."

"Listen, she's going through some shit, and I'm the last person who would be angry at her for having some big feelings where I'm concerned. If she needs some time to wrap her head around everything, I'm not going to judge."

"You're a good woman, Lucy." She's handling Nova's perspective on the situation a lot better than I am.

She offers me a half smile. "When I want to be. And if you want to check on her before you boys go off and do whatever it is you're going to do, go down the hallway and make a right. Third door on the left."

Lucy turns around and picks up a dart, handing it to Charlie. "Alright, my sister from another mister. Let's see if you can actually hit the board this time."

"Bitch," Charlie replies with a smile.

"When I want to be." Lucy turns and winks at me before I take off in search of Nova.

When I reach the door to the room Lucy directed me to, it's closed, but after standing here for a few moments, soft murmurs of a conversation float through the wood. She must be in there with Harper. I have a strong feeling neither will leave the other's side during their stay, but I'd like to speak with Nova alone. Thoughts of leaving without a word race through my mind. Would she care if I did? She did a damn good job of icing me out over the last couple days. Not that I didn't deserve it after the way I acted in the hotel the night of the rescue. But I would regret leaving without saying something, without some sort of conversation.

Inhaling a deep breath, I knock on the door.

"Yeah?" she calls.

I open the door a crack and peek my head in. "Mind if we talk for a minute?"

Harper looks at me, then glances back at Nova, who keeps her eyes trained on me. I have no idea if she's going to allow me in or tell me to fuck off. It doesn't look like she even knows the answer.

Finally, she turns to Harper and nods. Her best friend rises from the bed and offers me a small smile when I open the door a bit more, allowing her to slide past me and into the hallway.

"Can I come in?"

Nova waves her hand, and I step inside, closing the

door behind me. The room feels small, with the air around us charged with that kind of electricity that's unique to the two of us. It's crazy to think I can be in a room with several trained killers and criminals, but as soon as I close the door of this one, my first inclination is to unbutton the collar of my shirt so I don't feel this stifling weight that's sitting on my chest. Is this...guilt? Because this feeling fucking sucks.

"I'm going back to Boston in a few minutes."

"Figured you would," she replies with no emotion.

"If you need anything, you can call me."

"Kind of hard to do without a phone."

"Right. I'll talk to Ozzy about getting you and Harper set up with new phones before I leave."

"Thanks." The way she practically chokes out the word makes me feel like shit.

"I was an asshole," I blurt out.

Nova's head rears back as though she's just as shocked as I am at my admission.

"Trust me, I'm as surprised as you. I don't often find myself in the position of feeling the need to apologize to anyone."

"I haven't exactly heard an apology yet."

Inhaling a deep breath, I let it out slowly through my nose. Why is this so damn hard?

"I'm sorry for behaving the way I did at the hotel a couple nights ago. I was pissed about everything and let that singular emotion overrule any consideration for you. I'm not trying to make an excuse for it. What I did was wrong and you didn't deserve it."

"Holy shit...you're really bad at apologizing. That was an incredibly clinical way to say you fucked me because you were mad at me and then treated me like the dirt on the bottom of your shoe afterward."

If she had any idea that her reminding me about the way I fucked her made my dick twitch in my pants, she'd really hate me.

I close my eyes and shake my head a bit, trying to clear my muddled thoughts. "Nova, I'm not good at apologizing. I've never had to. You were in a bad spot when we were talking in my hotel room, and instead of being the man you needed me to be and have a fucking heart, I practically attacked you and—"

"Whoa, there. You were a long way from attacking me, Cillian. I was a very willing participant and loved every second. At least until the end."

I hang my head for a few moments then look Nova in the eye, imploring her to see how sorry I am since I'm apparently shit at saying it. I don't bring up what I was about to say and her complete lack of response. It wouldn't do either of us any good.

"The last thing I want is for you to think I'm the asshole I was acting like in that room. It's not me. Actually, scratch that. It is me. But it's not who I was with you. It's never who I want to be with you. Honestly, I haven't been myself since we met, and here's even more honesty for you...I like not being myself around you. I loved every second of the time we spent together in New Orleans...until that last part." The corner of my lips tip up and she returns my smile with a small one of her own.

"Yeah, me too."

The phone in my pocket vibrates, and I pull it out, seeing Finn's message.

**Finn:** *We're leaving.*

**Me:** *I'll be right there.*

"I have to go. We'll be back tomorrow. Try to stay in one place." I say it as a joke, but the thought of Nova bailing again has crossed my mind a time or six since pulling up to the clubhouse.

"I'll see you tomorrow. Promise."

The urge to kiss her goodbye nearly overwhelms me. It seems like it could be so natural to walk over and press my lips to hers. To feel her melt into me like all the times before. How can I be mad one minute, full of regret the next, and want to feel her soft lips all in the span of what seems to be barely more than a heartbeat?

Instead of acting on the urge, I twist the knob and walk out of the room before shutting the door behind me.

When I make my way into the main room, Finn and Eoghan are apparently already at the car because they're nowhere to be found. I walk outside and see Finn talking to Ozzy next to his car that's parked beside the one I drove here.

They clasp hands as I walk up to Ozzy, and the man turns to shake mine as well.

"Can you get Nova and Harper set up with new phones? I'll pay for whatever it costs."

Ozzy shoots me a knowing grin. "You got it." He doesn't comment further on my need to make sure Nova is taken care of while I'm gone before walking back to the clubhouse.

"You ready to finish this?" Finn asks as he opens his car door.

"Yup."

"You know, once these assholes are taken care of, she's going to be free to take off into parts unknown. You ready for that, too?"

"I don't have much of a choice. Nova and Harper need this over as much as we do."

"Have you thought about what it's going to be like for her to leave again?"

I shrug. "Guess it'll be back to business as usual." The slight melancholy tone of my voice doesn't escape my attention. Or Finn's, by the way he's looking at me.

"Just as long as you don't punch me in the face again," Eoghan chimes in from the passenger seat.

"Fuck off, asshole," I tell him.

Finn releases a huff. "Yup. Business as usual."

# CHAPTER TWENTY
## NOVA

HARPER KNOCKS ON MY door and peeks her head in not long after Cillian walks out. She makes a spectacle of looking around the room like she's checking for something.

"No bloodshed. That's a good sign."

"He took my gun away, remember?" I ask dryly.

The corner of her mouth tips up. "Oh yeah." She walks the rest of the way in and closes the door behind her then has a seat on the bed next to me. "How did it go? I didn't hear any yelling or loud moaning, so I'm not sure when it comes to you two."

"We had a conversation."

"And…" she prods.

"And, it was fine. He apologized for his behavior, and I let him. I'm too tired to hold shit against people today." And too tired to talk to her about what he was going to say to me before I tried to bolt again the other night. I still haven't wrapped my head around that one. Bigger fish to fry and all that, I guess.

"Does that go for Ozzy and the rest of the Black Roses?"

I lie back against the fluffy pillows at the head of the bed and scrub a hand over my face. "I don't know. What you said earlier was pretty spot on."

"Because everything I say is spot on."

I roll my eyes. "It's not that I haven't blamed Cooper or been mad at him. Trust me, I've done my share of screaming at him." My mind wanders to the night Harper called me for help when I was at the lake doing just that. God, what was that? Only three, maybe four nights ago? The hours and days have blended together since Tony found me outside that house in the middle of nowhere. "Sometimes it's just easier to blame something or someone I don't know or have any emotional attachment to, maybe? Like it's easier to take it all out on the Black Roses rather than admit I've been angry with Coop for a lot of things, including leaving me. Logically, I know dying wasn't his fault, but that's one more thing that enrages me. It was easier to blame Ozzy for his death than be mad at my dead brother for leaving. Does that make sense?"

Harper rests her hand on my knee. "Of course it does, babe."

"The fact of the matter is, I don't really know Ozzy or anyone here except Cash, and I've shut him out since Coop's death, too."

"Well, I'd say the fact that the president of an outlaw motorcycle club who knew you hated him was willing to let you come here and was willing to protect the both of us says a lot about him. And it says a lot about Coop that this was who and what he pledged his loyalty to."

My eyes fill with tears, and Harper scoots up the bed and lies down on the pillow next to me, turning her face toward mine.

"I need to let that anger go, Harp. I need to move on. It's been eating me alive, and I need to put it to rest. I'm so fucking tired of being mad about Cooper. I just want to be able to remember him without this black pit of rage in my chest." I rub the spot right above my heart.

"Maybe it was some sort of twist of fate that we ended up here. Maybe you were supposed to be here so you could finally let this go."

"You think the universe had a hand in you getting kidnapped by a man who pretended to be your boyfriend to gain your trust, only to sell you to some Russian piece of shit? Then, me coming to your rescue, only to get taken right alongside you? Oh, then having a gunfight at Port NOLA and needing a place to lie low until Cillian can find your ex and put him six feet under?"

"Well, when you put it that way, it sounds crazy." Harper groans. "Jesus, I couldn't make this shit up if I tried."

"Please, never try," I say, deadpan.

Harper laughs as a quiet knock sounds on the door.

"Come in," I answer.

A girl with dark-brown hair and big blue eyes peeks her head in. "Hey, I'm Charlie, Linc's girlfriend."

I smile at her kind voice and the way she seems

unsure about disturbing me. This girl can't be much older than Harper and me, if at all.

"Nova," I say, pointing to myself. "And Harper." I point my thumb at my best friend, who's wearing a warm smile on her face as well.

"Linc and Knox's mom made some food. It's in the kitchen if you're hungry. I would definitely suggest getting some before the guys find out she dropped it off. They're like feral animals when Tanya cooks."

"Sounds good. Did she happen to make anything vegan?" I ask.

Charlie looks uncomfortable with the question like she's about to disappoint me.

"This is a clubhouse full of bikers, so I can say with one-hundred-percent certainty, no."

"Oh, thank God. I need some meat and potatoes. Oh, and some giant rolls with like three pounds of butter on each."

Charlie shakes her head and laughs. "Well, you're in luck because Tanya is famous for her roast, which is what she made, and Cece, Lucy's sister, makes the best damn baked bread..." She looks at me with regret in her gaze.

I know the name but have yet to meet the woman who was with my brother when he took his final breaths.

Charlie was right about these guys acting like a pack of feral dogs when they realized the food was out. Had Harper and I not grabbed a heaping plateful before they ascended on the table that sits to the left of the kitchen door, we'd be eating crumbs.

Chatter around us is constant, and for the most part, the guys keep their eyes on their plates or talk among themselves. I've caught a few glances thrown in my direction, but when I make eye contact, there's nothing but a sympathetic smile in their eyes. Not the hardened looks I'd have expected considering I didn't exactly walk into the clubhouse with the best attitude.

It's when Charlie and a girl I don't recognize walk over to the table Harper and I are sitting at by ourselves that the room quiets. I saw her sitting with a biker who looked an awful lot like the man who helped us escape Tony in New Orleans. This guy is a smidge taller, with longer hair, and looks to be a few years younger, but he has the same air of unbothered confidence that I saw in his brother, Liam. Now, the man's eyes are fixated on the interaction that's about to take place, along with just about every other person in this room. That's not intimidating at all or anything.

"Hi," the woman says, nodding toward Harper and me. "I'm Lucy."

I offer her a tight smile, unsure of what I'm supposed to say here. This moment feels more monumental to me than walking into the clubhouse did. She was the last person to see my brother alive.

"Mind if I sit?" she asks.

I stare at her for a beat. The thought, *you were the last person with Cooper; you were the last person to see my brother alive* running over and over in my head. Then I realize I haven't answered her and probably look about as welcoming as my old neighbor, Mrs. Givens, who lived down the street from Cooper and me when we were kids. That woman's sole purpose in life was to sit on her front porch and yell at us for causing a racket during her "stories." I don't even know if she actually watched soap operas or just sat on her rocking chair all day every day to holler at us.

"Of course," I finally reply, shaking my head a bit.

Lucy smiles and sits across from me with Charlie taking the seat across from Harper. "Thank God. I didn't want to ambush you in your room while you were getting settled, so I told myself I'd wait to see if you would come out. I figured you probably have...I don't know, questions? Maybe you want to scream at me? Figured we should get it out of the way so our men aren't worried that as soon as they leave, we'll be pulling each other's hair out or something."

"Are you a hair puller?"

"No, I prefer a more direct approach, like a punch to the nose."

My lips quirk in a small smile. "So their eyes water and then you can go in on them?"

Lucy laughs. "Exactly. I take it you've been schooled in the art of street fighting?"

"I grew up with a loud mouth and a protective older brother, so yeah, he taught me a few things."

Lucy's smile drops when I mention my brother. "I was there with him. When he died."

"I know. Cash told me when I talked to him after it happened." The only time I talked to him, actually. After that conversation I was firmly in the I *hate the Black Roses and anyone associated with them* mindset. "Did he...did he say anything before he died?"

Lucy shakes her head. "No. It happened so fast. It was instant, though. I doubt that helps, but he didn't suffer. I wanted you to know that. He went for his gun so he could get us out of an impossible situation. But Otto got to him first."

"Did Otto suffer?"

A chilling smile spreads across Lucy's face. "Yes. They all did."

"Good." I'm not a particularly violent person by nature, but when it comes to my brother, had the people truly responsible for his death not paid the ultimate price, I would have no problem making it my life's mission to see them rot in hell.

"I don't blame you," I say. "Cooper made his choices and I have to learn to live with them. I think...I think my anger was misplaced for a really long time." My gaze cuts to Harper who is wearing a soft, knowing smile as she reaches over and squeezes my arm.

"I blamed myself for a long time. What if I hadn't needed something as stupid as a change of clothes? What if I'd been keeping a better eye out for someone following us? I should have known that crazy asshole would've tried something the first chance he got. They were after me. The men who ran us off the road. I don't know how much you know about what happened, but they killed Cooper so they could take me back to the cult I grew up in. Punish me for leaving and all that. I was supposed to marry Otto's son, but I ran before the wedding. He wanted me back, so he came to Shine to take me."

I knew Cooper was protecting her from some bad people, but I had no idea she ran from a fucking cult or that they hunted her down.

"Jude said when he found Cooper, he made a promise to him to exact retribution for what they did. He rode back with Cooper's"—she pauses and visibly swallows—"with Cooper from the crash site. He didn't want him to be alone."

When I look just beyond Lucy's shoulder, I see Jude watching us. The look in his eyes isn't menacing, but he's definitely keeping a close watch on the situation. I send him a small smile of thanks, though I'm not sure if he can hear the story Lucy's telling me.

"Liam came with them when they rescued me. Well, all of us, really. The men tried to defend the compound, but they were no match for the Black Roses or Liam's team. The leaders were taken out in the old church, and the rest of the men died pretty much the same way. We took the women back with us, and they live in a women's shelter not far from here. Except for my sister Cece. She lives with us. Jude and I go there every week to teach a self-defense class."

"Wow. I had no idea the Black Roses took an interest in helping women like that," I say.

"They aren't upstanding citizens. But they are good men, and they don't stand for anyone hurting women or kids. That's how I knew Charlie and I were safe here when we came. I knew they wouldn't let anyone hurt either of us and get away with it. And that includes you and Harper. After tomorrow, you won't have to worry about that piece of shit coming after you. You'll be free to live the life you want. You also now have several older brothers to watch out for you. Even though they'll never take the place of Cooper."

"No one ever could, but I appreciate it all the same."

It's not lost on me how odd it is to be sitting here and *not* wanting to crawl out of my skin being around the club I blamed for so long. I also didn't know the details surrounding Cooper's death—or that they exacted revenge for it. I was too wrapped up in my own feelings. I imagine Cooper looking down at me and saying, '*See, I told you so,*' or something otherwise annoying like any older brother would. It's also not lost on me how I feel so comfortable here surrounded by people who knew and loved my brother, people who thought of him as family. God, I wasted so much time being so damn mad at them. I didn't allow myself to have this, to be able to grieve with them, to be around people who loved him. I may not have plans of sticking around, but to know there are people in this world other than me who loved my brother as their own brings me a comfort I didn't know I needed.

"Thank you for sharing that with me." I reach over and cover Lucy's hand with mine, giving it a light squeeze before releasing it.

Lucy smiles, and it's as though the rest of the room lets out a collective sigh of relief.

"Now, how about after dinner, we play a game of pool?"

Charlie groans and I nod. "Sounds like a plan."

The next day, Harper and I are sitting out behind the clubhouse, drinking a cup of coffee and enjoying the chillier weather. That's not something either of us are used to. One of the guys gave us sweatshirts. The clothes we came here with aren't exactly made for cooler weather.

"Cillian comes back today," Harper says as though I needed the reminder.

It was all I could do last night to not text him

after Ozzy gave Harper and me new phones. Each is programmed with Cillian's number—and Ozzy's. Charlie and Lucy also put their numbers in my phone. Hopefully when all this is over, Cillian can transfer my contacts from my old phone onto the new one. There are phone numbers in there that aren't exactly publicly listed.

"Yup," I reply before taking a sip of coffee and looking out at the property that spreads as far as the eye can see. This place is so out of the way, and from what Lucy was saying, they recently acquired a farm that butted up to their property. I don't know how many acres they own, but it's enough to have an outdoor shooting range and not have to worry about nosy neighbors in any direction.

"Any thoughts on what you're going to say to him?"

I shrug.

"Wow. You're really forthcoming today." Harper smirks and turns her attention to the expanse of nothing we're looking at. Usually when we share a cup of coffee in the morning or afternoon when we roll out of bed, there are noises of other families in their houses or in their yards, sounds of life around us. It's so damn quiet out here. It's as though if I say anything, it will disturb the peace of where we are. But Harper is apparently in an uncharacteristically pushy mood this morning. Not that I'm surprised. She knows I can stew in the unknown or hard things for far too long and usually, she lets me. Guess that's over.

"There really isn't much to say, Harpy. We came to a

truce. He felt bad for fucking me and being a complete asshole, and I felt bad for fucking him over in New Orleans...even though I kind of didn't."

Harper shoots me a look with her lips pursed and brow quirked in that, *What the hell are you going on about?* look she does so well.

"Well, it's not like he wanted a cut of anything. And he knew where I lived, so he was able to find his car. I even left the keys in there for him."

"Do you actually believe half the bullshit you say?"

I bark out a laugh at her bluntness, but I'm far from surprised by it. "Not really, no."

"Thank God because I was not about to cosign that load of garbage."

A loud sigh escapes as I pull my feet onto the chair and wrap my arms around my thighs. "The fact is, I never planned to stay in New Orleans for the rest of my life, but to get to where I wanted to be, it was the best choice for my...profession."

"I don't know that I would have considered pickpocketing a profession."

"Don't be a judgmental bitch."

"I'm not. I'm just saying I wouldn't reference it as a profession. It's not like it came with benefits or a retirement."

"No, I have my retirement in a bag under the bed in my room."

Thankfully, all the rooms in the clubhouse come with a key. It would get really awkward carrying a bag full of stolen jewels everywhere with me.

"Cillian and I were never endgame. I wasn't looking for anything long term. And he was...well, he was Cillian."

"What does that mean?"

"Irresistibly charming without meaning to be. A gentleman and a criminal. The master of orgasms. Take your pick."

Harper lets out a tinkling laugh. "I'll take the first two. You can keep the last."

I smile in her direction, but it's hollow. When I left the first time, I never expected to see him again. I was lonely and missed him a lot more than I expected, but there was so much anger. It was easy to ignore the pit in my chest left by his absence. It's harder now, though. And I hate that.

"If he's all those things, why don't you tell him?"

"Because I have a plan and it doesn't include living in Boston. Besides, he may have forgiven me, but he's a long way from trusting me."

"Seems to me the distrust you have toward each other is because of a misunderstanding and *you* handling it horribly wrong."

I can't exactly argue with that.

"I'm pretty sure he was going to tell me he loved me that night he rescued us."

"And you're just *now* telling me this? You should have led with that, my friend. What did he say?"

"We were fighting, I was pissed and about to leave,

and he was about to say it, but I tried to move past him then he grabbed me and...unfortunately, you heard the rest."

"I don't get it. How did you end up back in our room that night then?"

"Because he was a complete asshole afterward. I don't know what changed between him giving me the best orgasm of my life then getting cleaned up to him treating me like I meant nothing to him. Hell, less than nothing."

"Did you say anything about him dropping the L word or even acknowledge it in any way?"

"Not exactly," I reply.

"Nova..."

"No. I didn't. But he didn't give me a chance before his personality pulled a one-eighty, and he was back to being angry with me. And now we're here, and neither of us has brought it up."

"Jesus, you both are shit at communication," Harper says under her breath. "Do you feel the same about him? Isn't this something you can work through together? When I saw you two at Geraldine's, it was like the man had stars in his eyes every time he looked at you or you opened your mouth to spout off some random fact. And you looked at him the same, Nova. You can't deny that."

"Doesn't matter. Men like Cillian aren't quick to forgive and forget."

"You never know. You just have to prove he can trust you again."

"How do you suggest I do that?"

"By staying. Not running."

I usually love my best friend's optimism, but she's missing the mark on this one.

"I'm not running. I'm moving on with my life. I want to find a little beach bar and spend my days in the sun and my nights laughing with regulars and creating a happy, stress-free life. Doesn't that sound better than working at Geraldine's?"

"I like Geraldine's. And…I kind of talked to Damon last night."

Now it's my turn to raise an eyebrow with the *what the hell are you talking about* expression on my face.

"I called to tell him I had a family emergency and lost my phone. That's why I didn't call. We got to talking for a while, and he opened up about some stuff. Mostly about why he was so closed off when we were together. I don't know, hearing his voice and his laugh, it reminded me of when we first started dating. Before he started acting like an asshole, and before I wanted someone more flashy and exciting. I've firmly decided that shit is overrated. As soon as it's safe and this is over, I'm going back to New Orleans."

"And you get on me for burying the lead. Are you two getting back together?"

Harper shrugs. "I don't know, but I want to give it a shot. Shit changed for me in that room when none of us knew what was going to happen. I know you think Damon is a boring stick in the mud, but I think he's...steady. And I need that more than a flashy car or some guy with a sexy East Coast accent." She shakes her head. "God, I was so damn stupid to date that piece of shit."

I reach over and rest my hand on her arm. "No, Harper. He was good at fooling you. Jesus, even I had no idea what a monster he was under the smooth exterior, and I pride myself on being a great judge of character."

"What about Cillian's character?" she asks.

I think about her question for a moment. "He's a good man. But our timing is off. And I don't think we can put it right."

The back door opens, startling us out of our conversation. I look over and the man himself steps on the patio in a devastating black suit, looking deliciously sexy—and every inch the mob lieutenant he is.

He looks toward the two of us and nods. "I wanted you to know I'm back and brought some people with me. This will be over by morning."

# Chapter Twenty-One
## Cillian

WHEN I MET FINN at his penthouse this morning to pack a cache of weapons to bring with us, the last thing I expected was for his wife or her best friend to be there. Or that they were making the trip to Shine with us. When I raised my brow at Finn, he replied with a small shake of his head and pursed lips. Looks like he had a few opinions on the matter of Alessia and Gemma coming along, and by the look on his face, he was overruled.

The marriage between Finn and Alessia is not particularly common in criminal organizations, but completely on par with what we grew up around. Though Cormac Monaghan was the head of the organization for years, Maeve was the head of the family and we all fell in line, including her husband. Finn could always lock her in a safe room like he's threatened to do before. However, Alessia has better aim than her husband—though I would never tell him that—and he probably has an only somewhat irrational fear of losing a certain appendage.

We walk into the clubhouse late in the morning, and

Liam and his team aren't far behind us. There are still a lot of details that need to be hashed out as far as where Farina is and then find the best plan of attack. Our sources are telling us he's holed up in his home, but we have no way of confirming that. At least until Liam shows up with Sawyer. My hacking skills aren't too shabby, but Sawyer has ways of getting satellite footage I could only dream of learning. Not that he'd teach me. Hackers are notoriously tight-lipped about their bag of tricks.

"How was last night?" I ask, walking up to Knox, who's sitting at the bar.

"Fine." He's about as much of a wealth of information as I am on any given day.

"Harper and Nova come out of their room?"

"They did."

That offers some relief. Though he's not divulging what happened when they did, which does nothing to relieve the tension that's been plaguing me.

"You know where she's at?"

"Out back."

"Thanks."

Usually, his less-than-chatty personality is appreciated. Today, not so much.

I walk out to the back of the clubhouse and find Nova and Harper sitting at a table with giant coffee mugs in their hands. The first thing I notice is the sweatshirt Nova's wearing. She's curled up on the chair with the too-large sweatshirt pulled over her knees and calves.

A Black Roses sweatshirt. Another man's sweatshirt. My jaw, along with my chest, tightens in irritation. There's no reason for me to be vexed. Nova isn't the type to jump into another man's bed only days after having sex with me. Or maybe she is. Truthfully, I don't know her well enough to make that call. And here's another truth; seeing her in another man's clothes doesn't sit right with me. Not at all.

The two turn their gazes in my direction, but I can't quite read the expression on Nova's face. There's a moment when she looks me over, a flash of something in her green eyes, but it's gone in an instant.

"I wanted you to know I'm back and brought some people with me. This will be over by morning."

She and Harper share a look before Harper stands. "I should go get ready or...something," she says and walks past me into the clubhouse.

That wasn't awkward at all.

"You look refreshed this morning," Nova says as I stand here like a fucking idiot.

"You look comfy." My head tilts to the sweatshirt she's curled up in.

"Oh, yeah. One of the guys let me borrow something a little warmer. Charlie and Lucy said they'd bring some stuff by for Harper and me today since nothing we brought is really suited for this weather."

Damnit, I should have thought of that yesterday.

"Good night?" I ask.

"It was, actually," she replies with a slow nod. "I had a

few…epiphanies, shall we say."

"Care to share with the class?"

One thing I learned about Nova the second we met—not when she was playing Charity but when I met the real her—is that all kinds of things fly out of her mouth. It was fascinating if I'm being honest. Like every thought she had needed to be shared. I loved the way her mind worked and the off-the-wall shit she would say in the unlikeliest of situations. But since that night in the hotel, there's been a wall between us. I realize I put it there, but I hate it all the same.

Nova considers whether or not she should share personal information with me as I stand and stare at her. Anything and everything used to flow freely from her lips, but she's not open with me like she was just a month ago.

It doesn't seem as though she's going to confide in me until she exhales a deep breath and opens her mouth to speak. "Harper helped me look at where my anger was really coming from. It was never something I admitted to anyone, and actually just recently kind of admitted to myself. Then I talked with Lucy and got a better feel for what Cooper's life was like here and how his death affected everyone. Not because they lost a member, but they lost a brother, too. I don't know. I guess I realized I had more in common with the club than I would have thought. And it was nice being around people who knew and loved him. Kind of like we could share the grief."

"Wow, that *is* quite the revelation."

She lets out a disbelieving huff of laughter. "Trust me, no one is more surprised than I am."

"I'm glad being here helped, Nova."

I offer her a smile and she returns it, but there's still this heavy unease between us. There was a natural camaraderie I felt with her from the start, and it's broken now. I don't know if we can ever get it back. I don't know if she wants to try, if it's all that important to her.

Jude peeks his head in from the doorway. "My brother's here," he tells me. "And Lucifer and Charlie just got here with some things for you and Harper," he says, turning toward Nova.

Good, she can change out of that sweatshirt.

"Thanks, Jude," she replies. When he walks back inside, she lets out a real laugh. The one I haven't heard for far too long. "Those two are something else. I don't think I've ever seen anyone so in love but so intent on pissing the other person off. It was like watching a tennis match last night."

The fond smile on Nova's face does something to my heart. Her face, her energy, it's so much lighter than it was yesterday when I left her here. She came here because she was out of options and wasn't willing to accept my help. But coming here has lifted something from her, and now she's found the family her brother was searching for, even if she doesn't realize it yet. I recognize it because that's what I found with the Monaghans.

"I need to go inside and talk to Liam. Finn's wife and Eoghan's fiancée are here too if you want to meet them." Not that she's going to have much of a choice. Making the trip to be close to their men wasn't the only reason Gemma and Alessia came with us.

"Sure, I'm just going to head to my room first and get changed."

"Okay, see you in there."

I turn and head back inside, wishing we could stay out here and I could enjoy this other side of Nova I haven't seen since everything went to shit.

But things need to get done, and plans need to be made. Today isn't the day for enjoying the beauty in front of me. It's for making sure she's safe and taking out the motherfuckers that threaten it.

Walking back into the main room of the clubhouse, I see Gemma and Alessia talking with Lucy and Charlie. The women have formed a friendship since the first time they met at a fight night a few months ago. Liam is at the bar talking with Finn and Ozzy as everyone else says their hellos.

"Sawyer here?" I ask, walking up to Liam.

"He's grabbing himself a cup of coffee and a donut from the kitchen," Liam answers. "He had a long night of getting into some footage and tracking down a few people. Seems Tony is at the Farina compound, and as far as we can tell, he hasn't left since yesterday afternoon."

Finn nods. "Makes it a bit easier for us."

"Trust me, nothing is going to be easy about this," Sawyer says, walking over with a coffee in one hand and his laptop in the other. "The guards are working in shifts of six. From what I can tell, they switch every twelve hours. In my experience, it's going to be best for us to go in about four in the morning. The shift change happens at five, so the guards on duty will be tired enough that they may not be particularly alert, but the ones relieving them also won't be up and ready yet. That will get us in. It doesn't look to me like the guards are leaving the property. Farina has a house separate from his where the guards go after their shift to get some rest. They're expecting something, unless that's standard protocol for them."

"That's not standard for Farina," I hear someone say as they walk up to our little group.

I turn and see Luca—Finn's cousin.

"I wasn't sure if you were going to make it," Finn says to his cousin, who has been traveling through Italy with his new wife, Giada, who is saying hello to Alessia and Gemma.

"I wasn't either, but glad I did," he replies before turning his attention to the rest of the group. "Farina never had more than four guards on at one time, and from what I saw when I was undercover with Cataldi, the guards never stayed on the property. They're definitely prepared for a full-scale attack."

"Well, I certainly hate to see them prepare for nothing," Liam quips.

Nova and Harper catch my attention as they walk from the hallway to the group of women sitting on the couches. I see Lucy introduce the two women to Alessia, Gemma, and Giada. Nova is wearing a smile on her face as she casually chats with everyone. Seeing her so friendly—and dare I say, relaxed—in this clubhouse and with the other women eases something for me. I hated the way she looked when we first walked in here yesterday, how stiff and ready to jump down someone's throat she was. Like the weight of the world was on her. Today is different. From what I can see, this is the Nova I met months ago who was quick with a smile and a joke.

Alessia catches my gaze, and the corner of her mouth tips up in a knowing smile. I know what she's thinking, and maybe in another life, she would be right. But Nova and I aren't in a place where it matters how well she gets along with the other women. It doesn't matter that her sense of ease around Alessia, Gemma, or Giada means so fucking much to me.

"Cillian, are you listening?" Sawyer asks. "I need to make sure everyone is aware of the plan and knows the roles they're playing, otherwise this whole thing will go to shit."

Finn casts me a worried look, but I ignore him.

"Yup, I'm here. Let's dial it in."

# Chapter Twenty-Two

## Cillian

Tensions are high when we pull up behind Farina's property. Sawyer is setting up while we gather everything we can carry on our bodies. It's your usual fanfare of guns, knives, and what look to be grenades strapped to Abel and Liam's vests. These men are quite fond of explosives.

"I'm in," Sawyer calls from one of the vans we took here. "And good news is, we're out of camera range." He'll be staying in the van for this operation. He's cut into all the camera feeds so he can be our eyes and ears until we have all these assholes neutralized.

"Jesus, is anyone else concerned that he wasn't sure of that until just now?" Luca asks.

"He's a little shit who likes to fuck with us," Liam says, coming up to our small group and clapping Luca on the back. "But don't worry, he's the best at what he does. If he wasn't, I would have dropped him in the jungle and left him for dead years ago."

"I can hear you, asshole," Sawyer says through the comms in all of our ears.

"That's why I said it," Liam replies. "Comms work."

Liam holds up a thumb along with every other member of his team.

Finn, Eoghan, Luca, and I, along with the Black Roses who came with us, all raise our thumbs in confirmation as well. Barrett and Wyatt stayed behind with Enzo, Alessia's personal guard. It was the one thing Finn asked so he would feel comfortable leaving his wife somewhere other than safely nestled in their fortified penthouse in Boston, and the men agreed to guard the women with their lives.

We've split into groups of five. Cash is the only member of the MC with us to make the tally of each group even.

"I've known Nova a long time," Cash says to me.

I nod and triple-check every last knife and gun on me.

"She's a good girl. Big heart."

"Yup."

"Don't break it," he says, holding my gaze when I finally look up at him. Little does he know, she's the one with the power to break me, not the other way around.

"This is all very adorable and heartwarming, but we have some Italians to kill," Eoghan says through the comms.

Liam walks to the center of the group. "Time to go in, boys. Let's go over this one more time. My team is Alpha. Finn, you're Beta. Ozzy, you're Gamma. That's how Sawyer will be referencing you and your team until we get in the house and cut the power. Then, he'll be blind. Is everyone familiar with the night-vision goggles?" We all nod. "Good. I want everyone to test them."

We do as he says as we pull them over our eyes and look around to make sure we have a clear field of vision.

"Jesus, this is a far cry from how we usually handle things. This is like a full-on tactical assault or some shit," Eoghan says.

"It is," Liam says. "We've run this sort of operation all over the world, and if you keep to the plan, we'll all get out of here alive."

Eoghan shuts up and listens intently to the rest of Liam's rundown.

"We know there are six guards out there. Three close to the house and three more closer to the perimeter of the property. Beta and Gamma will walk the perimeter and take them out before splitting up. Gamma, take the back of the house. Beta, take the front. Alpha, we're going to go to the house where the other guards are sleeping and neutralize that threat before entering the main house through the back patio door. We don't know how many guards are in the main house, if any, but if we don't have twelve dead bodies in the next ten minutes, we can assume some are inside with Farina. Tony is also in there with two of his own. My guess is that he's hiding out until they figure out what to do."

"Good thing we're answering that for him," Finn says.

"Once the guards in the other house are taken care of, we'll meet you inside. I want in Farina's office, where he hopefully keeps the information on the pieces of shit he works with. Everyone clear?" We all nod. "Alright. Be quiet, stay low, and don't get your dick shot off," Liam finishes.

We step into the trees lining the Farina property and begin our sweep. It's pitch black out here, so I'm pretty damn grateful for the state-of-the-art goggles that allow us to see what's moving around us. Within five minutes, we spot a group of three men in the distance. One is smoking while the other two walk beside him, all three with automatic rifles slung over their shoulders. Our two teams stop, still in the cover of the trees, and wait for them to get closer.

Ozzy motions for Jude and me, and we flank him on either side. He holds three fingers and begins a countdown. When the last finger is down, we aim, and each of us fires a nearly silent shot into the guards. Jude's bullet hits the one smoking square in the forehead, and he lowers his weapon with a smug smile on his face.

"Show-off," I whisper as we head toward the dead guards.

Linc, Braxton, and Knox pull the bodies into the trees so that the guards who are walking the house don't catch sight of three motionless bodies on the ground.

We wait behind the trees with the dead bodies until we see a guard walk around to this side of the house, staring at his phone. *Great work ethic, asshole.* He leans against the wall of the house and props up his foot against the brick behind him.

"Where are the other two guards, Sawyer?" Finn asks.

"Other side of the house, but closing in on your right. You have about one minute."

"You think you can hit a target that far?" I ask my boss.

"Are you...?" Finn looks at me then toward the man staring at his phone, thinking he's about to get some sleep. When Finn raises his rifle, he lets out a breath and fires. I see the shot hit the man in the chest, and he falls to the ground.

"Don't ask stupid questions, Cillian. It's beneath you."

"The other two are about to find their friend," Sawyer says into the comms.

We make our way toward the house with Linc and Knox leading the group. The second the other two guys come around the corner, both men fire their weapons. One is hit in the chest and the other in his head.

"Like fish in a fucking barrel," Linc says as the five Black Roses veer to the back of the house, and the rest of us take the front.

Once we're all in position, Sawyer gets back on the comms. "I'm going to disable the alarm and cut the power in three"—four beeps sound at the front door, and I see the light on the keypad turn green—"two, one."

The lights inside and outside around the entire property go dark, and I open the door, stepping into the large house, thankful once again for the night-vision goggles that allow us to see in the dark.

There's a giant marble table in the center of the foyer and two staircases on either side of the large room leading up to the second floor. Two hallways lead out of the foyer, one to the dining room and kitchen and the other to an office and the servants' quarters—according to the building plans Sawyer was able to find. Thankfully, Farina doesn't keep live-in staff any longer since his daughter and wife are hardly here except for holiday gatherings, where he tries to impress the other families. To the right of us is a large room that looks like a library and to the left is a formal living room. From the plans, I know that the patio has a separate entrance, and the Black Roses will be coming in from the hallway off to the left. As soon as I see Ozzy peek his head from around the corner, I breathe a sigh of relief. That side of the house is clear.

They'll be staying down here and clearing the downstairs while we sweep upstairs. Eoghan, Finn, and I begin walking up the steps on the right while Luca and Cash make their way up the other side. When we meet at the top, the duo moves down the hallway on their side and we do the same. No one is behind the first door on our left, so we move to the next room. The house is silent and the only thing I hear is my breathing before two soft pops sound.

"One of Tony's guys," Luca whispers through the comms.

When we enter the second door, there's a man sleeping on his stomach. I walk around the side of the bed to get a look at him. It's not Tony, so I put a bullet in his head before he has a chance to open his eyes. The third room is also empty which leaves two more on this side of the house.

"We're clear," Cash says.

I open the fourth door, and sleeping on his back is the piece of shit who had Nova in his grasp. I remember the fear in her eyes, the shiver of disgust that rolled through her when he had his hands on her. The rage I felt seeing him paw at her, thinking he was going to get away with her.

Eoghan walks to the other side of the bed, with Finn standing guard at the door. His handgun is pointed at Tony while I walk up to the man and raise my weapon, bumping the suppressor against the center of his forehead. His eyes pop open, and he lies in bed—motionless.

"Morning, fucker."

Tony, being the dumb shit he is, quickly turns in the opposite direction, but the fist to the side of his head stops him and he collapses back onto the mattress.

"Why do these dumb fucks always try to make a run for it?" Eoghan asks, shaking out his hand. Luca and Cash pop their heads into the room and take in the scene.

"One room left," Luca says, and Finn turns, leading Cash and Luca to the last door while Eoghan and I keep an eye on the soon-to-be dead man lying unconscious in the bed.

Moments later, Finn is dragging a very pissed-off-looking Massimo Farina from his room.

"You're dead. Every single one of you," he spits as Finn and Luca haul the man toward the staircase.

"You're not the first to threaten me, Farina, and I doubt you'll be the last," Finn says.

Eoghan and I grab an unconscious Tony from the bed and make our way out of the room to the staircase behind Finn and Luca. When we get to the bottom, Liam and his team, as well as the rest of the Black Roses, are scattered around the large foyer, watching Farina struggle and spit down each step.

When we get to the bottom, Eoghan and I unceremoniously drop Tony to the ground while Liam walks up to Finn and Luca, who are holding tightly to Farina.

"Massimo Farina, I presume," Liam says, looking the man up and down.

"Who the fuck are you?" Farina spits back.

"Liam Ashcroft."

"Never heard of you."

A sly smile spreads across Liam's face. "Then I'm doing my job right. You and I are going to have a little conversation, and you're going to decide how painful it's going to be."

"I'm not telling you shit, asshole."

"Oh, Massimo, that's what they all say. And yet I always get my answers." Liam nods toward Abel and Kingston who step forward and take Farina from Luca and Finn, then head down the hallway to Farina's office. "Come now, let's chat," I hear Liam say with an almost gleeful tone to his voice.

Tony begins to stir at my feet, and I take a step back, staring at the man as he comes to. He looks around at the rather large group and groans, realization hitting him as he catches his bearings. He knows he isn't getting out of this alive.

I've seen my boss ruthlessly murder people after torturing them. Nothing quite as gruesome as what he did to Orlando Farina, Massimo's son, but if I were a different kind of person, I'd probably have nightmares until the day I died. I've never been one for the dramatics. Any time I've taken a life, it's been in the service of my family and over quickly. But I can definitely see the appeal of torturing a man who's hurt someone you love before taking his life.

"Hope she sucked your dick good, Cillian. There's no way you're walking out of this alive." Tony's full of bluster and he knows it. Doesn't mean he isn't going to try to get under my skin while he can, though.

I cock my gun and point it at his head. "Who else knows about Nova and Harper?"

His laugh is almost maniacal. "Why should I tell you shit? I'm dead either way."

I smash the butt of my gun into his nose, which immediately explodes with blood running down his naked chest.

"True, but I get to decide how painful that death is."

"Fuck you." He spits a mouthful of blood at my feet.

I nod a few times then casually raise my gun and

shoot him in the hand.

"Motherfucker!" Tony yells, cradling his hand against his chest.

"Who knows?" I yell.

"Get fucked!" His face has gone pale, and beads of sweat gather across his forehead, but he's still being a stupid, stubborn son of a bitch, so I raise my gun again, this time firing into his kneecap, and he screams.

"Hurts like a bitch, doesn't it? You know, Liam has a guy who can keep you alive for at least another day. Think of it, Tony, twenty-four more hours of me putting bullet holes in you. Maybe I'll practice my knife skills while we're at it. It's been a minute since I've filleted human flesh." I raise my gun and point it at his other knee. "Who knows?" I yell again.

"Fuck, man. No one. No one knows except Massimo. I'm the only one who handles the skin trade."

I had a feeling that was the case. This is new territory for Farina, so it makes sense he was keeping his circle small for the time being.

I fire into his other knee anyways.

"Goddamnit, I told you what you wanted to know!"

"I know, but I like to see you suffer like those girls would have suffered."

I watch him for a few moments. He's a sniveling, bleeding mess, barely able to keep himself upright. And the sight brings me more satisfaction than any sane man should feel. Guess that says a lot about me.

I raise my gun once more and point it at his head. "See

you in hell, motherfucker."

And I pull the trigger.

Brain matter smears on the wall behind him as his lifeless body slumps to the floor.

"Goddamn," Eoghan says from beside me. "Remind me not to piss you off."

"I do. Every damn time you feel the need to needle me for your entertainment."

"It's brotherly affection."

I roll my eyes. "Wouldn't mind if you weren't so *brotherly* toward me then."

Eoghan's hand covers his heart with the dramatic flair only he can pull off. "Cillian, that hurts my heart," he says, wearing an exaggerated pout.

So I smack him in the back of the head. "There's your brotherly affection."

"Ow. Why does everyone always feel the need to hit me in the head?" he gripes, rubbing the spot.

"Jesus, Eoghan. Stop being such a damn crybaby," Finn says, shaking his head.

Just as Eoghan is about to open his mouth, probably to bitch some more, Liam walks out with Farina being dragged behind him by Kingston and Abel.

"Get what you need?" I ask.

"Of course," Liam replies with a cocky grin on his face.

I look at Farina—who has a few more spots that are sure to bruise on his face than what he walked in there with.

"Great. Let's get this fucker back to Shine. My

father-in-law would like a word with him," Finn says, then walks out the front door.

Liam and his crew stayed behind—along with Braxton and Cash. They're on cleanup duty, then Cash and Braxton are going to introduce Liam to a certain pig farmer who doesn't ask questions.

It's odd seeing a man like Massimo Farina tied to a chair with darkening bruises around his face and arms. We didn't run in the same circles, but any time I saw him, he was always dressed to impress in a three-piece suit with an air of authority. I've always thought he was an asshole, but at least he had a good tailor.

Eoghan and I stand inside the small room in the basement of the Black Roses clubhouse to keep watch on Farina. It's not like he's going anywhere, though, or doing much of anything except glaring at us from his one eye that hasn't swollen shut yet.

We didn't walk through the main room of the clubhouse, so I haven't seen Nova. The next time I lay eyes on her or talk to her, I want to be damn sure all of this is over and tell her she's free to live her life, find that little beach town, and open her bar without having to look over her shoulder or worry that the boogeyman is going to jump from the shadows and take her again. That particular boogeyman is dead, and this one is well on his way to meeting him in hell.

The door opens, and Finn walks through, followed by Mario Amatto, Finn's father-in-law.

According to Finn, Mario has been waiting for the day to end the Farina line. It would have caused a war ten years ago that Mario wasn't prepared for when he suspected Orlando killed his son Gio. Mario had no definitive proof back then, and he would have had the Farinas *and* the Cataldis to contend with. Now is a different time and an entirely different circumstance. The Amattos and the Monaghans hold the power in this territory. Mario knew Massimo's day of reckoning would eventually come.

And that day is today.

"Jesus, Massimo, you look like shit," Mario says, snickering to himself.

"Should have known you'd align yourself with biker trash, Mario. You already did with the Irish scum."

Mario chuckles. "They're pretty smart for scum. They have you tied up here, don't they?"

"Fuck you."

"Yeah, yeah. Fuck me." Mario waves his hand as though he's beating away an annoying fly. "You know," he starts, taking off his jacket and laying it on a chair on the other side of the room before rolling up his sleeves. "I've waited a decade for this moment. The point in time when you would have to answer for what you did to my family. Answer for your part in taking my son from me."

I've seen Mario several times throughout the years.

Usually at family dinners and celebrations where he's the doting husband and father. This is the first time I've been here to witness him as the ruthless Mafia don. I must say, I rather like this side of him.

"Your son-in-law killed Orlando!" Massimo yells in a rough voice.

"He did. But that was for what he did to Alessia. This is for what he did to Gio. What *you* knew about and helped him cover up. This is between us, father to father."

Mario slips a pair of brass knuckles from his pocket and slides them over his fingers. When he walks over to Massimo, he unleashes his rage, hitting the man in the face until the skin is broken and bleeding. Fuck, I think I might even see some bone.

"You took from me, from my family. Something we can never get back. My wife lost her son, my daughter lost her brother, her protector, and you knew what Orlando did!"

Mario grabs Massimo by the chin. If the man hadn't let out a groan of pain, I'd have thought him unconscious.

"You took and took. Then you tried to take girls and sell them to other monsters just like you and your dead son. You were never going to retire an old man and die peacefully in your sleep, Massimo. But fuck, I'm glad I get to be the one to end you."

Mario grabs Massimo's hair with one hand, pulling his head back while he takes the gun from his holster with the other, pressing the metal against Massimo's forehead. "Tell your son I said hello."

Then he fires.

The room is silent as Mario stares at the dead body of the man who allowed so much cruelty and was responsible for so much heartache for the Amatto family and others.

When Mario turns, he walks over to the sink in the far corner of the room and washes Farina's blood from his hands before putting his jacket back on and turning to face Finn, Eoghan, and myself.

"I'm going to give my daughter a hug and go home to my wife. I trust you will have this cleaned up?"

Finn nods. "Of course."

Mario walks to the door and opens it, but before stepping through, he turns to Finn. "Thank you for calling me, son. It's been a while since I got my hands dirty." He looks toward Farina again. "Damn, that felt good."

He smiles at Finn, who is wearing his customary smirk, before walking out of the room.

Ozzy enters moments later, looking from the body in his basement back to Finn. "Leave it for the prospects. They need to earn their shit. Go be with your women," he tells the room. As I move past him, he says, "Yours is out back."

"Not my woman," I reply, but Ozzy just shakes his head.

"Whatever you want to tell yourself."

Instead of answering, I walk out and head to the back patio where Nova and Harper were sitting this morning.

When I find her, instead of a cup of coffee, she's sipping on what looks to be a whiskey 7, and Harper is nowhere to be seen. Probably sleeping like any normal person would be at this hour.

"Hey," I say in greeting as I walk over and have a seat next to her. "Little early to be drinking, no?"

"Maybe if I'd been to sleep yet." Nova lifts the glass and takes a sip before handing it to me.

When I take it, our fingers brush, and it could be the exhaustion creeping in, but I swear I see a hitch in her breath at the contact.

Sipping from the glass, I wince. "Yeah, I much prefer it on the rocks." I set the glass back down next to her and lean back in my chair. "Everything is taken care of. Finn will have a meeting with the remaining Farina capos, but no one knows anything about you and Harper. Seems Tony was the only one who handled the skin trade."

Nova nods and settles back in her chair, mirroring my position. "It feels weird to say thank you for killing someone for me, but thank you."

I give her a soft smile. "Yeah, it sounds weird when you say it like that."

I have no regrets about tonight. What I don't tell her is I would hunt down and kill anyone who was a threat to her and her future.

"I'm going to ask one thing from you," I start, and Nova looks at me with skepticism in her green gaze. "I want you to let me take care of the jewelry."

She opens her mouth to argue, but I shake my head and hold up a hand, which she looks ready to cut off at the moment.

"Listen, I've been thinking about it. Moving it anywhere close to New Orleans is too risky. It was risky a month ago, it's risky now, and it'll be risky in another month. I have plenty of connections in this department and can make sure it's never traced back to you."

Nova sits in the chair and chews at her lip while she considers everything.

"I'll set up an account for you and send you all the information. I'll make sure if anyone digs into where you got your money, it will look like an inheritance from some rich, dead grandfather or something."

She's still silent.

"Please, Nova. Let me do one last thing for you. You know my plan is better."

A small smile graces her lips. "Well, you are the criminal mastermind."

A chuckle escapes me. "So I've heard."

Nova stands. "I feel like I can finally breathe. You know what I mean?"

"I do."

"That's thanks to you." She smiles again, and it's like the one I saw earlier. It's lighter. She's lighter, and the fact I had any part in that, big or small, makes those dark parts of myself a little lighter, too. "I'll see you in the morning."

"It is morning," I reply.

Nova shakes her head. "I'll see you later today, then."

She walks back into the clubhouse, leaving her drink on the table. I finish it for her, no use wasting good whiskey, and remember every time I kissed her with this exact taste on her lips.

# Chapter Twenty-Three
## Nova
### Two Months Later

"As you can see, the property needs work, but it's less than a block from the beach," my realtor says as she tours the third bar I've looked at since coming to Emerald Haven, a little beach town in South Carolina. I picked this place because it's right between Myrtle Beach and Charleston, South Carolina. I wanted somewhere quiet without the highs and lows of the tourism season. Somewhere I could feel safe and build a life for myself.

When Harper and I left Shine, I went back to New Orleans with her for a couple weeks. Even though Cillian assured us the men who took Harper and me were no longer a threat, it took a minute or two not to look over my shoulder every time I left the house. It actually helped that Damon was there every day, to my surprise. He and I never really got along, but when Harper said he wished he'd done a lot of things differently, turns out one of those things was the way he treated me. She seems happy, and that's all I can really ask for. Though I don't think he'll be moving in right away, the way she lit up whenever he was over has me thinking it won't be long.

About a week after getting home, a courier showed up with an envelope from Cillian. There was a letter from a lawyer regarding my nonexistent dead grandfather's estate, bank account information with my name on it, and a Louisiana driver's license with my real name on it. And that was it. Nothing from the man who hasn't left my thoughts for the last two months. I wasn't sure how to feel about it. I may have come a long way in figuring out how to process certain things without lashing out, but this one had and still has me stumped.

*I sit on the couch at our house and stare at the paperwork, which is where Harper finds me about an hour later.*

*She looks at the paperwork on the coffee table in front of me, then to my face. "You okay?" she asks.*

*I just shake my head. "I don't know why I can't stop staring at this. It's not like he's going to jump out of the envelope."*

*"Nova, if you miss him this much, call him."*

*I let out a slow breath and look her in the eye. "I can't. There's no way the man will trust me after what I pulled. Hell, I wouldn't trust me either. If there was even a slight chance he wanted anything with me, he would have brought the papers himself. Instead, he had a courier drop them off."*

*Harper looks at me with sympathy creasing her brow.*

*"Don't, Harper. It's okay, really." It really isn't, but it is what it is. "This is good. I'll go straight, and Cillian will*

*live his life just as he was supposed to. It was a great distraction and even better memories, but that's all it is."*

*Harper knows me well enough to know any arguments she wants to make will be for nothing. She's one of those sweet souls who believes in happily ever afters. I'm...not. I'll never hold ill will toward Cillian, but that doesn't mean I'm willing to change my entire life and all the plans I made for myself because of a few days of great sex and a connection that, when tested, failed miserably. I think the way I received all this information that I keep staring at is proof of that. And eventually, that will be fine with me.*

"It's a great space," I tell the realtor. "Give me a few days, and I'll think about it.

"Of course."

We part ways and I get into the little red car I bought before coming to South Carolina. I'm reformed these days, living the straight and narrow, as they say. And regular people do shit like that, right? Buy cars, rent houses, start businesses. The fact that the money is from a little heist we pulled off three months ago doesn't matter in the grand scheme of things.

Pulling up to the house I'm renting, I sit in my car and stare at the light-blue Craftsman-style home. It's only two bedrooms, which is fine because I only need one. Every time I come home from exploring the little town, I do this—sit in my car and stare. I was so damn excited to get out of New Orleans, I didn't stop to think what the reality of living here by myself would look like. I sit and stare and have no desire to go into an empty house. My time in Emerald Haven has been spent putting a house together—not that I've done much—and checking out the bar scene. I looked at the last bar that's for sale out here. It has everything I wanted. It's closer to the beach than the other two. It has a small kitchen that would be simple for one person to run, and it has an amazing patio that has a direct line of sight to the ocean. It's everything I dreamed of for so long, but instead of begging to sign the papers like I thought I would, I walked out still uncertain.

"It's just a house, and you just need time, Nova." Sometimes giving myself a little pep talk works, and I can walk in grateful for the changes I've made and the direction I'm going in. Other days, not so much. Today is the latter, but I can't sit out here all night.

I get out of my car and walk up the steps to my house. When I open the door, silence greets me, like it does every day. I've realized I truly hate a silent house. Harper and I usually worked the same schedule, her being a bartender and me usually not leaving the house until after dark, either. The first week I was here, I'd wake in the morning and the thought of what Harper was making for breakfast would cross my mind...until I realized she wasn't here. I'd have to shake the homesick feeling away and get out of bed. Then, my mind would inevitably wander to Cillian and his blue-gray eyes that were always a little darker when he first opened them. I'd remember the mornings I woke up to him staring at me and being tangled up with him after a night of exhausting ourselves with each other.

We only knew each other for a few months, and in those months, we only spent a handful of days together. Still, I'd be lying if I didn't say that was all it took for me to fall for him. I thought this feeling would go away. I thought it was because we burned so hot from the start, and this ache was just a remnant of that. But I was wrong. The pain of not being with him—of not seeing that smile I'd swear he reserved only for me—breaks my heart a little more with every passing day, not less. That's not how it's supposed to go, right? Time is supposed to heal all wounds or some such bullshit, but this one is only getting worse, and I don't have the first clue on how to fix it.

My phone rings in my pocket, and I pull it out to find Lucy's name on the screen. We've talked a handful of times since I left Shine. When we first exchanged numbers, I really didn't expect her to keep in touch. The only woman I've ever been close with is my best friend, but Lucy calls and checks on me at least once a week, which I find oddly comforting. My circle expanded when I let go of the anger over my brother's death. And surprisingly, I don't hate it.

"Hey, Lucy," I answer, falling back into the tan couch that came with the rental.

"You don't sound happy. What's wrong?"

For being a *loudmouth harpy*, as her boyfriend likes to call her, she's incredibly perceptive.

"Why would anything be wrong? I'm living my dream of being in a quiet little beach town about to buy a bar and have more money than I've ever had in my entire life."

"Then why do you sound like that?"

"Like what?"

"Like you're trying too hard to convince yourself."

"Damn, lady. Way to cut to the quick." A huff of unamused laughter leaves my lips.

"Who has time for bullshit?"

I'm silent for a few moments, and Lucy allows me the time to process everything. She may like to get right to the point, but at least she's allowing me to catch up a bit.

"I thought this was what I wanted. That starting over was going to be just that. A fresh start. New town, new me. But it's not. Or maybe the new me just needs to get used to being bored? I don't know."

"Or maybe you're trying to fit yourself in a role that isn't you. Someone you aren't meant to be."

"This is what I've been working toward since before Coop even went to live in Shine. I want this, Lucy."

*Right?*

"It's okay to admit that you don't. It's perfectly acceptable to change paths, Nova. Because from where I'm sitting, it doesn't sound like this is really what you want. You're out there away from everyone you love and care about. What's so important about being there instead of New Orleans?"

When I think about leaving Emerald Haven, it's not New Orleans that I think about going to.

"Your silence is deafening," Lucy says. "You know, Jude and I have been to Boston a few times in the last couple months."

"And?"

"And there's a certain mob lieutenant who's been a grumpy bastard every time, at least according to Jude. Me, on the other hand? I think he's a little heartbroken and doesn't know what to do."

"Oh, yeah? And who would that be, because it can't be Cillian. He sent me a bunch of paperwork by courier. That doesn't scream someone who misses me."

"Well, every time we've been to Clovers and Alessia or Gemma ask about you, he finds a spot on the wall that's much more interesting than our conversation, then he excuses himself from the table. And that screams someone who misses you and has no idea what to do about it."

"He could have come to New Orleans. Or he could show up any time down here. It's not like I'm keeping where I am a secret."

"Yeah, and it's not like you left him twice already. Tell me, Nova, how many times has he left you?"

"None, but the last time doesn't count. I had to go home and get things sorted."

"And who helped you do that?"

"Cillian," I answer through a clenched jaw.

"Nova, I'm going to say this with all the love in my

heart—you two need to pull your heads out of your asses and realize that neither of you is happy without the other, and you're both either too scared or too fucking pigheaded to do something about it. Someone who doesn't care about you wouldn't make sure you and Harper were safe from anyone who could have found out about you and used you against the Monaghans for funsies. They wouldn't sell off a load of hot jewelry and use their lawyer to draw up a bunch of fake paperwork so there wouldn't be questions about where the money came from. And as for you, stop being so damn stubborn. Trust me when I say this because I know a little something about being a stubborn asshole who's scared to go out on a limb and actually trust someone. Cillian has never let you down, even when he had every chance and, frankly, every right to walk away. Instead, he let you do the walking because he thought it was what you wanted, and he wanted to give you anything you could possibly want or need, the dumb bastard. If you want my opinion—"

"Hasn't this whole tirade been your opinion?" I ask, cutting her off.

"No, my sweet friend who needs to shut up and let me finish, it is not. This is me giving you the reality check you desperately need. It's your turn, Nova. You need to be the one to put yourself out there and get real comfortable with the idea that being obstinate doesn't mean being strong. And being strong doesn't mean you aren't allowed to be scared at the same time. Moving to a new town and starting over was quite the leap. And it's going to take another leap to admit it's not what you really want and go to Boston to get what you and I both know will make you happy. Are you strong enough to do that?"

"I don't know," I reply on a broken whisper.

"Bullshit. Do you love him?"

I'm silent again. Pretty sure we've already established that I'm shit at admitting things to myself. Especially things that have the potential to hurt me. But I'm also not a liar. The way he looked at me, like he was fascinated with everything I said, the way he always made me feel safe, protected, and *alive* just by being there, those moments when I saw his real smile and heard his laugh still make my heart smile as though he was standing right in front of me. There was a bubble the two of us somehow created together. I'd never felt anything like it. Never in my life had I been the center of someone's universe and vice versa. It was heady and intense, and nothing could have prepared me for it. But that's how it works, right? They don't say *falling* in love for no reason. Because that's what it felt like. We were in free fall, and we were happy, laughing, and holding each other as we went. Until it came crashing down, and I ran.

"Yes."

"Then what the hell are you doing in South Carolina?"

"What am I doing? This is crazy," I mumble to myself as I stand in front of a small bar on a chilly Boston street. Shit, I must look like a crazy person muttering to myself in front of Clovers if the side-eye stares I'm getting from random strangers passing me are anything to go by.

The day after my conversation with Lucy, I called the realtor and told her I wasn't interested in the bar. Then, ten minutes later, I had a plane ticket booked for Boston. And I'm scared, that kind of knot-in-the-stomach-might-puke-right-here scared, but like Lucy said, being strong doesn't mean you can't be scared. I have to at least try because I refuse to live with the *what-if*.

I open the door to the bar and take in my surroundings. An old jukebox sits against the back wall, and some classic rock plays in the background. The brick walls and beer signs, coupled with a large Irish flag hanging on another wall, seem pretty typical of what one would expect in an Irish neighborhood tavern in Boston. I walk up to the bar and have a seat, noting the prominent placement of Cillian's favorite Irish whiskey. The mirror behind the bottles makes me smile, remembering the first night I met Cillian and the rundown I gave him about mirrors and bars and the night that ensued.

God, this is ridiculous. Who shows up at a bar to find a guy who may not want anything to do with her?

"What can I get you?" the bartender asks as I'm still arguing with myself about whether I should stay or hop back on a plane to anywhere else.

"She'll have a whiskey 7," a smooth voice says from behind me.

I turn and my gaze collides with the blue-gray one I've been missing desperately for two months.

"Awfully presumptuous to assume you know my drink," I reply.

"I'm sorry. Would you prefer a daiquiri?"

My face scrunches in disgust. "God, no."

Cillian has a seat next to me, his eyes never leaving mine. "What are you doing here, Nova?"

"Well, Cillian, I'm having a drink at a bar."

He shakes his head and the corner of his mouth tips in a small smile. "That fucking mouth."

"I seem to remember you liking my mouth."

"I seem to remember you living in a small coastal town in South Carolina."

"I do—or did. I'm not sure at the moment." My gaze stays locked on his, waiting and hoping whatever he says next will help me make that decision.

"Hmm, well I guess I won't be needing this then." He pulls a piece of paper from his pocket and tosses it on the bar next to me. When he nods toward the paper, I pick it up and open the folded sheet. It's a confirmation for his flight that was supposed to be leaving in two hours. A flight scheduled for South Carolina.

"What is this?" I ask, looking at the paper in my hand then back to him.

He tucks a loose strand of hair behind my ear and hits me with one of those soft and sweet smiles. "Pretty sure everyone around here is sick of me being a surly asshole. Quite frankly, I'm sick of it, too. So I decided to book a flight." The bartender sets my drink in front of me, and Cillian orders a whiskey on the rocks for himself. "I'm so damn tired of this, Nova."

"Of what?" I breathe out.

"Of this hole in my chest. The one that only seems to be filled when I'm around you. Before I met you in New Orleans, there was something missing. Something that had been missing for a long time. I don't know...I thought working with Liam would fix whatever it was. And it did, for a while." He shoots me a crooked smile, and my heart does that double-beat thing that only seems to happen around him. "But then, I met this enchanting little thief with green eyes and a smart mouth, and I was smitten. I thought it would pass. Thought it was just a bit of excitement, and I'd go back to my regularly scheduled life. But the more time I spent with you, the more places inside of me you managed to sneak into, the harder I fell for you."

The bartender sets Cillian's whiskey in front of him, and I watch the way his throat moves while he takes a long sip from the glass. It's an odd thing to miss, but sitting here, I realize how much I missed every damn thing about him, even the way he drinks his bourbon.

I blow out a breath and sip my own cocktail. "It can't be this easy. Nothing in my life has ever been this easy." But nothing in my life has ever felt this right, either.

"It's not going to be. Not by a long shot. But I'm willing to show up every day and prove that you can trust me. That you've always been able to trust me. I'm not going to leave you, Nova. But that means you can't leave either. I don't care about a fresh start—I want a *real* start. I think we both deserve that, don't you?"

I nod and swallow around the lump in my throat. "Yeah, I do."

Cillian slides his hand to the back of my head and brings his mouth to mine, kissing me like he's missed the taste of my mouth as much as I've missed his. His tongue sweeps in and tangles with mine, neither of us giving a shit that we're in a bar full of people in the middle of the afternoon.

"Thank God," he says when he pulls a breath's width away. "Because I was ready to beg, had a whole speech and everything."

"Damn, I wish I would have been able to hear it."

"It started with *please* and ended with *let me love you.*"

Tears fill my eyes, and when one drops, Cillian swipes it away with his thumb and presses his forehead against mine.

"I think...I think that would have worked. And I would have told you that I love you, Cillian, and I can't think of anything I want more than letting you love me back."

"Yeah?"

I nod as a fresh wave of tears fills my eyes. "Yeah."

# Epilogue

## Cillian

### Five months later

"**O**H, FUCK, RIGHT THERE!" Nova screams as my mouth is buried between her thighs. Her fingers tangle in my hair while mine pump in and out of her as my tongue circles her clit at a furious pace. Seconds later, her wet cunt tightens around my fingers and the taste of her orgasm floods my mouth. *Fucking delicious.* I slow my pace, following her down as her entire body melts into the mattress.

"God, that's better than any alarm or cup of coffee in the world," she moans with that doped-up smile on her face as I prowl up her body.

Then my fucking phone rings on the nightstand.

Nova groans as I look at the screen and see Eoghan's name flashing.

"What?" I bark when I accept the call.

"Alessia's on her way to the hospital. She's having the baby," he says excitedly.

"We're on our way."

I disconnect the call and look down at Nova's sated smile. "We should shower and head to the hospital."

Nova glances at my hard cock jutting out between us as I hold myself above her. "You wash my back and I'll wash yours?"

I lean down and kiss her. "As long as you let me fuck you in the shower, I'll wash anything you want.

"I'm a great multitasker."

I hop off the bed and head to the bathroom while Nova is still lying in a mess of orgasmic bliss. "Come on, we need to make this quick."

"Just what every girl wants to hear."

"That mouth will get you in trouble one of these days," I reply, walking back over to the bed.

"You know, you keep saying that, but—" She stops short to let out a loud squeal when I bend down, haul her up, and throw her over my shoulder, smacking her ass on the way to the bathroom. I open the shower door with her still over my shoulder and turn the water on.

"Hold on, you big brute! Let me take this off."

When Nova gets her feet under her, she slides the three-carat ring from her left hand and places it on a little dish that sits next to the sink. When I sold off all those jewels from our heist in New Orleans, I held onto one. Of course, I made up for the money I would have gotten for it with my own deposit in her account since it was one of the more expensive pieces we lifted that night.

When I popped the question a month ago at the little bar she bought here in Boston, Nova's eyes went wide as saucers as she looked at the ring.

"Is this…?" she asked, her eyes darting from mine then back to the ring.

"It is. Figured I'd hold onto it if I was ever in a position to nail down the little thief who stole my heart right after she stole my wallet."

"That might not be the story to tell our kids one day."

"We can tell them whatever you want, as long as you say yes."

"Of course it's a yes," she said, and I slid the ring on her finger.

I smile, remembering that night. It's right up there with the day she officially moved into my apartment and the day she opened the doors to her little bar with a distinct New Orleans flare to it. She wanted to bring Boston that crazy New Orleans voodoo that she obviously enraptured me with.

Turning toward me, she cocks her head to the side. "Why do you have that look on your face?"

"What look?"

"That one with the mushy smile."

"You know why the wedding band goes on the left ring finger?" I ask, and her mouth quirks in a smile.

"Why?"

"Because people used to believe that the vein in that finger traveled directly to the heart. Of course, with modern science, they found out it wasn't true, but I still like the sentiment."

Nova cocks her head to the side and smirks. "You know, for a big, bad mob lieutenant, you sure are a softy."

"Woman, that mouth…"

"This one?" She points her finger to her lips. "You love this mouth."

"You're lucky I do." My arm wraps around her as I press my lips against hers. Kissing Nova is a high that no heist or territory takeover could compare to. She excites me and keeps me grounded in a way I never thought possible.

"You ever think about what would've happened if you hadn't caught up to me at Geraldine's?" she asks as I step into the shower, pulling her behind me.

"The only thing that would've happened is I'd still be looking for you."

"To get your wallet back?"

I shake my head, bringing both of my hands up to cup her cheeks as I lead her under the spray. "To find the woman I want to spend the rest of my life with."

And thank fuck for both of us that I found her.

"Now about that back washing…" I say, and Nova shoots me one of her wicked smiles as she leans up to take my mouth in a heart-stopping kiss.

We make it to the hospital about an hour later. Alessia's bodyguard, Enzo, is sitting with Gemma and Eoghan, while Luca and Giada are standing with Mario Amatto,

Maeve, and Cormac.

Giada spots us first and has a wide smile on her face as we walk up to the group, and she grabs Nova in a hug.

"Isn't this exciting? We're going to be aunties," Giada exclaims.

In the last few months since Giada and Luca have been back from their extended honeymoon in Italy, the women have formed a close bond that Nova never had with anyone other than Harper. Giada and Gemma even went with Nova to New Orleans for a girls' weekend with Harper. Alessia had to stay home because of doctor's orders, but she made the girls promise to plan another trip after she had the baby, on Finn's dime of course. Watching Luca fret over being away from his wife was honestly hilarious to watch, but he's adamant that Giada gets to lead the life that she was never allowed to when she was under the oppressive thumb of both her father and brother. Eoghan reassured him that he had it covered, probably putting trackers on all their phones or some shit.

Cormac pats me on the shoulder and hands me a cigar. "The next generation of Monaghans. I'm so fucking lucky to be here to see this day."

"If you light that cigar, Cormac Monaghan, you might not live to see the next one," Maeve says, pulling it from his hand.

Cormac laughs and kisses his wife square on the mouth. "Yes, dear."

"Is there any news?" I ask Maeve.

"A nurse came out about thirty minutes ago, since Lilliana and Finn didn't want to leave Alessia's side, and said everything was moving along. We should hear something soon," she replies.

"Uncle Cillian has a nice ring to it," Nova says, leaning up and kissing me.

"So does Nova Doyle," Maeve interjects.

"Leave them alone, Mom," Eoghan chimes in with a laugh. "They just got engaged."

"You're right," Maeve replies. "Let's talk about when you're going to slide the wedding band onto Gemma's finger instead."

Gemma laughs and Eoghan sits back in his chair. "Never mind," he says and waves his hand at his mother. "Proceed with the inquisition."

Maeve turns her attention back to us just before Alessia's mother walks into the waiting area.

"She's here," Lilliana announces.

Mario walks up to his wife and envelops her in a strong hug as tears of joy run down her face.

"Let's go see our granddaughter," Cormac says. He grabs Maeve's hand as Lilliana leads us to Alessia's room.

"Aren't there rules about how many people can be in the room at once?" Nova asks me as we follow the herd of our excited family.

"Sweetheart, no one in Boston is going to say no to the Monaghans," I reply, kissing her on the forehead.

The suite they put Alessia in is huge but still crowded with the amount of people packed in it.

Finn is lying on the bed with his wife and daughter as we walk in, and when he looks at us, he's wearing a smile bigger and brighter than any I've ever seen.

"Everyone, meet Isabella Lilliana Monaghan." He looks down at his sleeping daughter in his wife's arms and gently trails a finger over her cheek. "Izzy, this is your family," he says in a soft voice.

In all the years I've been a part of the Monaghan family, I've never seen my best friend cry. But when he looks from his wife to his daughter, his eyes shine with the kind of tears you only have when you're immeasurably happy. And I'd be lying if I didn't feel my own eyes begin to well up.

The moment is broken when my phone begins vibrating in my pocket, and I pull it out to see Liam's name flashing on the screen. I duck out of the room before accepting the call.

"Hey, kinda busy here. Alessia just had her baby," I say.

"Good news, mate. Give them my congratulations."

"Will do. What's going on?"

"Well, since New York and New Orleans went so well with you working with our team, I was thinking you'd like to do it again. I could even use your girl's skill set of relieving people of their belongings." That's a very Liam way to put it. "It will require a passport this time around, but good news is, I have my very own private jet now."

"How is that good news for me?"

"Fair point. I may have wanted to brag for a moment."

I shake my head. *Fucking Liam.*

"I'll talk to Nova and get back to you."

"Right, right. Check in with the missus. I'll need confirmation by tomorrow if she agrees."

"Jesus, you don't give us much time."

"Yeah, sorry about that, but it doesn't always work that way."

"Okay. I'll call you later."

I disconnect the call and head back into the room, taking my place next to Nova.

"Everything okay?" she asks, looking down at the phone in my hand and back to me.

"Liam wants us to help him with something that he apparently needs a pickpocket for."

Nova's lips tip up in a smile. "Good thing you know one."

I lean down and press my lips against hers. "Correction. It's the best thing."

The End

Thank you so much for reading Cillian and Nova's story. I hope you enjoyed living in their world as much as I enjoyed writing them. Did you guess which song I was obsessed with when I wrote the scene in the hotel bar? If you did, message me!

If you loved the book, I would be incredibly grateful if you left a review where you purchased the book.

Reviews help indie authors like me spread the word about our stories and mean the world to us.

Want to learn more about the Black Roses MC? They have a series too. In fact, we're headed back to Shine next, so now's a good time to catch up! I even have a little novella that my newsletter friends get for free. If you're interested, you can sign up by visiting my website at www.katerandallauthor.com.

### Stalk me on my Socials!

TikTok

Instagram

Facebook

Goodreads

BookBub

Or you can scan the QR code to find my socials and sign up for my newsletter!

# Also By Kate

**The Ones Series**
The Good One
The Fragile One
The Other One

**The Black Roses MC**
Linc
Jude
Ozzy
And more coming...

**The Boston Syndicate**
Finn
Luca
Eoghan
Cillian

# Acknowledgements

THANK YOU so much for going on the journey with the Monaghan family with me. Finishing this book was so bittersweet (I hate saying goodbye) but what a ride! With the millions of books out there, the fact that you picked up one of mine means the absolute world to me.

Thank you Kiki, Megan, and Anna at the Next Step PR. You ladies are absolutely amazing and I couldn't imagine doing this without you. Honestly, I *know* I wouldn't be able to do any of it without you. LOL

Huuuuge thank you to Victoria, my badass editor. Thank you for pushing me, thank you for educating me, thank you for understanding my voice and polishing it until it shines. You are stuck with me forever.

To my sister from another mister, Molli. You mean the world to me. Thank you for your calming wisdom and reminding me to breathe and just being an all around cheerleader. None of this would have happened if you hadn't turned to me and said, "I think you should do this." It's all your fault, and I love you for it.

And always, thank you, Matt. Your support means the world to me. You and I created a life where I'm safe to be me and hide in my office (aka our bedroom) to hang out with fictional characters that talk to me. I love you with all my heart, babe.

# About Kate

Kate is a lover of all things books. It doesn't matter what sub-genre, as long as there's a HEA, she's in. She started reading romance in high school and would hide novels in textbooks to read during class. Becoming an author was always a dream she had and finally decided to put pen to paper (or finger to keyboard) and write what she loves. She grew up in the beautiful upper peninsula of Michigan then became a West Coast girl where she lives with her amazing husband and hilarious son. She would love to hear from readers so check out all her socials and sign up for her newsletter so she can keep you up to date on her books and whatever other ramblings come to mind.

www.ingramcontent.com/pod-product-compliance
Lightning Source LLC
Chambersburg PA
CBHW061111310726
48974CB00002B/480